# The
# *Deeper*
## the *Water* the
## *Uglier* the
# *Fish*

a novel by
# **Katya Apekina**

*Two Dollar Radio*
Books too loud to Ignore

# Two Dollar Radio
## Books too loud to Ignore

**WHO WE ARE** TWO DOLLAR RADIO is a family-run outfit dedicated to reaffirming the cultural and artistic spirit of the publishing industry. We aim to do this by presenting bold works of literary merit, each book, individually and collectively, providing a sonic progression that we believe to be too loud to ignore.

**TWODOLLARRADIO.com**

*Proudly based in*
**Columbus**
**OHIO**

 @TwoDollarRadio

 @TwoDollarRadio

 /TwoDollarRadio

**Love the PLANET?**
So do we.

Printed on Rolland Enviro.
This paper contains 100% post-consumer fiber, is manufactured using renewable energy - Biogas and processed chlorine free.

*Printed in Canada*

100%   **PCF**   **BIO GAS**   PERMANENT

**SOME RECOMMENDED LOCATIONS FOR READING *THE DEEPER THE WATER THE UGLIER THE FISH*:** In a bathtub of your own tears, or pretty much anywhere because books are portable and the perfect technology!

**AUTHOR PHOTOGRAPH→**
Andrew Wonder

**COVER DESIGN**
Two Dollar Radio

**IMAGES→**
*Spray Paint*, DesignM.ag;
*The Ladies' Home Journal* (1889)

To David

"...but life is a trick, life is a kitten in a sack."
—Anne Sexton, "Some Foreign Letters"

# The Deeper the Water the Uglier the Fish

**PART I:**
*New York*

# Chapter 1

It's our second day in New York City. We're with Dennis Lomack. Mom is in St. Vincent's, resting. She has recently done something very stupid and I'm the one who found her. Dennis has been taking us around town, trying to get our minds off of everything, trying to make up for the last decade.

Tonight, he brought Mae and me along on a date with a redhead to a dance recital. Mom would take us sometimes into New Orleans to see *The Nutcracker*, but this isn't like that. We're in the basement of a church. It's cramped and damp. On stage a woman in a white sundress dances by herself. She looks like a feral cat. Her rib cage shows on the sides and down the front. She has thick dark hair that sways at her waist as she moves. The stage is covered in folding chairs and she dances with her eyes squeezed shut. She seems aware of nothing, banging her legs and arms and not even noticing. The chairs collapse and fall around her and she keeps going. She slows and cocks her head at an angle as if she's listening for something, then makes little twitchy movements with her hands. Even from my seat, I can smell her dirty hair. It wafts with each spin.

She blurs and I realize I'm crying. I don't know why.

That's not true. I do. It's because she reminds me so much of

Mom. The way she dances, so desperate, but also so closed off. She isn't dancing for us. She's somewhere deep inside herself and the seats could be empty and still she'd dance like this.

Mae looks terrified. I squeeze her hand but she doesn't notice. I don't know Dennis well enough to guess what he's feeling. Probably nothing. In the dark theater his face looks like it's carved out of a rock. His date has fallen asleep on his shoulder.

Outside, Dennis pries the redhead off his neck, twirls out from under her, and puts her in a cab. It's almost a dance too, the way he does it. His movements are so calculated. Obviously, he has a lot of practice getting rid of people. As the cab pulls away, the woman looks at us through the glass like she's a sad golden retriever. Mae waves. I already don't remember her name. Rachel? Rebecca? It doesn't matter. I doubt we'll ever see her again.

We walk back to Dennis's apartment in silence. He walks between us, holding our elbows. It's a long way, 30 or 40 blocks. The air is cold and most of the stores are closed with the metal grates down over the windows. The benches we pass have men lying on them. Some have sleeping bags, but others are just wrapped in newspapers. The ones who didn't get a bench lie in doorways or on the ground. Dennis leads us around the men in silence. I've never seen so many homeless people before. At an intersection, a group of women walks by us, laughing and licking ice cream cones. They don't even look at the people on the ground as they step over them.

"I'm sorry," Dennis says. His words hang there. Mae and I glance at each other. I wish he'd be a little more specific about what it is exactly that he's sorry about.

At the apartment, we sit at the kitchen table to have tea. When I think about the woman swaying on the stage, I start to cry again. Mae strokes my hair, rubs my temples with her cold fingers. Dennis hovers behind her. He helps her out of her coat, tries to help me with mine, but I shake him off. "What have we done?" I say. "How could we have left her?"

"Please calm down," he says and hands me a napkin. I blow my nose. His face is stiff and unreadable but his hand is shaking as he pours water into our mugs and he has to steady it so he won't spill. I look away at the box of teas Mae is holding. I don't like that his hand is shaking. He has no right to lose it. I take a deep breath and focus on the box. It's wooden with carvings of elephants and full of tea bags—*ginger lemon, rooibos, açaí berry*, shit I've never heard of. Mom only drinks coffee. I pick one that smells the least like grass. I bet the box was left here by a woman, just like the small sock we found balled up in the corner of our room.

Dennis wedges his chair between the table and the refrigerator. He buries his fingertips in his beard as he stares at us. I look away, but I see Mae staring back at him. He shakes my shoulder until soon I'm looking at him too. It's strange because his eyes are the same eyes that I see in the mirror. I feel momentarily hypnotized, like I'm outside my body.

"Listen to me," he says and his voice is wet. "I understand that you might feel, at first, that I'm a stranger. But I'm not a stranger. I am your father." And then his rigid face collapses and he pulls us into his chest and holds us until the tea gets cold.

# MAE

This is the kind of thing my mother liked to do: she'd pick a person and follow them for hours. Through the mall, to the garage, to their house. Once, we drove all night through the woods with our headlights off to somebody's hunting cabin. Sometimes, if it was during the day, she would let Edie come too, though when Edie was there it would become something fun and toothless. A game where she and Edie would share a bag of Twizzlers in the front seat and speculate about the people we were following.

But when it was just Mom and me at night, the trees and swamp rushing past the windows in the dark, it was not a game at all. I was submerged in Mom's reality. Sometimes she'd get out of the car and I'd have to go with her. Once we walked for a long time down an overgrown path to somebody's deer stand. The air was thick and cold. The sound of crickets and tree frogs was deafening. I was 10, maybe 11, and I remember this unpleasant recurring feeling I'd get every few steps like I was waking up and waking up and waking up.

The deer stand was a plywood shack on stilts. I don't know if we stumbled on it, or if Mom had been leading us there deliberately. I followed her up the ladder because I was scared to stay on the ground alone. It was like a treehouse, but it smelled of mold and blood. Mom went through an entire book of matches, reading the headlines of old newspapers covering the floor. We got lost on the way back to the car. I was terrified that we would get shot at or chased by dogs. These things had happened too. It was light out by the time we got home, and then I had to go to school and pretend like nothing out of the ordinary had taken place. I'd have to try not to fall asleep in class or draw attention to myself in any way.

I don't know how much Edie knew. She would say I was Mom's favorite, but it's not true. It was more that Mom saw me as an extension of herself, while Edie was free to be her own person. Edie would be out with her friends, riding her bike, sunbathing, sneaking into the movies, and I would be trapped upstairs in Mom's bedroom, buried under blankets despite the summer heat, my grandmother's fur coat draped over both of us. The coat was made from nutria—swamp rats—and Mom would make me lie under it with her for hours, sweating and itching, while she sucked the sleeves bald.

Yes, Mom dragged me with her to every terrible place. I needed to get as far from her as I could. She was consuming me. That day when she tried to hang herself from the rafter in the kitchen, I'd been lying on my bedroom floor. My mind was a radio tuned to her station and her misery paralyzed me. I must have known what she was doing, but I did nothing to stop her. It was Edie who saved Mom's life.

When Dad appeared out of nowhere to rescue us, it felt like he'd been summoned by magic. He took us out of school—I was a freshman and Edie was a junior—and brought us back with him to New York City. It was our first time out of Louisiana. We didn't know how long we'd be staying because everything was up in the air, but I understood that I was being given an opportunity to start over, and I wasn't going to squander it.

Everything about Dad felt like déjà vu. I would see an object and feel inexplicably pulled towards it. A pair of brown leather shoes at the back of his closet, for example, worn soft and in need of resoling. I didn't remember them exactly, but my body did. I'd shut the closet door and hold them in the dark, cradling them in my arms. I didn't want Edie to know that I did these things, and it was hard to hide from her in such a small apartment.

I loved that apartment. It was like a tight, dusty womb. Edie was constantly sneezing because the dust was so hard to clean out of all the books. The shelves in the living room overflowed onto the floor and there were stacks of books everywhere, against all the walls, on top of the piano, under the kitchen table. Dad was a writer, so books found a way of multiplying in his apartment. He got new ones in the mail every day, mostly from young authors hoping for a blurb. A blurb from Dad went a long way. He was a cultural icon. Once he'd even been a clue on *Jeopardy!*.

Mom had been a writer too, a poet, though not nearly as well known. She read to us a lot. One of my earliest memories is sitting on the floor of the kitchen with Edie, watching as Mom towered above us with her eyes closed, swaying, stomping, intoning, her notebooks covering the counters. Sometimes she would send her work out to magazines and have Edie and me lick the envelopes for luck. She rarely got published. At some point she stopped writing, and then eventually she stopped reading. The books became props. She could spend entire days sitting in the breakfast nook, staring glassily at some volume of poems open in her lap, her oily hair staining the shoulders of her nightgown. She would stare and never turn the pages. Her fingers, disconnected from the rest of her body, would be tapping something out against each other.

# EDITH (1997)

The sound of traffic gets louder when I close my eyes. I bet this is what the ocean sounds like. Our bedroom is like a cabin on a cruise ship. It used to be Dennis's study and it's so tight that if you're standing in the middle of the room you have to make sure not to "talk like an Italian," as our French teacher would have said—or you'll jam your fingers against the bunk bed or the dresser or the paper lantern.

Mae is lying next to me on the bottom bunk. We're scared to leave each other's side. All night we take turns drifting in and out of sleep.

"It's like we're on a cruise ship," I whisper to her, but she doesn't open her eyes. She shakes her head and her thick, dark hair falls over her face. She's like a little furnace when she sleeps. Her neck gets wet and her hair sticks to it. Her hair is just like Mom's. When she turns away from me to face the wall, I comb it with my fingers and pretend it's Mom lying there with me. *Sorry, Mom. I'm sorry.* We've been here for almost a week and the doctors still aren't saying anything. They tell Dennis that it's too early to know for sure. When I call, they tell me that they aren't authorized to discuss her condition with me. They treat me like a little kid, as if I haven't been the one taking care of her all these years.

Dennis still hasn't told us when we're going back. I don't mind a break, but I'm on student council and on the homecoming and dance committees and the longer we stay here the more likely all that shit is going to be usurped. Plus, I miss Markus, and it's only a matter of time before he gets usurped too, by one of the Laurens or worse.

I've asked Dennis, will we be back on the 3rd? The 4th? But he just smiles like an asshole and tells me how happy he is to have me here. I don't know how much more I can take of him following us around and making incessant observations about stupid shit. How we hold our spoons! How we drink our water! We are so similar to him! Oh, the wonder of genetics! I wouldn't be surprised if right now it turned out he's actually standing on the other side of our bedroom door, listening to us sleep, making notes on how similar our sleeping sounds are to his own. Maybe he can put *that* in his next book. We are such exciting material! Little mirrors in which he can stare at himself even more.

"Don't you think it's strange," I whisper loudly, "that Dennis never took any interest in us for 12 years and now, suddenly, he can't get enough?" If he's on the other side of the door, I hope he hears me.

Mae doesn't open her eyes but I can tell she's awake. Anyway, I already know what she thinks. She doesn't think it's strange at all. When I brought it up before she defended him. She was only two when he left, so what does she know. I was four. I actually remember it. I remember missing him, waiting for him by the front window every day like a dog. He never called, not on birthdays or Christmas. He never sent letters or postcards. He's this famous writer, or whatever, and I have no idea what his handwriting even looks like. And then there's also what Mom told us. Even when we were little she'd talk very openly with us, since we were all she had. She'd tell us how he'd taken advantage of her, of her youth, and how he'd been jealous and rageful, and slept with all her friends, not even because he wanted to, or was particularly attracted to any of them, but because he didn't want her to *have* friends. And she didn't have friends, not really. She had Doreen and she had us and we hadn't been enough.

"This isn't gonna last," I whisper. I don't want her to get her hopes up only to have them crushed. "As soon as we go back home we'll never hear from him again."

Mae is so bad at pretending to be asleep. She holds her breath, that's what gives her away. I don't say anything else and soon the sound of traffic fills the room until it feels like I'm floating on it. I drift off. I'm back home, in my own room. Mom is fine. I hear her in the shower, singing. See, she's fine. I knew she'd be fine. Her singing turns shrill. Sirens wake me up.

Mae is by the window. The lights from an ambulance seven stories below are making her face a blue then red mask.

"Mae," I whisper, but she doesn't budge. She goes into trances sometimes, that's why the kids at school called her Spooks.

"Mae," I say again, and put my hands on her shoulders. We both watch someone on the street below get strapped into a stretcher.

There was a torrential rainstorm the day I found Mom in the kitchen. The EMTs and firemen left puddles all over the carpet when they carried her out. It was like God made me and Markus get into a fight, so that I'd come home early from his lake house and find her. Mae says that she doesn't believe in God, but how else would you explain my being there in time? Just five minutes later and she would have died. I can't imagine her dead. It's like an eclipse, where if you look directly at it you'd go blind.

She hadn't really wanted to die. I know this for a fact. You know how I know? Because she'd put the hot water on and set the percolator up to make coffee. The whole wall was wet with condensation and the kettle was still whistling when I found her. I don't know how Mae hadn't heard anything. She must've been in one of her trances.

I walk Mae back to the bottom bunk and tuck her in. She reaches over and strokes my face.

"Don't cry," she says and closes her eyes.

I hadn't realized I was crying. Tears have been leaking out of me since we got here, like my face is incontinent. "I'm not," I say and wipe them with her hair.

"Don't you wish it could go back to how it was?" I ask. Before this happened, before Mom got depressed. She wasn't always sad. Sometimes she was happier than anybody I've ever seen. She would laugh, doubled over, unable to stop, and we would laugh too, even if we didn't get what was so funny. And then there were other times, when she wasn't happy or angry or sad. When she was just Mom, when she would take us to the park or to the parades, and when she'd stay up late, sewing us elaborate Mardi Gras costumes.

Mae doesn't answer me, turns to face the wall. Finally, when I'm almost asleep I hear her say: "Sometimes it feels like you and I grew up in different houses."

## MAE

The first couple of weeks Dad didn't let us out of his sight. He'd take us on epic walks, trying to cram in as much as he could to make up for lost time. We covered hundreds of blocks on foot. He said that when he moved back to New York he missed us so much that it felt like his internal organs were crawling with fire ants and walking was what brought him back to sanity.

It wouldn't have occurred to us to walk in Metairie. There was nowhere to go and you couldn't get very far without eventually ending up where you started or hitting the interstate. There were the terrifying night walks through swamps and woods with Mom, but that was its own thing. In New York, we walked like pilgrims and when our shoes wore down, Dad bought us fancy sneakers, designed to mimic the strut of a Maasai warrior. We'd wear them as we walked from the Cloisters to the southernmost tip of Battery Park, stepping around junkies nodding out on the sidewalks of the Lower East Side, sampling dumplings in Chinatown and pizza in Little Italy, fingering the bolts of fabric in the Fashion District and buying bouquets in the Flower District that wilted by the time we got home.

We'd walk through neighborhoods right as schools were getting out. Girls would pour into the street, wearing similar uniforms to what we had at St. Ursula's—gray-and-green plaid skirts and button-down white shirts—though, of course, these girls made them look a lot more sophisticated. We'd see them standing in long lines outside bakeries in Greenwich Village, rummaging around in their big, fancy purses.

Dad would try to steer us away from those girls because seeing them would inevitably put Edie in a foul mood.

"You've basically kidnapped us!" she would scream at him, and some of the girls would turn and watch us uncertainly, not knowing whether to take her accusation seriously. Once she took off her new sneakers and threw them at him. Dad looked so befuddled and surprised that it only made Edie angrier.

"When are we going home?" she screamed, and the only way to calm her was to invoke the doctors and Mom's health. Then she begrudgingly settled down, and after several blocks put her shoes back on.

My favorite was when Dad would take us on ghost tours of all the places from his childhood that had been effaced, places where he had lived and gone to the movies and drank malts and played pinball. I liked seeing another layer of the city under the immediately visible one. Metairie was a static swamp. Nothing there felt like it could ever change.

One time he took us to Morningside Park to look at the caves he'd camped in to protest attempts to segregate the park. Columbia had wanted to build a gym there with two separate entrances for "Whites" and "Coloreds." Anytime he talked about the Civil Rights Movement, Edie would forget she was supposed to be angry and would listen to him with her mouth hanging open.

## Letter from
## Dennis Lomack to Marianne Louise McLean

April 24, 1968

Dear M—

I sat down with the intention of working on a novel but everything I write turns into a letter to you. I'm under your spell, girl. Why fight it?

Fred and I are in Morningside Park. The Pigs are patrolling the park's perimeter but they won't do anything. Even the Mayor knows we're right. We're drunk and singing, celebrating Columbia's capitulation. Goodbye, Gym Crow.

Fred spilled our water bucket over the wood, so it wouldn't light (poor Fred, no depth perception). I had to climb down and look for more wood. From below the view is very satisfying: caves pockmark the side of the cliff, each one with a campfire burning in it. The side of the cliff is thus transformed into: a primordial skyscraper. A CAVEMAN SKYSCRAPER (this phrase came to me in your father's voice). Oh, how I wish you could both see it! It's better than a sit-in, it's a camp-in! It's a CAVE-IN! This isn't Mississippi! Not on our watch! etc. etc.

How is your father? I've been meaning to write him. I heard from Ann that the case against him is a mess, a total farce, though she did not go into specifics. I'm happy to talk to my sister for advice. She's a lawyer, you know. I just saw her earlier this evening, as a matter of fact. She brought us pork and cabbage, and that drip of hers, Stewart. Friends came over from the cave next to us, two Puerto Rican sisters. Stewart tried to talk to them about Gandhi but they were not impressed. They left. Stewart says if he could kill me and wear my skin, he would. Stewart's face is what you'd call a "bouquet of pimples." He blames this for his poor luck with women. Why my sister tolerates him is beyond me. Mosquitoes are flocking to the candle so I'm going to blow it out.

Goodnight, goodnight, my little m.

## EDITH (1997)

"I'm too old," Dennis says and waves us on. He's standing by the barbecuers in the grass below.

Mae and I climb under the railing and crawl along a narrow ledge to the caves along the side of the cliff. I don't look down. The caves have small openings. As we crawl into them, our hands brush against dirt and trash. Candy wrappers or is it condom wrappers? Dennis is shouting directions at us from below.

"To the left, to the left," he's saying. I stick my head out and see he's pointing to the cave next to us. That's the one he camped in back in the day.

We climb over to it. I hoist Mae in and then she pulls me up. The cave is deeper than the others and darker. It takes a while for my eyes to adjust, and then I see an outline of a figure. I can feel Mae tense but before she can do anything, I cover her mouth with my hand. There's a man very close to us. Asleep. He is naked, lying on top of a sleeping bag. Even in the dark I can see his dick. It's draped on his stomach, looking directly at us with its eye. Mae and I nearly fall out of the cave, crawling backward. I bet it's the first one she's ever seen.

"What happened?" Dennis says. Mae and I are both out of

breath. Her face is smudged from where I covered her mouth. A Snickers wrapper is hanging off her knee and Dennis peels it off.

"We saw a snake," I tell him. I don't know why I lie. It just comes out.

"Oh," he says. "Was it green and yellow?"

I nod.

"A garter snake. Don't worry, they're harmless," he says.

There's a woman standing next to him. Not the one from the theater, a different one. The way she smiles at us makes her look like a horse. When she tries to compliment Mae on her hair, Mae growls.

## MAE

Dad had a lot of women. It was better not to encourage them. The worst was when they tried to act motherly, and then it felt like some awful community theater production where they were auditioning for a part that didn't really exist. Edie and I both made a point of being rude to them, though we had different reasons. I had finally been given a father and I didn't want to share him, while Edie thought these women were an insult to Mom.

I don't think Dad knew how to keep all the women at bay. His whole life he got a lot of female attention. Growing up, he was the youngest, and his mother and sister doted on him. And then, as an adult, he was handsome and charismatic, tall enough to have to stoop through doorways, talented and famous. Of course women liked him! But it didn't seem like he took any of them very seriously. He was completely focused on Edie and me. Being in the center of someone's world like this was intoxicating. The way he looked at us... I've never experienced anything like it.

One night when Edie was asleep, I snuck out of our room and crept up to Dad's door. I stood there for a while, gathering my courage to knock. I needed to tell him that I couldn't go back, that I couldn't leave him, but I was afraid to say anything in front of my sister. I was nervous to break rank and go behind her back.

I remember as I tapped on his door, it pushed open and I found him sitting at his writing desk, staring at a photograph. I startled him, and he quickly slid the picture into a drawer.

"What are you doing up?" he asked.

I lost my nerve. I didn't know what to say. And what if Edie was right? What if his love for us was an illusion, and my words would expose this and scare him off? So, I said nothing.

But I didn't have to. "Come here," he said, and pulled me onto his lap.

"Are you scared?" he asked me.

I nodded, and he kissed me on the forehead.

"Who wouldn't be," he said.

## EDITH (1997)

"My two beautiful daughters, my beautiful, beautiful girls," Dennis says at breakfast. My shoulder is warm under his hand. His eyes are soft like we're his baby birds.

I look at Mae looking at him and I can see things, important things, slowly shifting around in her like plate tectonics.

I'm not gonna lie. I also felt a moment of sudden complete-ness when he touched me, like the wires in my Bullshit Alarm had been cut. But at least I recognize it for what it is. Two weeks have gone by since Mom disappeared into the hospital and we're betraying her already.

"I thought I would take you to the Met today," he says. The phone rings but he keeps smiling at us. I squirm out from under his hand. It's Markus, probably, calling me back. I've left him three messages. That, or one of Dennis's ladies. So many ladies. They call and call. One showed up the other day in a trench coat with nothing on underneath. She'd been out of the country and came straight from the airport to surprise him. Surprise! She couldn't even sit down, just held the coat closed tight around her neck with one hand as she shook our hands with the other. I almost felt bad for her.

"Hello?" I say into the phone.

It's a male voice. "Could I speak to Mr. Lomack, please?" It's the doctor, I think.

I hand Dennis the phone. I watch his face as he listens.

"Yes," Dennis says. "How is she doing?" He looks down at his hands. "Yes," he says, "yes." He turns from us, and the cord on the phone wraps around his back. "What about the medication?" he says. "I see," he says. "Yes." His voice gives away nothing.

My heart is beating in my throat.

"I'm sorry to hear that," he says, but he doesn't sound particularly sorry. I can't see his face. What is he sorry to hear?

Mae shifts in her seat, and the chair creaks. I must be giving her a mean look because her lips are quivering. She's sensitive. That's what Mom always says. *Be careful with your sister, she's so sensitive.* I smile at her, or try to, then take a deep breath.

"Yes," Dennis says again, about three thousand times. They're keeping Mom there against her will. She's probably tied to a bed, screaming. She's lost her voice. That's why they won't let me talk to her. She has no voice. I picture her face screaming and no sound coming out. This scares me so I take Mae's hand.

"Ow," she says, and rubs where I touched her. She can be a real brat sometimes.

Dennis hangs up the phone. His eyes are shining and he doesn't say anything until he sits down at the table with us.

"The doctors think it would be best," he says, burying his fingers in his beard, "if you moved here on a somewhat permanent basis. Your mother is not doing well. She needs more time."

"No," I say.

Dennis nods. "I know this isn't what you were expecting," he says.

"What about school? We can't just leave in the middle of the spring quarter. We can go back and live there by ourselves. I'm 16. Who do you think has been taking care of things this whole time?"

"Legally, you couldn't do that," he says.

"We can stay with Doreen." Doreen is like Mom's sister. Not biological, but they grew up together. She owes it to us.

"She hasn't offered."

I try to stay calm because I know that is the only way to win an argument, but I can hear my voice growing shrill. "I don't agree to this."

Mae interrupts. She glares at me and says: "I think you're being very selfish." It feels like she has reached across the table and slapped me.

## DENNIS LOMACK'S JOURNAL

[1970]

Last night I began… something. Something big, alive. I don't want to speak too soon, but maybe finally a book (!). I typed and Marianne lay on the mattress on the floor, watching me. With her I am an open glove welcoming a hand. It is her energy working through me, I'm certain of it. I wrote all night. Outside, it rained. Marianne lay on her back, raised her arm, squinted at her ring, fell asleep. Yesterday, my sister came into the city for a visit and as we were passing City Hall, I felt compelled to get married. We bought carnations, dyed bright blue, from the deli across the street. "Look," Marianne had said, running her thumb along the stems, veined like arms. We stopped a tourist on the street, asked him to take a picture of us with his camera. He promised to mail it. And since our marriage, the urge to write has consumed me. Beneath all my words, like subway clatter—*my wife, my life, my wife*. It was already light out when I stopped and crawled in beside her. I needed more of her to keep going.

"They bit me all night long," she told me, sleepily showing me her arm. A row of small red welts. The bedbugs live between the floorboards and inside the electrical sockets.

"I'll bite you too," I said. And I did.

Then after, in the bathroom mirror, as I washed my face, I caught sight of my earlobe—two uneven lines, marks from her crooked front teeth. And again, that zap of desire.

I ran back to bed, unbuttoned the blouse from the bottom that she had begun buttoning from the top. She's shy but about all the wrong things. I moved her hands off her breasts and kissed her wrists. Pinned her down.

And then, her whispered refrain: You can save me?

For which there is only one answer: Yes, of course, yes.

## Edith (1997)

Dennis and Mae are banging pots around in the kitchen. He's teaching her how to make dumplings from scratch. It's his grandmother's recipe from Poland. I guess that makes her our great-grandmother. I did most of the cooking back home and kept the batteries out of the smoke alarm by the kitchen because of Mom and Mae. All our pots had outlines from burnt rice on the bottoms from when they would try to make red beans and rice. I was thinking about that yesterday, when we got a special tour of the Metropolitan Museum of Art by some woman Dennis was/is/will be putting it into, and she was showing us the swirly night sky in a painting by Vincent van Gogh. It looked just like the bottoms of all our pots in Metairie. It makes me sad: those pots, stacked and unused in the cabinets of our empty house. I don't know how much longer I can take being away.

I heard someone say once that if you visualize what you want, like really picture it with all the details, it'll come true. Sort of like prayer. So, I try it. I close my eyes and concentrate. I'm not in this cramped shithole anymore. Instead, I'm back home, standing in our living room. To the left is the shelf with the gourd sculptures filled with my grandfather's ashes. In front is the window with its lace curtains. It's the middle of the day and light is streaming in, casting patterns on the green velvet couch and the coffee table.

I try to imagine the smell of the neighbor's trees. It creeps in, despite the closed windows and the humming air conditioner. Those trees were just starting to bud when we left, by now they should be in full bloom. Little white flowers that smell like fish sticks. Last year people complained and signed petitions to have them cut down, but I liked them. I've always liked those kinds of smells—fish, skunk, gasoline, armpits, dirt.

Mom and Mae are in the other room. I stretch my arms out and walk towards them. But then, as I'm getting close, as I'm almost at the threshold of our kitchen, the floor creaks and ruins everything. Our house has thick carpet. The floor never creaks. I try to stand still, hoping that if I focus hard I can start again where I left off, but it's not working. I can't figure out how to teleport entirely, how to be in Metairie for more than a few seconds at a time. I open my eyes and there is Mae, the real one, standing in the doorway, watching me. She has flour on her face and on her shirt. She's holding the cordless phone.

"It's Markus," she says. "You want to take it?"

I'm embarrassed, but then I think, why should I be? She doesn't know what I was doing. All she saw was me with my eyes closed. Mae always acts like she knows everything, but what does she really know?

"Finally," I say into the phone, shutting the door in Mae's face. "Didn't your mom give you my messages?"

"I'm calling you, aren't I?" He sounds annoyed. We broke up the day everything happened with Mom, but we got back together the day after, and the day after that I came here. "So," he says, "what's up?"

"I need your help," I say.

"Okay…"

"I need to stay with you."

He doesn't say anything for a moment so I rush to fill the silence. "I don't have anywhere else to go. Dennis wants me to move to New York, and Mom isn't better yet."

"I'll ask my parents," he says.

"Please," I say, because I don't think he will.

"I'll ask them."

"I could live in your guest room," I say.

"Okay," he says. It sounds like there are people in the background, voices, laughter. I feel a pang.

"Where are you?" I ask.

"At the lake house," he says.

"Who's all there?" I ask.

"Lauren B, Lauren S and Drunk Mike."

"Why are you hanging out with the Laurens?"

"Don't..." he says, but then someone grabs the phone from him.

"Edie!!" Mike slurs. "Why aren't you here??"

I hear Markus wrestling the phone away from him.

"He doesn't know?" I ask Markus.

"He probably forgot," Markus says.

"So, you'll ask your parents?" I say.

"Jesus," he says, "I said I would."

He sounds so annoyed with me. Neither of us say anything. I sniffle loudly into the phone. I know he can hear it and that he feels bad, because his voice goes low, and I feel like it's Markus I'm talking to again, not this other person he has become over the last few months.

"Edie, come on, stop. I'm sorry. Stop crying."

"I want to go home," I say.

Someone picks up the phone on his end and starts dialing.

"Hello? Hello?" It's Markus's father.

"Hi, Dr. Theriot," I say.

"Hello? Hello? Markus, is that you? I need the line—the hospital is paging me," he says, seeming not to have heard me.

"I'll call you later," Markus says and hangs up. I hold the phone for a moment, listening to the dial tone. In the other room Mae is laughing. It's a weird sound, ugly.

I come out into the living room and see Dennis on the ground and Mae standing on his back.

"Bend your knees! Arms out! Eyes on the horizon!" He's shouting the commands as he wriggles around and bucks under her. They're both covered in flour. Mae is trying to balance, but she's doubled over with that hideous laughter.

"I can't... I can't..." she gasps.

"I'm teaching Mae how to surf," Dennis says when he sees me. They look about as idiotic as this sounds.

"Stop sticking your butt out like that. You look like you're about to take a dump," I tell her.

She keeps smiling, but doesn't look at me.

Dennis yells: "Wave!" and bucks under her. She squeals as she flies off and lands on the couch.

"You wanna try surfing?" he asks me. He's got to be fucking kidding. This is the kind of shit he should have been doing 12 years ago when he abandoned us, not now when I'm 16.

"You know, we've never even *seen* the ocean," I tell him. But how would he know this? He's a complete stranger. I knock a stack of books off the coffee table for emphasis and there's a cloud of dust. Dennis gets up, streaks of dirt on his belly and legs, flour in his hair.

"You don't know anything about us," I try to say, but I can't stop sneezing.

## MAE

I think Edie was so scared of Dad leaving again that she wanted to preempt it. If she drove him away, she'd feel like she had some say in the matter.

Well, she's done it, I remember thinking after Edie threw her first fit. Every little mean thing Edie said, I would think, this is it, because everything in New York felt so precarious. We weren't in school. We had no routine. We didn't know anyone. We were just floating there.

Even though I'd get mad at her, I'd hold her until I could feel her rumbling rage subside, until finally whatever it was inside her would grow silent and still.

People who didn't know Edie very well were always surprised to find out that she had a temper, because of her voice, and also, because she had this look, like a blind baby animal, a leggy calf or a freshly hatched chick—all bones and matted fluffs of yellow hair. One of my earliest memories, though, is of her wailing on me. She claims not to remember, but whenever she was feeling contrite, she'd pet the tiny white scar in my eyebrow with her finger. I don't have it anymore, but it was over my right eye. She'd given it to me by kicking me in the face with an ice skate.

Once, after an argument when I told her to stop making trouble with Dad, she took a handful of my hair and jammed it in my mouth, enough for me to choke, and said: "He's going to leave us again. He's going to leave us as many times as we let him." In that moment I believed her, despite Dad doing everything he could to convince us otherwise. Like when she threw a fit because she wanted to go to the beach, and within minutes Dad was in his swim trunks, carrying towels, herding us onto the Q train to Brighton Beach. It was a long subway ride and because it was the middle of the day I remember the car being empty. It had felt like it was our private train, and even though Edie was trying not to enjoy it, I know she did. It was my first trip to see the ocean and I didn't even know that I was dying to see it until I was on my way there. People are always surprised when I tell them this because we lived by the Gulf, but the coast of Louisiana is all swamp. We'd go up to Lake Pontchartrain, but there were no ocean beaches—for that you'd have to drive out to Alabama or Florida, and we'd never left the state. Mom traveled, but she never took us. She'd disappear for weeks at a time, leave us with Doreen, or when Doreen got sick of us, with the Wassersteins, an older couple who watched crime shows all day and fed us nothing but hotdogs. Edie and I loved to hate the Wassersteins.

In a recent show, I tried to recreate the feeling of that first trip to the beach, but it was hard to capture the intense and simple joy I'd felt. It was windy and full of seagulls and it was Brighton Beach, so I'm sure the sand was full of wrappers and trash, but I didn't notice any of that. I was bowled over by the horizon line! All that water! Water, stretching out forever, and those waves! The way the water gathered itself and suddenly rose up! The force of it as it pulled the sand out from under my feet. It was cold, but of course we all went in. Edie looked like an animated broomstick in a bikini. The coldness of the water just made her broomstickier, hopping from foot to foot. The cold water was a shock to our systems. It made us momentarily euphoric. Our teeth practically fell out they were chattering so much, but it was really lovely. The Atlantic Ocean in March.

After the beach, we went to a Russian dumpling restaurant and met Aunt Rose, our dad's sister. We didn't even know we had an aunt. Mom had never mentioned her. She looked like Edie, if Edie had been left out to sour. It must have been strange for my sister to be surrounded suddenly by so many approximations of herself.

## EDITH (1997)

I'm sick of strangers acting as if they are continuing some sort of conversation with me, as if they'd just stepped into the other room for a minute as opposed to, you know, abandoning Mae and me completely for over a decade. With Dennis you'd think he'd tripped and fell into a time portal. *Oops. I forgot all about my daughters and made my wife go crazy. My bad.*

His sister is just like him. Looking at her face makes me want to die young.

"I didn't think I'd get to see you again," Rose says with a quavering voice. And, "You probably don't remember me," but she says it like she thinks we should.

When the waitress brings Dennis extra dumplings "on the house," Rose rolls her eyes but you can tell she takes some weird pleasure in her brother "having this effect on women." She keeps reaching over and picking food out of his beard. If he'd gotten a steak I bet she would've insisted on cutting it up into small pieces for him.

"You poor girls," she says after we finish the appetizers. She tries to take my hand, but I quickly move it onto my lap. "Your mother. What that woman put you through!"

Mae is sucking the salt water out of her hair, not saying anything.

"She's not the one who abandoned us," I say and glare at Dennis. He stares back at me.

"Your father did not abandon you." For a public defender Aunt Rose is not a very good liar. She blushes in the same blotchy, grotesque way that I do, and noticing this makes my ears burn.

I tell her: "Mae doesn't remember, so go ahead and tell her, but I was *there*, Rose. He never called or wrote. I waited for him for months."

"I'm sorry," he says. "You're right. I'm sorry. You can be mad at me as long as you need to be."

Like I need his permission.

Rose grabs his sleeve. "It's not right for them to think that." She turns to us. "Marianne drove him away. It's how she wanted it. Your mother—"

"Stop it!" Dennis slams his fist against the table hard enough to make the dishes rattle.

We're all silent. Rose takes a sip of her ice water, her eyes thick with tears.

Then Dennis says: "I did a horrible thing. I can only hope that eventually you'll forgive me." The words come out practiced, like he's been saying them every morning in front of the mirror for the last 12 years.

He is staring at me, waiting for my reaction, and when I don't give him one, he stands abruptly. Rose tries to stand too, but he pushes her back down into her chair. He goes outside to smoke a cigarette. We watch him in silence through the window. His back heaves, the smoke appears in a cloud over his shoulder like a thought bubble.

Rose dabs her eyes with a napkin. I finish the dumplings on Dennis's plate out of spite, shove them all violently in my mouth, try not to gag as they slide down my throat. The waitress is watching us. Mae gets up slowly and goes outside. Through the glass, I watch her comfort Dennis. She looks so gentle and serious.

"If you'd only seen what your mother put him through," Rose murmurs to me, but I don't take the bait. She gestures to the waitress for the check. "My poor Denny."

# ROSE

The first thing that struck me when I saw my nieces after all those years was how much Mae looked like her mother. It was uncanny. That pale skin, that long, thick black hair. Girls used to get burned at the stake for looking like that. My choice of words… all I meant was that Marianne *had* been a witch. A witch and a bitch. And in the end, even she didn't want to live with herself.

I remember Denny writing me to say he'd met the girl he was going to marry, but that he would have to wait a while. He fell in love with her instantly when she was a kid. Not in a perverted way, but he just knew. He waited for her to grow up and then he married her.

How sad that I had not been able to help those girls when they were little and living with Marianne. But Denny told me not to meddle. It was his life. What could I do? Especially after they moved back to New Orleans.

Stewart and I couldn't have children, and when the girls were born I thought of them as my own. I know it drove Marianne crazy, especially when the first one came out looking nothing like her. She said I was like one of those parasitic birds who hides her eggs in other birds' nests. It was a joke, sort of. But that's what her sense of humor was like. Not exactly "ha ha." Always an edge to it.

She would say Denny took advantage of her. She was 17 and her father had just died, and she was left all alone. A barefoot orphan. For God's sake, Denny saved her by marrying her. How is that taking advantage? He probably saved her life. He loved her since she was a child. It was very romantic.

Thirty-two and 17 seems like a big age difference, but it's only 15 years. And she was no innocent. He loved her more than anything. She broke him. She wore him down and broke him. Drove him out of their house. When he got off that plane I fell to my knees. What she did to him. There was no Denny in front of me, just broken pieces. His neck was so thin it could barely hold up his head. His skin was the color of a corpse's. Stewart and I nursed him back to health. Fed him, found him an apartment. But he couldn't write, and when we tried to introduce him to someone else, to get his mind off Marianne and the girls, it was no use. I don't mean to say there weren't other women. Sure. There were. Women loved him. How could they not? Talented, handsome, and now also damaged.

# Chapter 2

Dmitry Appasov
Detstvo Publishers
St. Petersburg, Russia

February 2, 1997

Dear Mr. Appasov,

I am a PhD candidate at the University of Wisconsin and I have a question that I was hoping you might be able to help me with. I am writing my dissertation on the work of the American writer Dennis Lomack. One of his books is a translation of Russian folk tales. There is one story in particular that fascinated me, but when I showed it to some colleagues in the Slavic Studies Department they did not think this particular variant sounded familiar. One of them suggested that I get in touch with you, as you are an expert in the field.

The story is about a raven-haired beauty living in a hut perched atop a set of chicken feet. She spends her days making tapestries out of flowers. Then, one day, a boy and a girl who got lost in the woods appear on her doorstep. These children cast a spell and turn the beautiful woman into a bald witch, a

*Baba Yaga*. She has no choice but to put the children in a cage and make soup out of them. Unlike the Baba Yagas of other stories, this one returns to her true, beautiful self after she eats the children.

If you could point me to the original story that was being translated, I would be extremely grateful. I have attached the text and included a carton of Marlboro cigarettes.

Sincerely,
Amanda Singer

# MAE

Dad would take us everywhere, even if he was only going downstairs to check the mail or to the post office up the street to buy stamps. He never left us alone at first. I would wake up sometimes and see him silhouetted in the doorway. I think he checked on us several times a night. Just being near him did something for me, and as long as he was there I almost didn't think about Mom, about the darkness that was in her and also in me, waiting. The only times I couldn't help thinking about her were in the moments right before falling asleep. There'd be the sensation of falling into her body, and then the hospital sounds—the other patients moaning, the stern voices of the nurses, the canned laughter from the television. But this lasted only a second, maybe two, and then was obliterated by sleep. I'd never slept so well in my life. After years of being woken up in the night by Mom, forced to go God knows where, it was a relief to wake up in the same room as my sister, to hear lip smacking and light snores coming from the bunk below. We'd never shared a room before, unless we were at Doreen's or at the Wassersteins'. I loved it.

Since we weren't going to school, Dad made a point of filling our days with an assortment of enriching activities. Once, we spent a whole afternoon riding back and forth on the Staten

Island ferry. Dad taught us a poem by Edna St. Vincent Millay: *We were very tired, we were very merry, we had gone back and forth all night upon the ferry.* The ferry didn't run all night. And I don't know that we were merry exactly, but joy found a way of squeezing through, even for Edie. Dad had bought us a netted sack of navel oranges and we peeled them and sucked on the slices as we floated by the Statue of Liberty, watching her green face change in the light. It's how immigrants must have felt, coming to Ellis Island. All that water around us like a baptism. Yes, it was a rebirth, the fresh start I'd been longing for.

And then, on our way home from the ferry terminal in Battery Park, we saw a cardboard box with a "Free Kittens" sign in front of it. When we opened the box though, there weren't any kittens; there was just one adult cat. We had assumed it was the mother, abandoned there after everyone had taken her kittens. White paws, white nose, white tail. Heartbreaking!

We were instantly attached to it. I could picture the cat slinking around in Dad's apartment, or spread across all our laps—it was that big. It would be the first thing that belonged to all three of us.

One of the women Dad was dating met up with us in the park. It was Rivka, an art curator from Prague who had dyed pink hair that was so garish it managed to make her ugly face somehow transcend itself. She was so strange to look at that it got confusing after a while, why it was you were staring at her—was it because she was ugly or because she was beautiful? It was extreme to the point that it basically looped around the spectrum and became its opposite.

Rivka insisted that Dad shouldn't let us touch the cat until it got its shots, so we brought the box to an animal hospital on 7th Avenue. The cat had not expected to be moved. It was difficult carrying a box for over a mile with a clawing and squirming cat inside of it. Edie and I nearly dropped it at several intersections. We told the vet the whole story of its discovery, and he lifted the cat's tail and told us there was no way this cat was the mother of those kittens. It was a male. Maybe all the kittens had been taken and he was a stray who just found the box? Though he was pretty fat for a stray. Maybe he had eaten all the kittens? We named him Cronus for the Greek god who ate all his children. We'd never been allowed to have a pet before. Mom had been allergic, or that is what she'd always said.

## CHARLIE

I met Edie for the first time the day they brought home the cat. I'd been living in my grandmother's rent-controlled apartment directly below Dennis Lomack, but I'd been too shy to introduce myself. As a teenager, I'd devoured his books. At 16, everything I knew about sex came from them. I'd read them in a frenzy until the pages stuck together. It's funny because I looked at *Yesterday's Bonfires* recently, and it wasn't even that smutty. What strikes me now about that book is its sense of freedom, in the broadest sense. Maybe this is what inspired me to become an adventurer, an urban explorer.

I usually take the stairs, but I didn't that evening because I saw Dennis Lomack and his daughters standing in the lobby, waiting for the elevator. The two girls were huddled over a cardboard box. What was in the box? It's in my nature to be curious about such things. And then Edie glanced up at me and she had this look and that was what gave me the nerve to finally introduce myself.

"I'm Charlie, your downstairs neighbor," I whispered, as I followed them into the elevator. And because they were looking at me strangely, I added: "I've lost my voice."

This was a lie. I had not actually lost my voice. I stutter and whispering is one of the few things I can do to hide this. I've whispered through job interviews. It's awkward but it works. It's how I'd landed my gig as a substitute teacher.

Before I got out, Edie lifted the cat up from the box and showed it to me with such pride. It was a beautiful cat, probably part Coon cat, judging from its size, and Edie was beautiful too, of course. That night I went out on a shoot with an NYU film guy I met online. I was giving him a tour of the decommissioned subway stations, but I was distracted and kept getting us lost. I couldn't get that image of Edie holding that cat out of my head.

## Rivka

Poor Dennis. He tried very hard with them. "We're a package deal," he said to me, a daughter on each arm.

Not for me. Not my kind of a package. I tried, but it did not work.

That is okay. For some time it was very nice. I had a gallery. I traveled. I was busy. I did not fear being alone, but sometimes I became lonely. Dennis was gentle and constant. He did not demand from me emotionally. This is a hard quality to find in a man. I kept an apartment key in the flowerpot and he would come by a few times a week to make love. But after his daughters arrived, it became too difficult and we made love only once. The daughters were in their room and I begged him to take me on the kitchen floor. I pulled him down onto the ground. He was distracted. I knew it was to be our last time.

## EDITH (1997)

Dennis is leaning on our windowsill, smoking a cigarette. The ugly Czech woman is in the living room, moving around, dropping things, making her presence known, but he doesn't seem to hear her. He's telling us about how he had tuberculosis as a boy, and how he almost died. After he got over the worst of it, he still had to stay in bed for a very long time. Running a low-grade fever for months, he discovered *The Count of Monte Cristo*. This is when he learned to love books.

I drift off, thinking about that cozy feeling, the warmth from a fever before it gets high enough to make you shiver. When I was eight and got the chicken pox, Mom never left my side. She read to me and fed me soup. I remember looking at her through my crusted-together eyelashes and thinking she was the most beautiful person I had ever seen. I recognize that look in Cronus now when he looks at me, purring and squinting.

Dennis puts his cigarette out and closes the window.

"Tell us more," Mae says.

"Okay," Dennis says. "What do you want me to tell you about?"

Since Mae is too scared, I ask: "Tell us about how you met Mom." On the rare occasions that Mom talked about this, I always felt like I was missing something important.

These were the facts as I knew them: Dennis had known Mom since she was a child, he married her when she was 17, and eventually, he left her. Left us. But why? And what had he done to her to make her the way she is? I want to hear him tell it.

"How I met her, or how I fell in love with her? Those are two different stories," he says.

They had loved each other? This hadn't even occurred to me. He sits on the edge of my mattress and I scoot back into the wall to balance his weight.

He closes his eyes. "I'll tell you how I met her. She was nine, I think. Nine or ten. I didn't know much about kids but I could tell that she was special, already a fully formed person. And so smart and kind and perceptive. And disarmingly sweet. Her father, Jackson McLean, was a friend of mine. What an amazing human being. He took me and my friends into his home and nursed us back to health after we'd been attacked and that's when I met your mother."

"Attacked how?" I have only a vague idea.

He tells us about how he joined the Freedom Rides to desegregate the interstate highways in the South. He'd gone with his friend Fred, who was black, and they'd driven together to Chicago from New York and boarded a Greyhound bus with the other members of the student group they'd been a part of. The first bus driver refused to take them, said he didn't need that kind of trouble. They eventually got another driver, but outside of Lafayette the bus was stopped by a white mob. Dennis and the other passengers were dragged off the bus and beaten, and the bus was set on fire. Remnants of the bus are in a museum now in Mississippi. Fred was beaten so badly he lost an eye. I mean, he lost the use of it. Dennis was beaten too. His front teeth were knocked out with a bicycle chain.

My grandfather had been a medic in the war. He scooped up Dennis and Fred and the others and took them to his house in the woods where he patched them up as best he could. Of course, this didn't make him popular with the neighbors. Mom was teased a lot at school. A boy held her down while some older girls cut her hair, all while the teacher watched and egged them on.

He describes her coming home with her hair hacked off and how she tried to pretend that she'd wanted the girls to do this to her, that it had been part of a game they'd all been playing. And then my grandfather had evened it out and Dennis gave her a big magnolia blossom to put behind her ear and told her that she looked beautiful, just like a silent-film star.

I'm waiting for Dennis to say something, some combination of words that will work like a spell, that will make what happened to our family make sense. But the more he talks the further away I feel from understanding anything.

"People were doing such horrible things, it was easy to feel like the world was a hopeless place. When Marianne was around though, even the angriest and saddest people felt a little less angry and a little less sad," he says.

The ugly woman in the other room puts on a record too loud then lowers the volume. It's a singer Mom plays sometimes. A woman who sounds like her throat is full of splinters.

"But Dennis…" I start. I want him to skip ahead, get to the part when they are in love.

"Please, call me Dad," he interrupts me. "Could you?"

For a moment I don't say anything. The song coming from the other room seeps in:

…*Why not take all of me, can't you see, I'm no good without you. Take my lips, I want to lose them, take my arms, I'll never use them…*

"No," I finally say, "I don't think I could." I feel Mae kick the mattress above me, like she's warning me, but I don't care.

"Okay," he says, standing up, "fair enough. I won't rush you." The mattress creaks as it releases him. The music playing in the other room stops.

"Goodnight, Dad," Mae says. I hear him kiss her goodnight,

a loud smacking sound. Then he squats next to me and looks for a moment intensely into my face, like he is trying to read my thoughts. It makes me shy and I look away.

"Goodnight, darling," he says, and squeezes my shoulder.

"Finally," I hear the woman in the living room say as Dennis shuts the door. Mae tosses angrily in the bed, making a lot of noise as she gets "comfortable."

*Dad*? No, I don't think so. Sorry, Mae, you can toss till you fall off the bed. I'm not calling him that.

# DENNIS LOMACK'S JOURNAL

[1961]

This morning Jackson McLean made us grits. A bunch of us have broken teeth, so grits are about all we can manage. Grits and milk.

The adrenaline is still pumping, which is why I don't feel the pain fully yet. Yesterday was as close to death as I have ever been. Max is at the hospital in a coma. Fred's eye is swollen shut and his arm is broken, but there are Citizens' Council thugs waiting around the black hospital, and the white hospital won't treat him. Jackson worked as a medic in the war, so he set Fred's arm himself. He used the plaster from his workshop to make a cast. Fred asked Jackson's daughter to draw something on it. She's shy, but she took out a paint set and is drawing what looks like a three-headed cat. She says that we're not to look until she's finished. She sticks her tongue out and breathes loudly through her nose when she's concentrating. I like watching her work because she's so absorbed in it, so serious. When I look at her I'm able to not think about last night. Or, at least to not think about it for long. Faces through the flames like jack-o-lanterns, and then I'm back in Jackson's kitchen where the curtains are drawn, and where his daughter is painting on Fred's broken arm, turning something horrible into something beautiful.

I will try to walk to the gas station this afternoon to call my sister. Jackson doesn't have a phone and his neighbors are not... sympathetic to our cause. That is how Jackson put it. He's careful not to badmouth his neighbors. They're no different than anywhere else, he says. I hope he's wrong.

Even with all the chaos in the house, Jackson still manages to escape into his studio and paint every day. What's my excuse for not writing? I try to keep notes, but I can't seem to make them come together into anything intelligible.

April 17, 1997

Dear Fred,

It was good to hear from you! It's been too long. We have quite a bit of catching up to do. Diane told me that you were made department chair. Congratulations! As for my giving a lecture this spring, it seems unlikely. Everything is on hold at the moment because my daughters have come to live with me. I believe when you met them Edie was in diapers and Mae was gestating. Well, despite my absence from their lives (or maybe because of it), they have turned out to be quite lovely almost-adults. You'll see for yourself—you'll be flying in for the *Freedom Fighters* book party, won't you?

As for your graduate student, things here are a little crazy, but tell her that I'm flattered and that she should feel free to get in touch. I'll try to be as helpful as I can. Not sure I can tell her anything very useful about my own work, but I'll do my best.

Keep On Keepin' On, Right?
Dennis

## EDITH (1997)

I'm standing on the threshold to Dennis's room. His door is ajar but it feels like an invisible velvet rope is holding me in the hallway.

He'd gotten a phone call (from some woman) and based on his responses full of false modesty, it appeared that she was flattering him. When he finally hung up, he told us he'd be right back. It's the first time he's left us alone since we got here, and it's true, when the front door closed behind him, I felt a surge of panic. *Gone again?* I didn't look at Mae. I didn't want her to see that I cared.

It's ridiculous. No, of course I don't care! I feel freer with him gone, without him following me around, watching my every move. I push open the door to his bedroom. I can imagine it recreated in a museum somewhere, on display next to that piece of burnt-out bus. "The Writer at Work." Look! His unmade bed, where he sleeps and dreams! An empty glass with a moldy lemon wedge! And that enormous desk with the typewriter! The very typewriter that he uses to type!

I put my finger on the letter *D*, watch the metal arm slowly rise and fall back down before it touches the blank page. I take a seat in his chair and roll myself forward.

*Dear Dennis,* I begin typing invisibly. *Did you ever think about me...*

I don't know why I'm doing this. I stand up and slam a few keys at random. The metal arms tangle together, catch in midair. Good. I leave them like that.

There's an ashtray on the windowsill. A cigarette burnt down to the filter. I touch it with my finger and the column of ash collapses into a pile. There's another cigarette in there, half-smoked. I pick it up and look at myself holding it in the window's reflection. I put the unlit cigarette to my lips and inhale. Sometimes, I'd wake up and find Mom sitting on the porch, smoking in the dark. I'd want to come sit by her but I knew better than to bother her. When you have a mom like our mom you develop an instinct for this sort of thing. Bother her too much and she'll leave.

"Where does Dennis keep the matches?" I call to Mae. Maybe in his desk?

One desk drawer is filled with used-up pens and paper clips. The other one is locked. I jiggle the handle, try to pry it open with a pen. It doesn't work. Then I take a paper clip and untwist it. I saw a girl at school do this one time, though I don't know how exactly. The paper clip jams in the lock.

"Mae, help me in here." Where is she anyway? I'd think she'd be curious.

"Mae," I start again, but then something clicks and the drawer slides open.

No matches. Papers. For a second I think: What if he's been writing to us this whole time, but never sending the letters, and they're all stacked here, neatly in this drawer? How dumb is that? Of course there are no letters. It's a manuscript. I start skimming it, but then put it back. Who cares what it says. I haven't read any of his novels, so why start now? I'm about to close the drawer, when something glossy catches my eye. A photograph. I pull it out from between the pages.

It's a picture of Mae from a few years ago. Black and white, not one I've ever seen before. She's looking at the person behind the camera with the kind of smile Mae only uses on special occasions. She's wearing a weird dress. It's plaid and has a round collar. I don't know where she would have gotten it. A thrift store? Was it from Halloween? No. No. I would've remembered it. And that fountain behind her, it doesn't look familiar either. Where was it taken?

The photo is bizarre. Totally bizarre. It's just like her to have this secret life. She would say that Mom took her places when I was sleeping but I never believed her. And how had Dennis gotten the picture? She must have sent it to him. So they had been in touch before we came here. For how long?

"Mae," I call, as I go into the living room, holding the evidence.

But Mae isn't in the living room. The front door is ajar and I can see Cronus standing in the empty hallway, paw lifted. He looks back at me and twitches his tail.

The first time I met Dennis Lomack was at a basement Italian place across the street from where I was staying. I was a PhD candidate at the University of Wisconsin in Madison, writing my dissertation on his work. My advisor was an old friend of Dennis's back from their Civil Rights days together, and he'd helped me arrange the meeting. I got there early and was so nervous that I drank two glasses of wine to calm myself down. Maybe it was the wine, or maybe it was the sense of familiarity I had with him because I knew his books so well, but I felt an instant connection.

Appearance-wise, Dennis was not what I'd expected. He was older than the pictures on his book jacket, and bigger. Not fat, but tall and broad shouldered. He had a beard. He was less handsome, but I think that was also what made him more attractive, more brutish. Next to him, Barry looked like a pencil neck wrapped in corduroy. Barry was the graduate student I was engaged to back home.

I remember the first thing I thought when I saw Dennis. After: *Holy shit, that's Dennis Lomack!* and *I hope my teeth aren't stained purple from the wine I've been swilling.* It was: *Barry and I are over. Done.* I'm sure that realization would have come on its own eventually, but seeing Dennis sped it up.

I'd prepared a long list of questions, but I didn't quite know where to start. I mentioned how I had been trying to track down the original of his Russian folk tale translations with no success. It's funny because as I was saying it out loud it finally occurred to me that there was no original source material. In retrospect, it seems pretty obvious. I asked Dennis Lomack about that and he shrugged and said that he might have taken some liberties. He asked me how I had gotten my hands on the book at all, seeing as it had come out with a tiny press with a tiny print run. I told him Prof. Fred Jones had been very generous with his personal archives.

I asked him if he had written the story when his ex-wife was pregnant with their first child. The date of the publication seemed to indicate this as a possibility. He took a sip of his drink and didn't say anything.

"Was the story prophetic?" I asked him.

"In what sense?" He put his hand down on the table close enough to mine so I could feel the heat off of it, but not quite touching. "Did my wife become a witch? Did she eat our children?" His voice was low, hypnotic; patient, but not. He was straining to keep things light.

"Did having your children change her? Did she love you less afterward? Did you want her to get rid of them to help her return to who she used to be? And did you say the story was a translation to avoid taking responsibility for your feelings? For these implications?"

I had no experience interviewing people. The whole thing was preposterous. I'd used up my entire summer stipend to fly to New York and stay in a by-the-week motel in Midtown, purely in the hopes that Dennis Lomack would meet with me. I'd tried to seem casual and told him I was visiting an aunt, but I had no aunt. I was only there to see him, and after begging my advisor to put in a good word, ten minutes into the meeting I managed to botch it all completely.

Dennis Lomack held the silence long enough for me to feel my missteps, but I think at that point my questions had crossed over from uncomfortable to so absurdly inappropriate that the equilibrium of power was again restored in his favor. He must have felt sorry for me.

"Fred didn't tell me your dissertation was on my ambivalence around having children," he said after a while.

My dissertation was about anachronistic temporalities across Lomack's novels and essays viewed through a Foucauldian lens. Or, that is what it was going to be about. I never finished it.

At that point in my life the thing that really interested me was exactly what I had been asking him about: How would having children change a person? Or more specifically, how would having children change *me*? I was two months pregnant and had not told Barry.

As we were leaving, I remember Dennis Lomack helped me into my jacket. My arm got momentarily stuck in the sleeve, and I remember standing with my back to him and feeling a rush of excitement at the thought that I was trapped and that I could feel what I imagined was his breath on the nape of my neck, like the scene in his book with Cassandra. When I turned around, though, he wasn't even facing me. He was turned away, looking up at something in the window.

## Mae

The first time Dad left us alone in the apartment, I followed him. I waited for him to get a block ahead like Mom had taught me. In those days, Mom was always with me whether I wanted her in my head or not. I could feel myself descending into a trance, and even though my body was on the street, following Dad, my mind was being trampled. She knew how to draw my attention to all the things that were ugly—a hypodermic needle, a man peeing, a woman talking to herself. She had me convinced that Dad was meeting with someone in order to discuss sending us away, even though I knew this wasn't the case. I was so relieved when Edie appeared by my side. Once she was there, my mother's grip on me loosened and I could pretend that my sister and I were running down Broadway on a fun adventure.

It turned out I was right to worry—Dad was meeting a woman, Amanda, who would eventually prove to be a very troublesome person. They met in a dank-looking Italian restaurant in the basement of an office building. Patrinelli's. It doesn't exist anymore. Edie and I kneeled by the ankle-level windows in the alley and watched them sitting at a table with a red-and-white-checkered tablecloth. We watched them slowly eat spaghetti in real time. There was no way for us to hear what they were saying, but it didn't look like Dad was all that engaged by the conversation. When he gestured to the waitress for the check, Edie and I ran back to the apartment, laughing as we ran.

## EDITH (1997)

Mae and I lean against each other, trying to catch our breath. Luis the doorman is asleep at his desk with a baseball game playing quietly on the transistor radio.

*...Nice-looking pitch right there, curve ball gets the inside corner, that's gonna even up the count...*

"We can ask Luis to let us in," I say between gasps. "We should have propped open the door." Luis doesn't stir at the sound of his name. I notice a man standing by the mailboxes, looking at a coupon booklet.

Mae shakes her head and jabs several times at the elevator button. "No, don't. He'll tell Dad that we went out," she says.

"So? We're free to go wherever we want. We aren't his prisoners," I say. The man is still staring at his coupon booklet. It must be the most interesting coupon booklet in the world. He's obviously eavesdropping.

"Excuse me," Mae calls to him. He looks up like he's been waiting for this invitation. I've seen him before. Something is strange about his face. No eyelashes. But as he comes closer I see that he does have them, they're just the same color as his hair, yellow-white. "You live here, right?" she asks him.

He nods. Oh God, Mae. What is she about to do?

"I-i-i-i-in…" he stops and clears his throat. "In the apartment under yours," he says through his cough. "We met the other day. Charlie." He shakes her hand as he coughs into his other elbow.

"Can we climb through your window to get to the fire escape?" Mae asks. The elevator doors creak open before I have a chance to contradict her or laugh it off. He's going to think we're freaks, not that Spooks has ever cared about that. Standing up for her in school was a full-time job.

An old woman limps out of the elevator with a balding Pomeranian. We stop talking and wait for her to pass. She moves between us slowly like a barge, eyes straight ahead.

"Sh-sh-sh-sh-sure," Charlie says after the woman has gone, and follows us into the elevator. I'm embarrassed that we've invited ourselves over to his house. I stare down at the floor. Charlie's shoes are the strangest things I've seen—a wetsuit type of material with each toe separated out. Like gloves for his feet.

"We locked ourselves out," Mae explains.

"Of course, it h-happens," he says. He pauses between his words, like he's swallowing air.

His apartment is the same layout as ours but feels smaller. All of the furniture has been pushed to one end of the living room and stacked to the ceiling—wooden tables with doilies, ceramic lamps, a plaid couch, a rolled-up rug. It's darker too, because cardboard boxes are blocking one of the windows. It smells like cigarettes, B.O., peppermint, and something else.

"Did you just move in here?" Mae asks, eyeing his boxes.

He nods. "A few months ago. My grandma used to l-l-live here."

A telescope is set up by the living room window. I stop and look through it. The lights are off in the apartment across the street.

"There's too m-m-m-much light pollution to see any stars," he says and playfully taps the telescope so it swings out of position. I'm not sure if it had been aimed at that apartment on purpose or not. "Can I get you guys s-s-s-s-s…" He stops, swallows, tries again. "Water?"

"No, thanks," Mae says. She's in a hurry.

"Sure," I say.

He fills a mug for me from the tap. The door to the room that's under Dennis's bedroom is ajar. The ground is covered in sawdust. That's what the other smell is—sap.

"That's my wood shop," he says, handing me the water and pushing the door open all the way. Piles of 2x4s and plywood boards. A table saw. "If you ev-v-v-er want to build anything."

What could I possibly want to build?

Mae tugs me towards Charlie's bedroom, the room directly below ours. It's empty except for a sleeping bag on the floor, a stack of books, a box of tissues, an ashtray, and an Altoids box. I wonder why he doesn't build himself a bed.

Mae pushes the window up and crawls out onto the fire escape.

"Come on," she hisses at me. I'm looking at the books. One of them is by Dennis—*Cassandra's Calling*. "Hurry up."

"Thank you," I say to Charlie. I pass him back the empty glass and crawl out his window.

Through the fire escape steps I can see his face looking up at us. It's an interesting face. He's definitely a weirdo, but that's not necessarily bad.

"Help me," Mae says. She's trying to pry our window open. I squeeze my fingers into the crack under the frame and push.

"Go in a little, and then up," I tell her. The window loosens and creaks as we finally get it open from the outside.

I scrape my leg on the sill as we crawl back in. It stings. I limp into the living room where Mae is already sitting on the couch, pretending like this is where she's been all night. I sit next to her and we both pant quietly, ready for the sound of the key in the door. A few minutes go by and nothing. I've caught my breath. Maybe Dennis isn't coming straight home. Maybe he's going to that woman's house.

"What'd you think of our neighbor?" I ask.

Mae shrugs, eyes still on the front door. "He seemed fine."

I drape my injured leg over her lap and inspect the tiny beads of blood already beginning to clot along the surface of the scrape.

"Fine or fiiiiiine?"

"Ew," Mae says, ignoring the question. "Stop picking at it."

"But I've been in-jured on the job," I drawl, lifting my shin towards her face. "How'm I gonna find a law-yer to get me the settlement that I de-serve?" Personal Injury Law Call and Response. A game we started when we had to live with the Wassersteins, since those ads played on endless loop in their living room.

Mae pulls the scarf off my neck and ties it around my leg like a tourniquet. "Why, it's just as easy as picking up the phone!" she says dutifully, and then whistles the jingle.

"Do it in a bow," I say, pointing my toes.

"You're ridiculous," she says but ties the ends in a bow.

"What do you think the Wassersteins are doing at this very moment?"

"Choking on a hotdog," Mae says.

"Just one?" I snort, picturing the two of them gagging on opposite ends of the same hotdog like Lady and the Tramp.

Cronus emerges from Dennis's room and stretches.

"Was that open before?" Mae points past our cat to Dennis's door.

"Oh, right," I say. The photo. I fish it out from my back pocket, and smooth it against my thigh. Looking at it now with Mae beside me, I feel very stupid for having thought it was her.

Of course it's not Mae. It's Mom. Obviously it's Mom. I've just never seen any pictures of Mom from when she was Mae's age, and they do look exactly alike.

"What is that?" Mae says.

I pass her the picture.

"Where'd you find this?" she asks.

"In his desk."

She stares at it. "I think I saw him looking at it the other day. He must think about her still," she says finally and makes me put it back exactly where I found it.

Then I join her again on the couch and we wait.

## LETTER FROM
## MARIANNE LOUISE MCLEAN TO DENNIS LOMACK

June 14, 1962

Dear Mr. Dennis,

Daddy says, long hair or no long hair, it's impolite to call you Dennis. So, now I will call you Mr. Dennis. I went up to the lake yesterday with Cynthia and her little brother and I saw the burial mounds! I told her what you said about the Indian bones inside and her little brother Gus, who is a pain-and-a-half, heard and started to try to dig them up with his hands. He thinks he found an arrowhead but I think it was just a sharp rock. He kept sneaking up on us and poking the back of our necks with it and telling us we were cursed. Then he got stung by a bee, so I guess he got what was coming.

Then we saw girls from our school and they didn't talk to us, but Cynthia's mom said we just had to keep our chins up, and that we were on the right side of history, and that when those girls grew up they would be deeply ashamed of what their parents had done to our daddies. Then Cynthia's mom gave us chicken grease sandwiches and I ate mine and pretended to like it. I think Cynthia was embarrassed. Daddy says you are coming back in September to help register people to vote.

I miss you! I miss going on our walks and your stories and having you and all your friends on our living room floor. It was like a slumber party and there was always someone to talk to. The house is so empty now and Daddy just paces back and forth. Here is the photo of me you took with Daddy's camera.

Don't forget me!
Marianne Louise

# *Chapter 3*

[1997]

my dear daughters,

please ignore my previous letter. a familiar itch behind the eyeballs, words not my own.

can you even read this? it's the medicine that makes my hands shake. please do not be alarmed. tremors & earthquakes in my hands & feet & face. they'll keep deforming me until there's nothing left to deform.

every morning, they put me in an ice bath up to my neck. i have never been so cold. a nurse, sadistic bitch, sits & watches my teeth chatter. i've developed a nasty cough, pneumonia? but they say some of the fog has lifted. i am writing you girls a letter, after all. my two lovelies. my ribbit & rabbit.

i forgive you & try not to think about you. i'm ashamed, of course. i want to keep you, even thoughts of you, away from this place. the suffering is in the walls, in the floor, under the tables.

it's mixed into the paint. it smells like shit & fear. it gets into your nostrils & then it's too late because it's in you. my neighbor can't stop crying (can't or won't?). i have only recently begun to distinguish between awake & asleep. i've started writing again. words repeat in my head, the only way to flush them out is to write them down. poems. your father is no saint, but he is a lot of things.

i love you, it's a bell in the fog, the only thing that still exists.

be brave,
mom

## EDITH (1997)

What have they done to her in there? What did I let them do? The paramedics and the police. I should have lied, but I was so stunned. I told them what happened, and then they twisted it.

The man with the gun holsters, pouring me an orange soda into a Styrofoam cup. He was younger than the detectives on television shows, practically my age, wispy mustache. He asked me question after question and stupidly I told him everything, and he rubbed my shoulders and wiped the orange from my mouth with a napkin. Why hadn't I kept quiet?

I put her in there. She thinks so too. Why else would she need to forgive me? And now they're torturing her because of what I said. Between the ice baths and the pills they're giving her, it's a miracle she can write at all. Her handwriting was always so small, neat, round. She would press down hard enough that it was almost an engraving. You could run your fingers over the paper and feel the words.

Here, though, her handwriting looks like a ghost sneezed. There is nothing in the way it looks that is hers. It could have been written by someone else. Her sobbing neighbor. Some fat slob in a turban. It makes me feel better to think it was somebody else's hand shaking over the paper, that Mom was just dictating.

I read the letter again, a third time, a fourth time. I start to hear the words and not see them. *my two lovelies. my ribbit and rabbit.* That sounds like her. The sound of her voice in my head calms me—*bell in the fog*—even though the things she is saying— *tremors… deforming me*—are not very calming. I get to the beginning of the letter again, and stop. *please ignore my previous letter.*

"Where's the other letter?" I ask Dennis. I never saw it. He must have hidden it from us.

Dennis doesn't answer me. He's busy reading over our shoulders. He's squinting because he's too vain to get glasses. Has he gotten to the part about him yet? *No saint.* If he has, he gives no indication of it. I don't know what she means when she says *he's a lot of things.* I assume it's bad?

"What did you do with the other letter?" I ask him again.

"What letter?" he says, looking down at me with his wet lamb eyes.

Is he lying? Where did he put it?

"She said she sent another letter. You can't hide things like that from us." I feel the blood rushing into my face. "It's not right."

"I'm not hiding anything! You're with me all the time. You see me get the mail." This is true, but it's not like we pay attention to it. He could easily have hidden it in a magazine, read it later in his room.

"She probably never even wrote it," Mae says slowly. "She probably just thought she did, or dreamed she did and got confused." That's Mae—she'll take any opportunity to make Mom look foolish. It's disgusting.

"Or, maybe the doctors held on to it," Dennis says. "They monitor her correspondence."

I imagine a doctor unfolding and reading my mother's letter, and then folding it back and putting it in a manila folder in her file, evidence against her, words she said to us in anger that will now be used to keep her locked up.

"I think you're lying." The chair falls backwards as I stand, bangs against the tile on the kitchen floor. Mae puts her hand on mine, but I shake it off. That little know-it-all traitor. No, thank you. She probably knew about the letter all along. Dennis must have showed it to her, and she told him it would upset me too much to see it. Well, I'll find it.

"Edie, what are you doing? Please don't touch my desk. Edith!" Dennis follows me into his room. He crouches, gathering the papers I threw on the floor.

"Enough," he says as I try to swipe at a stack of papers on his bedside table. I open the book he's been reading and shake it out. A bookmark flutters to the ground, nothing else. "Edith, that's enough." He holds me by the back of my shirt, but I leap forward like I'm on a leash. I'm looking at the windowsill. That's where he probably sat, reading it. Smoking, reading, crying.

"Why is there so much ash in the ashtray?" I say.

He burned it, lit the tip with a match and watched the words melt.

"Edie, stop," Mae's voice is quiet. She's embarrassed. I look at her face. No, she's not embarrassed, she's scared. Of me. I place the ashtray back on the windowsill, careful not to spill any of it.

## MAE

I was the one who threw out the first letter from Mom. I could hear the whistle of it hurtling towards us, so I intercepted it. This was difficult since I was almost never alone, but desperation makes you crafty. The envelope felt heavy and hot to the touch and it contained ten illegible pages, each word a barbed hook. I skimmed it, careful not to let any of the words catch in me, before I tore it up and flushed it down the toilet. I didn't want Edie getting any more agitated about Mom than she already was. I wouldn't say I wanted Mom dead, I'm not a monster, but I wanted her vacuum-sealed somewhere where she couldn't get to us. In New York I was happy. Happy and safe from her, I thought.

I failed to intercept the second letter. It arrived—narcissistic, well wrought, barely legible, and full of those elliptical riddles that get under your skin and tug. Edie became obsessed, analyzing it to death: What did it signify that nothing was capitalized? Mom's low sense of self-worth? Her aversion to order? Her artistic temperament? Was she a frustrated creative person with no outlet for her artistic energies? Was this the true source of her unhappiness? Would poetry prove to be her salvation? I let

Edie talk and talk about it. I didn't contradict her, even though I knew that none of what she was saying was true or relevant. She did not understand Mom at all.

The third letter came a few days after that. Edie was already wound up, and she pored over the new one like a cryptologist. It wasn't really a letter. There was no "Dear" or "Love." It was a poem. How coy of Mom, how opaque to communicate with us in this way, to demand that we guess what it was she was trying to say, like she was Sylvia fucking Plath.

"What do you think it means? What do you think it means?" Edie kept saying, standing too close and watching me as I read it.

The poem was gibberish, the unpunctuated words together unpleasant sounds, repeated, oppressive. *goatman's goatpelt fur mouth spackle choke grind down water in the throat ears choke.* But reading it filled my mouth with the fetid taste of lake water. It made me think of those night trips when Mom would disappear into Lake Pontchartrain and I would nervously pace the shore, waiting for her head to break the surface. I was dry and on land, getting devoured by mosquitoes, but I could only feel the algae squishing under my feet, the black water burning in my nose. Once Mom emerged from the water with an enormous catfish latched onto her arm. On the drive home the fish flapped and struggled in the backseat while Mom laughed so hard I had to steer. She was laughing, but what does that mean? It wasn't an expression of joy. It was just a sound, like something in her was trying to get out.

"What?" Edie said. "What?" She sensed that I had been able to decode it in some way.

It was clear to me the poem was a suicide note. It might as well have been an acrostic that spelled out: GOODBYE! FOREVER!

How selfish, how grotesque. Why pull us into all that again? We were children. And the text, the handwriting, jerky and weak, it forced me to imagine her in the act of writing, which I also resented. I did not want to imagine her at all, because if I allowed her in, I felt like I would lose myself again. It was better to take this rare opportunity that forced her off of me and leave it that way.

I never told Edie what the poem really meant. I think I made up an interpretation involving mythology and even tried to convince myself of it. But I couldn't get the images out of my head of Mom floating face down: in a lake, in a bathtub, in the neighbor's pool. I remember hugging Cronus at night and burrowing my face in his fur, letting his purring replace the static that her words had left in my head.

## Phone Conversation
## Between Edith and Doreen

**EDITH**: Doreen.

**DOREEN**: Yes, Edie baby.

**EDITH**: I need to go home.

**DOREEN**: Go home? Your momma's not up for that.

**EDITH**: Can't I stay with you?

**DOREEN**: No, baby. I have a lot on my plate right now. My brother's sick and he's staying with me. I couldn't be responsible for another human being.

**EDITH**: Doreen! I'm 16. You wouldn't have to be responsible for anything...

**DOREEN**: Did you call me just to cry on the telephone?

**EDITH**: Yes.

**DOREEN**: How's your sister?

**EDITH**: She likes it here. She's very *adaptable*.

**DOREEN**: Well, shit, honey. You don't adapt, you die. Why do you say it like it's a bad thing? You don't adapt, you die.

**EDITH**: ...

**DOREEN**: I'm not going to talk to you if you keep sniffling.

**EDITH**: Don't hang up!

**DOREEN**: I'm not hanging up, Edith. God damn.

**EDITH**: Have you gone to visit her?

**DOREEN**: I went yesterday.

**EDITH**: How was she?

**DOREEN**: Not great, Edie baby. Not great. It's hard to understand what she's talking about.

**EDITH**: Did she ask about me?

**DOREEN**: Sure, honey. Sure, she did.

**EDITH**: What did she ask?

**DOREEN**: Oh, you know, how you were doing. I told her you were doing great.

**EDITH**: We're not doing great. That's not true.

**DOREEN**: Edie, sweetheart, I'm tired. My brother kept me up all night, moaning. He's in a lot of pain. I can't keep talking in circles.

**EDITH**: She sent us a letter and a poem.

**DOREEN**: Well, that's good.

**EDITH**: Did she say anything else about me?

**DOREEN**: She said thank you for that fuzzy bathrobe you sent her. She was wearing it. I could tell she liked it.

**EDITH**: She wrote in the letter that the doctors are torturing her.

**DOREEN**: That's nonsense. You know that's nonsense.

**EDITH**: She said they're overmedicating and deforming her.

**DOREEN**: You gotta let her get better. You gotta let the doctors do their work. I have to go now, baby. Give Mae a kiss for me, will you?

**EDITH**: Yeah, okay. Tell Tyrell I said hi.

**DOREEN**: He's with his daddy, but I will when he comes back. Bye, baby.

Marianne left you with her messes. Most people walked away, but once in a while she'd find a fool, a fool like myself, who couldn't. I've known her since she was in diapers. My momma worked for her daddy, Jackson McLean. Everyone liked Jackson. After his wife died he hired my momma to help him around the house.

When I was little, my momma spent so much time over there, taking care of Marianne that, it's true, I got jealous. I had five younger brothers and sisters, and my momma was wasting all her love and affection on a white girl across town. She'd come home tired and lie down. People only have so much to give and Marianne was taking it all. My friends in school, their parents worked for white people and none of them got invested the same way my momma did. I wondered if she was in love with Jackson, and I know my daddy wondered too. Sometimes I'd hear them fighting about it at night.

Because I was the oldest, I was responsible for my brothers and sisters. I made them food when they got home from school. I sewed their clothes when they ripped them climbing fences or being wild. My momma would bring Marianne over sometimes and make me play with her and that was one more chore on my list. My momma never said it, but I was expected to treat Marianne like a little princess. We did eventually become close, just because we were similar ages and spent so much time together. We'd pick blackberries that grew wild in the bushes along the railroad tracks and my momma taught us both how to can them and make jam.

Marianne wasn't handy and she had no common sense, but she was good at making up stories. She'd even convince herself that what she was telling you was true and eventually you'd start believing it too. The swamps would become fairy castles and witches' lairs, that kind of shit. As I got older, though, her imagination started to bug me. I could never afford to be strange because I had people depending on me. Being weird is a luxury. I was embarrassed to be seen with her. She'd trail after me and my friends, floating, round-eyed, walking on her toes. It drove me crazy the way she would walk, her heels never hitting the ground. The girl could hardly make herself a sandwich. I finally got into a big fight with my momma about it.

I was my high school valedictorian and I already knew what I wanted from life. I was going to go to college and become a nurse, move out to a big city and make something of myself. I told my momma that I didn't need spacey Marianne, like a weight around my neck, dragging me down during my last summer at home. Oh, my momma got mad. She never usually laid a hand on me but that time she slapped me with the comb she was using on her hair. Here we were, all of us fighting for civil rights, and this girl was my responsibility? How do you figure? How is that fair? My momma felt we owed something to Jackson. But I think she would not have gotten so angry with me if she hadn't seen my point.

For years I didn't hear from Marianne. Both of us left town, got married, had kids. For a while the world had seemed big and anything was possible. I did what I had hoped I'd do: I moved to Atlanta, went to college on a full scholarship, and became a nurse. Then my momma got sick, and I had to move back home to take care of her. She passed away, my husband left me for someone else, and I stayed on here. Marianne had moved back too and I still felt responsible for her. Her weirdness got darker. She wasn't happy with her husband. They'd fight and fight, loud enough for everyone to hear. I'd run into him at the store, buying paper plates because she'd broken all their regular ones. Eventually he left after she put herself in a coma with pills. Her daughters stayed with me while she was at the hospital and he moved out.

God, she was so selfish.

She'd say, "You don't understand, Dor, it's hell."

Right? 'Cause that ignorant little bitch was the only one who'd ever felt pain.

And I'd say, "Marianne, choose the hell you know over the one you don't, because it can always get worse." It's what my daddy used to say.

She didn't believe in that, though. She'd say the only hell that existed was the one she was living in.

Her husband left and things got better and then worse again. She put me in charge in case anything happened to her, gave me power of attorney. But I had enough of my own problems, shit: a divorce, a teenage son who wouldn't talk to me, a little brother dying in my living room. When she tried to hang herself I did what I could. I kept her out of the state hospital, got her a bed in St. Vincent's, made sure she had good doctors. It's an expensive place, but I got her ex-husband to pay for most of it and I rented out her house to help pay the rest.

## EDITH (1997)

It pricks a little where the water is hitting me, but my skin has mostly gone numb. I am with you. Your eyes are the only things sticking out above the icy water. You are an iceberg. I am an iceberg. We are across the country from each other but our teeth chatter in unison—

"Edie, I really have to pee." Mae is banging on the door.

I turn the water off and wait. I count to five, shivering. My fingers are numb. They don't give her the towel right away, I'm sure. The nurses make her wait, those sadistic bitches. They make her shiver like this.

"Edie, come on."

I pull the green towel off the hook and wrap myself in it before unlocking the door.

Mae pushes past me to the toilet and starts peeing as soon as she sits down.

"Your lips are blue," she says.

They are. Like I just ate a blue Popsicle. I stretch my lips out over my teeth and look at myself in the medicine cabinet mirror.

"You look like someone just thawed you out of a glacier," Mae says as she wipes and flushes. I move aside and let her wash her hands.

"Jesus." She touches my arm.

I shrug her hand off. I don't need to get into it with her.

"Edie, what are you doing? Stop torturing yourself."

Why should I? Saints whipped their backs raw then wore shirts made of thorns to punish themselves. Cold water is nothing. Cold water is pathetic. But I don't say this because Mae doesn't like other people's feelings. Whenever Mom would get upset you could just see it in Mae's face, her shutting down. And that's the last thing I need. Better to be calm, to move slow, then she'll come back with me.

"Don't be stupid, Spooks. We ran out of hot water," I lie, then clench my jaw to keep my teeth from chattering.

## MAE

Anybody who's read Dad's novels could feel the intensity of his obsession with my mother. Obsession like that never really goes away, not when it's connected to one's fundamental sense of self. He never said anything about Mom's letters, but I'm sure he heard her whistle as loudly as Edie and I did, that piercing sound that made Edie come running and made me dig in my heels. How did her letters have this power over us? I don't know. The desperation was in the negative space of everything she wrote.

Before that spring, I'd never read any of Dad's books. It had never even occurred to me to track them down at a library or bookstore because until we came to live with him, he hadn't existed for me. But in New York, I started reading his books ravenously. I devoured *Cassandra's Calling*. I read his novels before bed. I wanted to have the rhythms of the sentences inside of me, so that I could dream about them. In my sleep though, all the characters were Mom. Sometimes Mom would turn into a strong wind and pull me somewhere, or sometimes she would jump on my back and try to wrestle me down to the ground. I barely ever saw her face. Sometimes—and these dreams were always the scariest—I *myself* would turn into Mom, and then I would be on someone else's back, or turning into a wind.

## Edith (1997)

Mae's lamp casts large shadows on the wall as she reads in bed. Her fingers rustle the pages of her book. Cronus is lying on my feet, keeping them warm.

"Do you think she's gonna stay here long?" I ask Mae. The woman from the basement restaurant is sleeping on the couch. She appeared in our lobby this afternoon, looking like a mess. A hospital bracelet on her wrist. That bracelet is the only thing she and Mom have in common but that seems to be enough for Dennis.

Mae doesn't respond.

"It's like what Mom said about him. He likes his birds with their wings broken," I say.

Mae isn't listening. She's absorbed in whatever it is she's reading.

"Kind of like you," I say to Cronus and he squints back. "You also like your birds with their wings broken. Don't you?"

Mae's breathing has gotten too quiet. She must have gotten to a juicy part.

"Read it to me," I say. She's holding her breath.

Mae turns the page and doesn't say anything. I reach my hand up to the coiled spring above and nudge her.

"Stop," she says. I watch her shadow on the wall as she sets down the book. "I don't think you'll like it. It's kind of…"

"I just want to hear your voice."

Nothing. I hit the bed again.

"Fine." She clears her throat, clears it again: "*At first she was like a blind kitten in bed. Just hopeless and rooting, always rooting for my,*" her voice flutters, "*penis, trying to put it in her mouth. She would practically sleep with it there. Or in her hand. It was like it formed a circuit, a closed circuit, our bodies…*" She trails off.

Something squirms through me and a weird giggle escapes. I'm thinking about Markus, and the way my throat would go numb when he came in my mouth, and then the footsteps in the stone chapel, or the footsteps on the carpeted stairs to the attic. Afterwards was always full of other people's footsteps.

"Can I see it?" I ask her.

She lies there, silent, too still. Why? Suddenly, I realize what she's been reading to me. My face goes hot. Disgusting. And that she hadn't warned me first. Let me lie there thinking about it, thinking about Markus and not saying that it was some disgusting thing Dennis had written about Mom.

Mae hangs over the edge of the bed and looks at me. Her eyes are in shadow, her hair a curtain. Upside down, in the dark, her face could be someone else's.

"Do you think that was about Mom?" she asks. That little pervert. "There were details that made it seem…"

Mae's big white forehead is inches from my face. I feel the snap of my knuckle, the thwack of my nail against her skull. She shrieks and nearly falls off the bed.

Mom like a fucking kitten, rooting around for the turkey neck in Dennis's disgusting pants. I feel nauseous. Mom in a white nightgown like a fucking kitten. Mom, Mae's age, writhing around like a fish on a hook, a big white fish, a ghost, her mouth and throat numb.

"It could be about anyone," I finally say.

Mae doesn't respond. She's not talking to me anymore. When I try to join her on the top bunk, she sticks her leg out to block me. There is a bump on her forehead, a red welt, it must be where I flicked her. I reach for it, but she bats me away.

"I'm sorry." I really am. Below us, the sound of a saw. Our downstairs neighbor Charlie must be building something.

"Mae, I'm sorry." I say it again, even though she won't look up from the book.

## AMANDA

I decided to get the abortion while I was in New York. I'd been waffling and my time was running out. I was worried that if I waited to do it until I got home it would be too late, or that Barry would somehow talk me out of it. I didn't have anyone in the city to pick me up from the clinic, so I looked up Dennis's address in the phone book and took a cab there after the procedure. I sensed that he wouldn't turn me away and that it might even be my "in." And it was. He very generously offered to let me stay on his couch and recuperate. It was an unpleasant procedure, but it was in no way earth-shattering.

I remember how completely surreal it felt, following Dennis Lomack and his daughters into his apartment, and then standing there surrounded by his things, feeling a little crampy and woozy from having lost so much blood and from the residual effects of the anesthetics. I remember standing in his bathroom, staring at the hairs in his hairbrush and the dirty Q-tips in the wastebasket and thinking that I'd made it into the reliquary.

All the details from my arrival at Dennis's house still exist for me in a magnified Technicolor brightness. That first night he made a lentil mash, which surprised me initially, but after thinking about it more it made sense. Indian food, of course! That's exactly what he *would* make. There were lots of moments like that. I had sat around in my basement cubicle at UW, day-dreaming about all of these little things. How does Dennis take his coffee? (with cream, no sugar); How does he hold his mug? (the usual way, I suppose, no stray pinkies); How does he sit? (legs crossed, sometimes); How does he walk? (not lumbering, for his size), etc.

His daughters felt like characters that belonged in the world of his books. They were not friendly toward me, which was fine. It felt more authentic that way. It was flattering, their perception of me as a threat. That night after dinner, his younger daughter sat on his lap, and the cat sat on her lap, and I remember thinking that they looked like a totem pole of familial bliss. And even the older one, Edith, wasn't arguing with anyone and they all seemed to get along quite well.

Edith was so headstrong. You could imagine her caught in a rainstorm, or leading oxen across a forded river. I would have cast her in a movie about pioneers. You know, stubborn, full of principles, but still delicate somehow.

I spent the next day recovering on his couch, making an inventory of his bookshelves. So these were his influences: All the Russians. And a lot of Germans. It was no longer empty speculation and lit-crit fiddle-farting, I had access.

That night after the girls had gone to bed, I followed Dennis Lomack into his room. He looked surprised, but he didn't kick me out. I touched every object on his desk while he got undressed.

"Well?" he said, after he had gotten under the covers and turned off the light, and I had continued to stand there in the dark, wondering if all of it was real.

"Well?" he'd said. Just like that. "Well?"

How many people can say that the heartthrob in the poster came to life for them? Because that is what it felt like: Mick Jagger stepping out into my childhood bedroom.

May 4, 1968

Dear Mr. Dennis,

I hung up the postcard you sent by my bed. I like to lie awake, tracing the outline of the skyscrapers with my finger and imagining you—tiny, walking through that city. All those little glowing windows have people living behind them. It's hard to believe. Maybe one day I'll visit you there?

How is the book you're writing? Did you start it yet? Am I in it? Name a character Cassandra. Or put in a secret message. Like maybe on page 32 have one of the characters eat an apple, and then I'll know that you were thinking about me when you wrote it.

It's been such a long time since we've seen you. I miss you! And so does Daddy. He hasn't been well. Ann told you about the trial? It's set to start soon, and though he tells me it's all nonsense, I know he worries. Mrs. Williams has been helping me take care of him. This last week Daddy has barely gotten out of bed but of course he refuses to see a doctor. School has been okay. Pointless but fine. Nobody talks to me. My only friend,

Cynthia (remember you took us waterskiing? She had a huge crush on you, which I'm sure you knew), she had to move back to Illinois because her daddy had a breakdown.

Something strange happened to me the other day, when I was walking back from Mrs. Williams' house. Maybe you could use it in your book? I keep thinking about it, but I'm not sure why. I guess because it scared me. It was last Thursday night when everyone was in town, watching the parades. I didn't go this year. Daddy wasn't feeling up to it. Anyway, I was walking alone in the dark on the dirt road behind the Hillhurst farm, the shortcut from our house to the river. Well, I was walking when suddenly I heard someone breathing, right by my shoulder. I could feel it on my neck. I was so scared I couldn't even scream. I opened my mouth but no sound came out. I turned around to see who it was, but there was no one there. I told Doreen and she said I was being stupid, that the sound probably bounced off the trees and created an illusion. It was my own breath I was hearing, or maybe the breath of a horse in the pasture, and it only sounded close. Maybe she's right, but that's not how it felt. Ever since then I've felt different, like I've been marked. I worry about Daddy a lot. Maybe you could hitch a ride down here soon? I know he wants to see you and I do too.

Yours,
M

## Edith (1997)

We're on a bus with Dennis and Amanda, somewhere in the depths of Queens. The buildings are squat and the signs are in Chinese. Everything looks flat and gray. Dennis hasn't told us where we're going. He says it's a surprise. Amanda wouldn't stop asking me questions, so I moved to the back of the bus, squeezed myself between a sleeping guy in a puffy jacket and a fat lady knitting.

*What kind of books did your father read to you when you were little? What pet names did he use for you?* Was she for real? And he wasn't doing anything to stop her, just looking out the window like we weren't there, like he wasn't the one dragging *us* out into the middle of nowhere. When I told Amanda to fuck off it only seemed to make her more cheerful. I tried to get backup from Mae but things between us have been weird. All she does is lie around reading Dennis's books.

The guy next to me, his head rolls onto my shoulder with the movement of the bus, then rolls back to his chest. What if I stayed on the bus with him? Begged him to take me home? Maybe I could sleep on his couch? Or what about our downstairs neighbor, Charlie? Maybe I could use his woodshop to build my own place. Something portable.

I can see Amanda across the bus, still talking.

*Had* Dennis read to me when I was little? I seem to remember something with pictures of a tiger. What difference does it make, though? And how is it any of her business? I caught her the other day trying to read one of Mom's letters over my shoulder. Good luck with that, Amanda. Even I couldn't decipher it. Mom's hand is now a seismograph. Soon she won't even be able to hold a pencil. The only part that was legible was Mae's name. Of course.

They stand at the next stop and Dennis gestures for me to follow. I bid a silent goodbye to the sleeping man, to the life we could've had together. Outside, the sky is low and the air feels strange and thick, ready for lightning. Mae has dark circles under her eyes and a tiny bruise on her forehead. From me. I watch her smile at Dennis, and it reminds me of the photograph I found. The photograph of Mom.

The thick air is making my heart beat faster. Amanda is talking, but I tune her out. Something is about to happen. Any moment now. But nothing does. We just keep walking. The buildings around us get uglier and more decrepit. No more brick, only vinyl siding. A moving truck idles across the street. All the furniture is out on the sidewalk. I see Mae notice it. I wonder if she's thinking of Inside/Outside too—a treat Mom would do for us sometimes, where, in a burst of super-human strength, she would drag all the living room furniture onto the lawn and then the three of us would sit on the velvet couch, feet on the coffee table, and look up at the sky through the branches of the oak tree.

"Remember…" I start to say but change my mind. Amanda is too eager for any scraps, and I don't trust Mae not to ruin the nice memory. That's exactly the kind of thing she's in the mood to do. I can tell by the way she's pressing her lips together. She'll find some way to take the three of us, curled up, looking at the stars, and turn it into additional proof of Mom's failures.

We get to a hill with a park entrance, a bronze plaque that

none of us bother to read. Amanda is giddy. She's not walking, she's skipping, despite having been laid up on our couch for the last few days. There's a patch of trees, a dirt path that snakes away from the road. Splintery green benches, cigarette butts, and beer cans. I kick a can towards Mae and she doesn't kick it back, doesn't even notice. When the trail makes a sharp right, Dennis stands to block our view of what lies beyond the turn. He looks awake now, alert, completely here.

"Close your eyes," he says.

I don't. What is he going to do to me? Amanda tries to cover my eyes with her hands, but I shove her away from me, so then Dennis makes us turn around and walk backwards. I feel like I'm being walked off the plank of a ship.

Something begins welling up in me, but then Dennis spins me around and it catches in my throat. We've emerged on a clearing. There, on the side of the hill, are thousands of yellow flowers glowing radioactively against the gray, overcast sky. The light is escaping from somewhere and making the ground yellower than anything I've ever seen. I feel lightheaded, dizzy. What had I thought would be here? Dennis looks triumphant. Mae is happy. Amanda looks back and forth between the two of them. I take a deep breath. The smell of dirt, the strange-looking glow of the yellow flowers on the hill. The emotions that have been building this whole walk are being rerouted. I don't want to cry but it's hard to breathe. Yes, this place is overwhelming. It's magnificent. How did he know to take us here? Why do I feel this way?

"Go," Dennis says, "go," shoving me forward.

I run into the field and down the hill. I'm trampling the flowers. Blades of grass whipping over my ankles. I can hear Mae behind me. She's running too, chasing me. She dives onto me and we roll through the tall grass down the side of the hill. Just like when we were little. The flowers crush under us, sharp stems and petals. It's the first time she's touched me in days. I am so happy to have her back. She's mine again. I'll do anything she wants to keep her. It hurts to breathe because I'm laughing so hard. She pulls me up, we run back to the top of the hill. She takes my other hand too, crosses it, and starts to spin. We grip each other tight and lean back. The flowers smear yellow, the sky a circle of gray.

Yellow, yellow, yellow.

We fall down and we're laughing like we share a set of lungs. The sky is so low that soon we'll be able to touch it. Our hands reach up for it at the same time.

Dennis hovers over us. Mae moves her hand from the sky to his shirt collar and pulls him down onto us. He falls. We're all rolling now. Someone's foot in my stomach, elbow in my face. We collapse at the bottom of the hill. Then slowly sit up, our limbs still tangled.

Amanda crawls towards us. A raindrop hits my arm. Amanda and Mae both look up at Dennis. I don't know why he needs me too. But he does. He peels a flower petal off my cheek and draws me towards him, presses me against his chest. I let him for a while to please Mae, inhale his smell of cigarettes and sweat, then pull away. He looks at me and I feel shy.

I remember: a plaid wool blanket, a lake, a Popsicle melting down my arm, Mom and him reciting poems together. This was before Mae, when it was only me. Something stabs through me, I don't know if it's joy or not, but whatever it is, it hurts and I don't want it.

I sit up. No. I don't want it. I don't want what he's offering me.

There's a big flat stone near us. Amanda won't stop talking. I see another flat stone, and then another. How did I not notice before that we're in a cemetery? We've been rolling around on top of people.

"…This is just like when Gregor takes Cassandra…" Amanda is saying.

Did I hurt Dennis's feelings by pulling away? He looks only

at Mae now. Her head is in his lap. They're staring at each other. It's probably not the best time to bring it up, but I do anyway because I can't stand watching them stare at each other like that.

I interrupt Amanda. "Mae and I have to go back," I say.

"No," Mae says.

"Yes," I say. "We'll take the bus home this week."

"I'm never going back," she says. She sits up. Her face looks crooked, dreamy. "I'd rather die."

I don't know what to say to this. It was her that Mom wanted, not me. There's a steady drizzle now. Amanda scurries under the trees for cover. Dennis stands and helps Mae up.

The rain is getting harder. It runs through my hair, trickles down my back. He offers me a hand but I don't take it.

"Mae," I try to coax her, "you know we have to. She needs us."

Mae shrugs. "Needs us for what." She walks away to join Amanda under the tree.

"To get better," I call after her.

"Mae and I are going home," I say to Dennis. His hand is still outstretched for me. Water drips down his forehead and into his eyes. "You have no right to keep us from her."

He squints. "I'm not keeping you from her. Your mother is not well," he says.

I stand without his help.

"She's not well because of you," I say. Who else? He broke her somehow. He changed her.

He wipes his face, exasperated. "What do you think I did? What do you imagine I did to her?"

I follow him under the tree, where Mae and Amanda are.

"You did something," I insist. He's about to lose it, I can tell, and then Mae can see for herself who it is she's siding with.

"Did something to whom?" Amanda says.

"Shut up," I tell her.

Mae is staring glassily at the rain hitting the grass. She isn't even listening. Whatever he did to Mom he'll do to her too.

"We're going back," I say to her again.

Her face quivers with irritation. "Are you deaf?" She walks away from me, out into the rain, up the hill where we came from.

Amanda stands there like a wet bobblehead, looking between us, back and forth. "Why are you even here?" I scream at Amanda because it's easier to scream at her than at my sister. She nods, she nods, she backs away.

## MAE

That afternoon was the first time I felt... I don't know how to describe it exactly. My head was in Dad's lap and all the happiness that I'd missed was being compressed into that moment. I looked up at him, and I was no longer me. I was Mom, but not as I knew her. This wasn't her forcing her darkness on me, like a bag over my head. No, this was something else. I'd become Mom from many years ago. Dad felt it too, I could tell. Maybe it would have lasted longer if not for Edie, talking and talking, pressing and pressing. She wanted to take me back to the other mother. The one in the mental hospital who needed me brought to her, tied and quartered, like a sacrifice.

# Chapter 4

**INTERVIEWER:** Thank you for talking with me. I was so excited when I figured out it was you in the mugshot. I'm a huge fan. Would you like to have a look? Hold it by the corners, please.

**DENNIS:** Oh, wow. Where'd you get this?

**INTERVIEWER:** I found it actually, on an auction website on the Internet. A whole box of mugshots. Do you remember having this picture taken?

**DENNIS:** I'm trying to think. I've been arrested more than once.

**INTERVIEWER:** They were from the Freedom Rides arrests. It's dated May 15, 1961. Opelousas, LA.

**DENNIS:** And they were just available on the computer?

**INTERVIEWER:** Yes. A lot of old documents are. Do you recognize any of the people in the other photos?

**DENNIS:** That girl looks familiar, but I can't remember her name. I think she ended up working with us on registering voters. Oh, and there's Fred! Fred Jones. Damn he looks young. I guess I do too, though in my mind that's still what I look like. And there's Diane. She and Fred got married.

**INTERVIEWER:** Can you talk about how you got involved with the Freedom Rides?

**DENNIS:** Sure. Fred and I knew each other from Columbia. We were both English majors, and we took a liking to each other right away. I was 24, old for an undergraduate, and Fred was one of the few black students at the school; neither of us quite fit in. We kept hearing about the boycotts, the sit-ins going on in Greensboro and Nashville and so on. We participated in some stuff like that in New York, but nothing large scale. Then Fred's cousin turned us on to the plan to ride a bus down South to integrate the interstate.

**INTERVIEWER:** Had you visited the South before?

**DENNIS:** No. I'd never been south of DC. But the fact that I wasn't from there, and of course that I was white, this gave me a level of protection others didn't have. I could swoop in and swoop out, and this gave me the courage I might not have otherwise had. The people who lived there, for whom this was their inescapable reality, they were the truly brave ones.

**INTERVIEWER:** Okay, so what happened on the ride?

**DENNIS:** Well, after we crossed into Louisiana, a mob stopped the bus and attacked us. Those of us who managed to escape were taken in by a man named Jackson McLean. The police came for us later at his house to arrest us. They made a point of breaking down his door, trampling his garden, scaring his daughter.

**INTERVIEWER:** Your wife?

**DENNIS:** Eventually, yes, she became my wife.

**INTERVIEWER:** Was this your first time getting arrested?

**DENNIS:** No, but this was different.

**INTERVIEWER:** How so?

**DENNIS:** In New York when I'd been arrested during protests it hadn't felt personal. Here they were trying to make a point. They stripped us, tried to humiliate us by making us walk up and down the hallway, naked. They put us in separate cells—blacks on one end, whites on the other—but it only made us more determined. We drove the guards crazy because we wouldn't stop singing "We Shall Overcome," our voices carrying from the opposite ends of the hall. They took away our mattresses and toothbrushes, and when that didn't stop our singing, they took the screens off the windows and let the cells fill with mosquitoes. We kept going, though. Up until the moment when Jackson McLean bailed us out.

**INTERVIEWER:** Were you scared?

**DENNIS:** That's a good question. I don't know. I was so angry, so righteous, I don't think I was scared of anything. I was on some sort of autopilot. It was only afterward when I wrote about it—

**INTERVIEWER:** In *Yesterday's Bonfires*?

**DENNIS:** Yes. It was only after writing about that time period that I was able to start processing it.

**INTERVIEWER:** Did you think as you were doing these things that they would make for good writing material later? Is that, in part, what motivated you to go?

**DENNIS:** I don't know who would admit to something like that. I was young. I wanted adventure, so sure, that was part of it. But it wasn't just some stunt so I could write about it and win awards. I believed deeply in what I was doing.

**INTERVIEWER:** And do you miss it?

**DENNIS:** It was an awful time in history. But, if you're asking me if I liked being a hero, doing the right thing and being completely confident that what I was doing *was* the right thing, no ambivalence, no vagueness, then, yes. That, I miss. I miss being young and sure of myself and pumped full of adrenaline. I miss being surrounded by brave friends who felt as strongly as I did about these things. I miss trusting people completely with my life.

**INTERVIEWER:** *Yesterday's Bonfires* is the only one of your novels that deals directly with social justice.

**DENNIS:** Sorry, was that a question?

**INTERVIEWER:** Do you feel a responsibility to promote social justice in your work?

**DENNIS:** Sure. But I don't write propaganda, if that's what you're asking.

**INTERVIEWER:** Is propaganda always bad? Couldn't it be good if it was being used to a good end?

**DENNIS:** I think propaganda is always bad.

**INTERVIEWER:** Can I ask you, is it true that *Yesterday's Bonfires* was autobiographical?

**DENNIS:** It's like what Flaubert said: *"Madame Bovary, c'est moi."*

**INTERVIEWER:** What?

**DENNIS:** All the characters are me. That's what the writing process is like. It's schizophrenic. A person talking to himself. Robert might've had biographical features similar to Fred's, but he wasn't Fred. He was me. They were all me. So, yes, it's deeply autobiographical in that sense.

**INTERVIEWER:** And what about your wife? What role did she play in *Yesterday's Bonfires* and the other books? Are the rumors true that she helped you write them?

**DENNIS:** She was my muse.

**INTERVIEWER:** What does that mean though? Like in practical terms. Was she your co-writer? Your editor?

**DENNIS:** No, she was my muse. She inspired me.

**INTERVIEWER:** That sounds romantic. And, what about current projects? What are you working on now?

**DENNIS:** I don't discuss projects until they're finished.

**INTERVIEWER:** Not even a taste?

**DENNIS:** Nope.

**INTERVIEWER:** Thank you so much for your time.

**DENNIS:** Happy to help.

Dennis first caught my attention back in college at a reading for a lit mag I edited. It was your usual fare: a Barnard girl read a story about her cat, an ROTC guy read a sonnet about his mother, I read a villanelle, a terrible villanelle, and then Dennis stepped onto the stage, cleared his throat and ACHOO!! Blew us all away, read a poem about trying to chop down a tree after his father died. Strange poem, surreal and sad, not like anything we'd heard before. He read it in that booming voice of his and sat back down. I don't even think he was aware of the shift in the room that happens at a reading when somebody is finally, actually, very good.

Afterward, I had to fight through a throng of girls to introduce myself. God, that talented prick—girls were always surrounding him and he just took it for granted. We became friends after that reading. We'd stay up late, drinking at a soul food joint where we'd talk and debate until it got light out. Dennis was usually the only white guy there, but that didn't slow him down any—in a loud voice, he'd happily pontificate into all hours of the morning on questions from the core philosophy class we had to take: Was man inherently good or evil? Was he motivated by reason or desire? Dennis always wanted to talk about Jung, and I always wanted to talk about Marx, but we could meet half-way at Dostoyevsky.

When the place closed, he'd usually get on the subway to Brooklyn, where he lived with his mother, or sometimes he'd sleep on the floor of my dormitory. The dorms weren't seg-regated, but our friendship raised some eyebrows, particularly from the Southern students in the cafeteria. They usually didn't say anything outright but they watched us. Dennis wasn't my first white friend, but he was the first white person who truly felt like my brother.

When we heard about the Freedom Rides, we signed up. I couldn't believe what I believed and not go, but I was scared. I understood what I was getting into. For me it was never a game. I knew that I was risking my life and that my life was worth nothing to a lot of people. At the same time, what kind of life could I have if things didn't change?

After the arrests, Dennis and I stayed down South and worked to help register people to vote. Then we came back to New York together and re-enrolled in Columbia. For a while we were as close as friends could be. And then we weren't.

To this day, my arm hurts every time it rains and I have no more depth perception, but I've never regretted going. I met my wife there. Our children's lives are better because of what we did.

## DIANE

Everyone was singing on that Greyhound bus. I'm tone deaf, but I sang anyway. Fred thought at first that I was singing poorly on purpose, that I was goofing around. Well, it was embarrassing but it got his attention. He asked Dennis to trade seats with me so that we could sit together. We talked for hours. By the time we had crossed the border into Louisiana, we'd been on that bus for several days. It was just starting to get dark out. It was hot, a summer day in Louisiana, you can imagine. I was half-dozing, my head on Fred's shoulder. I woke up because I felt him tense. The bus slowed down and stopped in the middle of the two-lane highway. And then I felt like there was an elevator shaft inside of me and I was falling down into it. I knew that I had no control over what was about to happen to us.

If Jackson McLean hadn't gotten us out of there, I doubt Fred would be alive today, or he'd be a vegetable. The way those men kicked and kicked his head. It was horrible. I don't think about that very often, so much has happened since, but seeing the mugshots at the book party brought everything back. It was strange, having our faces billboard-size at a trendy art gallery in Chelsea. We looked like Calvin Klein ads. What are we selling here? That's what I kept asking myself. That book, I guess.

Anyway, I sound like an old crank, which is probably what

I am. No, it was a great evening. It was great to see everyone we'd lost touch with. Even Ann Carter was there, using a cane and hoping nobody would notice. I guess we were all old. That was the point of the show, wasn't it? Living historical relics.

I don't know if I'd be willing to die for anything anymore other than my children. But I had at one point, we all had, and that night in New York together during the party it had felt like we were those same people we'd been decades earlier. I remember asking Fred on the cab ride back to our hotel, both of us feeling buzzed and exuberant: "Fred, why did we lose touch with all these people? We were such good friends. Why don't we ever see Dennis? What happened? We had all been so close."

And Fred said: "You know. Time. People drift apart." Of course, it was more than time. It was Dennis's damn book. It had hurt Fred and me. It had hurt a lot of people. It was hard not to feel like Dennis had used us up and then moved on. But who hasn't done something they regret? And overall the evening had been nice.

The one slight stain was Fred's grad student, Amanda. Fred claimed he'd told me she was coming but I know I would've remembered that. I don't know if Fred was having an affair with her exactly, but I don't think for a second that his interest in her was avuncular. I think he'd introduced her to Dennis as a way to show off, and that backfired because she was glued to Dennis's side all night. She was young and attractive, and God knows, attentive, but anybody not guided through life by their penis could see that something about her was not right. She was unhinged. Not the kind of person Dennis's daughters needed to have around them.

## EDITH (1997)

There's Dennis: huge, beardless, young, in black and white. Handsome. And there's the whole bad boy thing (it *is* a mugshot). He looks like he thinks he knows everything, like even with the cops he had the upper hand.

I look over at Mae and she's still staring at the picture. Every time I look at her, her eyes are suctioned on it. Amanda too. It's creepy.

"Stop," I tell Mae.

I pull her arm and she ignores me. I catch a glimpse of something in her face, something repulsive. I don't know how to describe it, but it makes me feel lightheaded. I glance to see if Amanda noticed. Maybe I'm being paranoid. I probably shouldn't have smoked a bowl with Charlie before coming here, but he'd offered and it didn't occur to me to turn it down. We'd spent the afternoon sanding wooden spoons in his apartment. He said he'd come by the gallery, but he hasn't. He was probably just being polite. The more I look at Mae the worse I feel. I look away. Dennis is spitting olive pits onto his cocktail napkin. Amanda is watching him like a dog.

A group of women have surrounded Mae. They recognize her as "Marianne's." They touch her face and her hair, and she smiles and lets them. They don't notice me. I take a step back and then another. I'm invisible. I walk backwards until I run into a woman in a tuxedo, holding a tray of champagne glasses. I take one. The bubbles tickle the back of my throat. I reach for another, but she pushes me away.

"You're gonna get me fired," she hisses and hurries off.

A small belch. Voices are echoing off the cement floors and bouncing around in the rafters. The front window is fogged up. I press my hand against it and look at the mark it leaves. Turkey.

I turn back to face the party. A cluster of "well-intentioned" women is looking at me. They'd asked about Mom, and I told them that Dennis locked her up in a mental hospital. The conversation ended quickly after that and now they're hugging Dennis and giving me pitying looks.

Fuck all of them. Having a party and calling each other heroes for something they did a million years ago. What heroic things have they done lately? Do they recycle? Did they adopt a fucking whale?

I write on the fogged-up window: "Fucking Cunts." I turn to see if they see it, but they are facing the other direction now. I look for Mae, but she's blocked from view.

She's been ignoring me since the cemetery. Last night it got so bad, I held her hand and cried. She let me, but I could tell it wasn't her hand really. She'd removed herself from it. Like when we were kids, holding on to each other's sleeves and slipping out of our shirts. Her hand was this limp thing I could have, but she wasn't *in* it, and it didn't *mean* anything. She was closed off to me, and I was nothing to her, and that was it. I am nothing to her now.

I feel the panic begin to radiate out from my chest. No. I press it down. I shouldn't have smoked. That was a mistake. It's making me dizzy. I wonder if Charlie is feeling this way too. I lean back against the glass, but this only makes it worse.

When I open my eyes I see a man across the room, staring at me. Snaggletoothed wolf.

"PERVERT," I write on the glass.

Through the letter *T*, I see the people on the sidewalk below, milling around, smoking cigarettes. A cab pulls up. A fat woman and an old lady climb out. The old lady is very short and has a poof of white hair like a troll doll. She leans on the fat lady and hobbles towards the front door. Someone outside takes a picture of her with flash. The smokers are watching her like she is someone important. She doesn't seem to notice them, just keeps hobbling towards the building.

Then, suddenly, she stops and looks up at the window. Our eyes lock and she smiles.

It's the first time anyone has really seen me all night. I quickly wipe the words I wrote with my sleeve and step back to hide behind the fogged-up glass.

## MAE

It's probably why I became a photographer—this power of a two-dimensional image to make you feel something so deeply. I looked into my dad's black-and-white eyes and felt like I understood him completely, like I had never seen anybody before who looked this good to me. And then I looked at him as he was at the party—old—and I couldn't help feeling like my mother had eaten the orange and handed me the rind. I noticed Amanda looking at that picture too. I wonder if she felt the same way.

That party picked a scab for me. Afterward, I lay awake with my menopausal insomnia, revisiting ancient slights. Dennis and that horrible book. "Claudine," the clingy sad sack. "Blundering and bovine," his exact words. And how he'd insulted me afterward when I confronted him, told me I was imagining things, that I wasn't worth writing about, basically.

"All the characters were made-up composites," he'd said and even had the gall to offer to sign my copy. Right. Composites. Then why was I so recognizable that my ex-husband followed me around the house, quoting lines about me from that book?!

I slept with Dennis and I liked him and I tried to make him like me. Is that really so pathetic? No. What's pathetic, *truly* pathetic, is my bad taste in men. If my daddy hadn't been a total asshole, I probably would've been able to see that Dennis was no good. I don't think he was capable of love. Not really. Why else a child bride and not a fully formed person? It's sick. That little girl was always following us around at Jackson's house. Even when I'd insist we go into the woods to get away from her she'd track us down and ask endless questions or offer to braid my hair.

I heard he wrote her letters and tried to groom her. Well, how'd that work out? I heard not so great.

## Phone Conversation
## Between Edith and Markus

**MARKUS:** Where are you? I can't hear you.

**EDITH:** I'm at a party.

**MARKUS:** Well, do you want to call me later?

**EDITH:** No. Obviously I wanted to call you now if I called you now.

**MARKUS:** Okay...

**EDITH:** Do you miss me?

**MARKUS:** Sure.

**EDITH:** What do you miss about me?

**MARKUS:** I don't know.

**EDITH:** Remember what you said to me after you fucked me on the couch in the attic? How you—

**MARKUS:** Edie, my parents are home.

**EDITH:** So what?

**MARKUS:** So, I don't want to talk about that right now.

**EDITH:** Fine. If your parents are home, then you can ask them about Mae and me staying with you for a bit.

**MARKUS:** About that...

**EDITH:** What do you mean, "About that..."? What, you heard someone say that in a movie?

**MARKUS:** You can't stay here. You just can't.

**EDITH:** Because you don't want me to?

**MARKUS:** It's just not going to happen.

**EDITH:** If it's because you're dating someone else, I don't even care.

**MARKUS:** Aren't you at a party. Shouldn't you be getting back—

**EDITH:** You're just like Mae. There's something wrong with you. You're a cold person. You have no idea what it means to love anybody, to care about someone other than yourself. Now that I'm not directly in front of you, sucking your dick, I don't even exist for you anymore.

**MARKUS:** Whatever, Edie. You've sucked my dick a total of like two times, and I didn't even cum.

**EDITH:** You're a coward and a liar and a terrible friend.

**MARKUS:** I'm a terrible friend? I can't even believe we're having this conversation. It's always you, you, you. You need this, you need that. You dumped me, let me remind you, and then I was supposed to just pretend like you didn't?... Hello? Hello?...

## TILLIE HOLLOWAY

My life changed after I got the part of Cassandra in *Yesterday's Bonfires*. At the time, I was married to my agent. We were very rich and I was deeply unhappy. My husband made sure I was cast steadily in small roles, but when something substantial finally came along, he balked. He wanted me to stay away from politics, stay behind my white picket fence. He was furious when I accepted the part and the studio flew me, and the rest of the cast, out to New Orleans for the weekend. The movie was going to be shot on a sound stage, but they wanted us to absorb some of the local color. They arranged a boozy luncheon with Dennis Lomack and Marianne at one of the oldest and fanciest restaurants in the French Quarter.

I was surrounded by actors and professional charmers all day long, but they were just mimics. Marianne and Dennis were the real thing. Marianne especially. She was… magnetic. Maybe it was her voice? She had a great voice, low and gravely. It made you want to lean in as close as you could.

I remember Dennis was holding court. He was telling everyone the story about how the restaurant made its turtle soup— supposedly it was prepared in one of Napoleon's very own pots and had been boiling continuously for centuries. I was listening, but it was Marianne who I couldn't keep my eyes off of.

Consciously or unconsciously, I was adjusting my posture to mimic hers, parting my lips the way she did. In that moment, I wanted so much to *be* her. We locked eyes and only when I was caught did I realize what I was doing. I felt deeply embarrassed but Marianne was kind. She took my hand and held it to her cheek.

"It's hard sometimes," she said, "to know where you end and where others begin. You're an actress, so you understand." I told her that I did.

Her husband called for a toast and she stood up, and only then did I realize how heavily pregnant she was. In his toast Dennis thanked the studio and the director, said he gave them his blessing to take his book and make origami or confetti or whatever their plans were for it and everyone, fairly drunk by this point, laughed.

The meal lasted through many more courses. I was so focused on Marianne that I wasn't too aware of anyone else. She had such a vivid way of talking and drawing you into her world. I only knew how to talk like that when someone else had written the words for me. She told me about her childhood, growing up in Louisiana, wandering the swamps, watching her father paint. Her mother had died when she was a baby, so she and her father had been very close. I remember being moved by the way she talked about him, and by the way she talked to her husband. They seemed very close. My own marriage was sexless, unbearable, and I remember seeing the way Dennis couldn't keep his hands off Marianne and thinking that this is what a marriage should be. At any rate, I was enchanted with her and thrilled when she agreed to let me spend the weekend with her. She even promised to take me to her childhood home.

But the next morning when I showed up at her house, as we had arranged, and rang the doorbell, nobody answered. I knew she was home. I could see her through the frosted glass, her pregnant form, as she disappeared up the stairs. It was the strangest thing. I knocked again, sat on the front porch, and waited. Periodically, I got up and knocked, on the off chance that she hadn't heard me and that it was a misunderstanding.

How tenacious I was! But I didn't know how else to be. The part was important. "Fame had begun to feel like something waiting for me on the table, getting cold," to quote the book.

Eventually, Dennis Lomack pulled up in front of the house. Had I done something to offend her? I wanted to know. She'd seemed so eager to help the night before.

"She's an unreliable person," Dennis said. In my world this is a very damning thing to say, but I think he was just stating a fact. He could tell I was upset, so he told me the part had nothing to do with his wife anyway. She'd been a kid at the time the events took place. The screenwriters just combined all the female characters into Cassandra. "You can play her any way you want," he said. And that ended up freeing me to bring more of myself to the part.

The movie was silly in a lot of ways, a product of its time and by no means a classic. But I ended up learning a lot about the Movement as a result. After living in the world of these brave young men and women struggling for social justice, how could I walk back into my stultifying and privileged life? I couldn't. I tried to model myself after Ann Carter and others. I opened up my enormous house, the one I got in the divorce settlement, to girls who needed a place to live. Some of them have been through unimaginable horrors. We became a tiny army up in the Hollywood Hills. And with Edie's help later, I turned this project into a foundation, and set up other houses like it throughout the state.

# Edith (1997)

"I would love to paint you."

The Pervert has me cornered. I don't understand how I got here. I'm still fuming about Markus. That shit. That shit, shit, shit. I was on my way to Mae but she slithered off. And now, the Pervert's arm is blocking me from passing. His fingers are in my hair. "Maybe you could pose for me sometime. I paint women's heads on animal bodies."

"Oh, Xander, stop. That's Dennis's daughter," a woman next to him comes to my rescue. "Dennis," she calls through a group of people. "Xander wants your daughter to model for him. Xander has discovered your daughter. My drunk husband's a regular Vasco da Gama!"

Dennis appears by my side, Amanda trailing after him. His lips are greasy from the hors d'oeuvres. He kisses that woman on the cheek, leaves a shiny smudge with his slug lips that Amanda stares at for a moment too long.

"My daughter? Discovered? My angel on stilts? My untrammeled continent? Discovered?"

The woman tilts her head back and brays, showing everyone her rotting back teeth.

"Your father," she says, and puts her hand on his shoulder

to steady herself, "has always had such a way with words." She starts to tell me about the good old days in Louisiana. Amanda moves in closer to Dennis.

And then, a blond woman sweeps into the room. I know her. Was she a friend of Mom's? She looks like a doll. Tiny and precise.

They're all looking at me like I just said something.

"What?" I say.

They laugh again. Ugly and insane.

I pry past the Pervert and move towards the woman. Where do I know her from? She's trailed by a group of girls, and this makes her look like a nun or schoolteacher. But she's too pretty to be either of those things. The girls look rough. They're dressed nicely, but their clothes look too new, like they don't really belong to them. These girls follow her through the room, a gaggle of them. Who is she? A pied piper. Could I join them?

"Do you know my mother?" I'm asking her.

"What, honey? Who's your mother?"

I feel the way I felt when I was little and Mom forgot me at the grocery store.

The woman's features flicker. She waves to somebody over my shoulder. Dennis's friend is shaking hands with all the girls. Some of them are so shy they don't even look up at him.

Oh. This woman must think I'm a real idiot. Of course I don't know her. She's that actress. She was in that '80s movie based on one of Dennis's books.

"I'm sorry," I say. "I thought you were someone else."

I hear some girls behind me, snickering. The actress squeezes my shoulder, smiles at me, makes a point of looking into my eyes. I can tell she's congratulating herself on how good she is at eye contact. She can go fuck herself too. The pressure is building in my brain. My mother: her purple face and tangled hair, feet twitching inches off the floor. A yellow puddle on the linoleum.

Dennis pulls me away. He's hurting my wrists. "You're hurting me." I can't hear myself say the words, but I feel my mouth moving. My ears are ringing. People are turned around, looking at us. Even if I wanted to change what is happening, I wouldn't be able to. I feel it coming. Mae looks away from me. She'll never look at me again.

And then, darkness.

## Mae

Edie's fit was terrifying and embarrassing. Her body jangled. Her voice became a horrible croak. Her eyes bulged as though something was forcing them out of her face from the inside. Before I would have made her a compress of frozen peas and whispered soothing things to her, but this time I hung back.

Dad tried to hold her as she kicked and thrashed, and the actress Tillie Holloway and her girls lifted Edie up and carried her off into the coatroom.

For weeks an unpleasant energy had been building around my sister and I wanted it to finally be over. I wanted her to go back to Metairie, to leave already and be gone. It's horrible to admit how cold I was, but I wanted more than anything else for my new life with Dad to begin with no interference from Edie or Amanda.

And I got my wish! It had only taken one word from me in front of his friends and Amanda was gone too. I had not expected it to be so easy. He must have already been looking for an excuse to get rid of her. I remember watching him through the gallery window as he put Amanda in a cab and I remember thinking: Life, real life, is about to begin.

## AMANDA

Of course it came as a shock, especially considering how well things had been going and what a marvelous time we'd all been having. It was a mistake for Mae to interfere. Nobody ended up benefiting from that. I think maybe my advisor's wife got involved as well. Who knows what that woman told Dennis, and he was in such a vulnerable state so I don't blame him at all for believing her. Maybe I would if things had turned out differently between us, but my leaving only strengthened our relationship because it gave me the opportunity to prove my commitment to him.

## Edith (1997)

The room feels crowded. Faces and coats.

"Here, drink some ice water. You'll feel better." The old woman I saw through the window now holds a shaky glass to my lips. I steady it, look at her poof of white hair. The actress and the girls back out of the room, one by one.

"Are you embarrassed?" the old woman asks after they leave.

Of what? Oh. That jittery feeling is back. I try to sit up more but can't.

"Don't be embarrassed. Look at me." I look at her feet. They don't even reach the ground. She holds my chin with her soft hands.

"Shame is useless unless it motivates you to do better. Usually it does no such thing. It only sucks up energy. Drink."

I drink.

"You must be dehydrated from all those tears," she says.

My cheeks burn under her cold hands.

"Do you know who I am?"

I do not.

"I'm Ann. I noticed you earlier, noticed you writing dirty words on the glass—"

I try to protest, but she interrupts me.

"That was you, Edith. Don't lie about it! You're not in trouble. It reminded me of something your grandfather said a long time ago.

"You knew my grandfather?"

"Sure. He was a good friend of mine. A dear friend. And he told me that he had a plan for all of the politicians, lobbyists, journalists who were ignoring him, who weren't returning his phone calls, or reading his letters. He decided he'd haunt them by writing messages in the steam on their bathroom mirrors. Everyone would be forced to either finally hear him out or to start taking cold baths. I hadn't thought about that in a long time."

The woman laughs at her own story and something about her laugh feels familiar.

"I never got to meet him."

"I know," she said. "He died too young. Are you feeling better? The color is returning to your face. Being brave is very difficult but being a coward is even more difficult. Trust me. Here. Put your head in my lap. I'm going to tell you a story. Close your eyes."

She begins to stroke my temples as she talks. It's nice to have someone touch me. After the mess in the gallery I feel hollowed out and now her words begin to fill me back up...

"When I was a few years older than you are now, I moved away from home. I was like you—popular, boys liked me. I wasn't as pretty as you are, but I was pretty enough. A debutant, all that. Had a coming out party at the hotel ballroom, a big deal. My parents agreed to send me to college, but they expected me to come back, marry and play bridge, maybe join a flower club. Instead, I ran off to Louisiana. I told myself—'I'm just visiting,' even as I walked into the newspaper office and got a job as a stenographer.

"When you grow up surrounded by so much wrongness, you don't know how to notice it even if you want to. It took your grandfather pointing everything out to me before I allowed these vague feelings I've always carried with me to take shape and be given names.

"For example, at the newspaper, when I typed up the crime blotter, the rule was if the person was white it was Mr. or Mrs. and if the person was black it was only the name, no honorific."

"That's crazy," I say. I wonder how it was I didn't know this before.

"Yes. It was. But I didn't make much of this at first. It had seemed like any other arbitrary grammatical rule. After I met your grandfather though, I began making more and more typos.

"Or, I'd be having lunch with the other stenographers in the cafeteria overlooking the courthouse across the street, and we'd be laughing, and joking, and suddenly my eyes would catch on the words: *Equality, Liberty, Justice,* engraved over the courthouse doors, and inexplicably I'd lose my appetite. I wasn't thinking consciously yet that those words were lies. I was raised with the unconscious assumption that a white life was worth more than a black one. I took for granted that a white man who walked through those courthouse doors would only get two months in jail for murdering a black man, whereas he'd certainly get the chair if the victim were white. Or that a black man wouldn't get more than a year for killing another black man either, but if he so much as looked at a white woman the wrong way, forget about it. I wasn't consciously thinking about these disparities because my brain had been conditioned my entire life to turn a blind eye and yet I felt the injustice of all this on a primal level."

Her saying this scares me. How is it possible to not know something that is right in front of you?

"My awakening came slowly. It didn't happen overnight, though from the outside that's probably what it looked like because one morning I couldn't get out of bed. I pulled the sheet over my head and lay there like a corpse for hours. And it's true, part of me had finally died. I was lying there thinking:

What now? What am I supposed to do *now*? Your grandfather came by to check on me while the landlady stood in the doorway, watching us. He'd recently been through something similar. It's a rite of passage for all Southern whites, you either open your eyes and deal with the fallout, which I should say is an ongoing process, or keep them shut, which is maybe more convenient, but also infinitely more difficult."

Will it be a rite of passage for me? I wonder. I think about the vague feeling of wrongness and shame that throbs under everything. No, I don't want to think about it. I focus instead on the old woman's story.

"Your grandfather coaxed me out of the house and took me to a party, which is where I met Lydia Van Horn. Has your mother told you about her?"

I keep my eyes closed but shake my head "no."

"Lydia wasn't the type of person I'd have known back home. She was white, but she was poor. She worked as a seamstress and lived with her sister's family on the other side of town. She had a plump, young face, but prematurely gray hair and a gentle manner. She was very attentive. I never felt judged, stumbling through all these discoveries in front of her. Your grandfather, though, he couldn't stand her. She was the subject of one of our first arguments. I was so excited to have a female friend that I was willing to overlook the little things that didn't add up. Your grandfather thought it was a mistake for me to try to fill my loneliness as quickly as possible."

I open my eyes and look at her. "Why?"

"It's uncomfortable, but it's a necessary step in a person's awakening."

Is it? It seems like not giving a hungry person food. She shifts under me, then keeps talking. "Lydia would come over to my rented room and we'd sit on my bed, drinking tea or sherry. She never took her shoes off—I think her stockings had holes in them. She wasn't a terribly good seamstress. She grew up in the country and, sometimes, I'd get her talking about that. Or, I'd talk about my family. Often, we didn't talk at all. We'd just enjoy each other's company, play cards, and then she'd rush off to take the trolley back to her sister's.

"Do you know about Willie McGee?"

I shrug. "His name sounds familiar."

"It's in history books now. He was a black man in Laurel, Mississippi, falsely accused of rape and given the death sentence. I say 'man,' but he was barely older than you. It was a lynching, plain and simple, only they were using the justice system to do it. Horrible things were being done to protect the white Southern woman's 'virtue.' So, as a white Southern woman when I heard about Willie McGee, I felt personally responsible.

"Men at work were joking around about the case like it was nothing—our paper wasn't even covering it. When I tried to say something, they laughed at me, but rather than feeling embarrassed, I felt a simmering anger. And, as I was sitting in my room, watching Lydia darn socks, that anger transformed into action.

"'Lydia,' I said. 'We have to protest the execution.' So she helped me get a few women together for a trip to Laurel and your grandfather and some others pitched in to pay our bus fare.

"We rode the bus for hours, but the time flew by. I felt close to these women in a way I hadn't before. We believed that since this was being done, presumably, to protect white Southern women, that when we got there and told them that we didn't need such protection, they'd listen. It seems strange, I know, that at 23, I could be so naïve."

I try to picture her young but I can't. A blank face.

"We marched straight from the bus station to the jailhouse, chanting 'Not in Our Names,' and holding up signs we'd stayed up late the night before painting. Passersby stopped and stared, some shouted insults at us. A journalist from the paper even took pictures, the same way he would have if a local farmer's pigs had gotten loose and stormed the courthouse."

I snort a little but she keeps going.

"Lydia was with the rest of us, holding a sign and chanting. She was not as clever or as loud as some of the girls, but I remember thinking how lucky I was to have her on my side because she seemed so solid. As Southern ladies we'd all been socialized to be timid. Standing in front of men dressed in suits and police uniforms, yelling at them, it didn't come naturally. But the sound of our voices, raised in unison, however awkwardly, was thrilling. We tried to get housewives who were out shopping to join us but of course none did.

"Eventually, the sheriff arrested us for disturbing the peace and put all six of us in one cell. When you're raised to believe that being arrested is a shameful thing, it's hard to ignore this. The married ones especially regretted coming. Lydia, though, her face was blank. While the others argued and cried, she stood there, leaning against the wall, saying nothing. I remember coming up to her and hugging her because I'd imagined she was distraught. It felt very unnatural, like hugging a mailbox. I realized that I'd never hugged her before."

I open my eyes and look up at the old woman's face. Her skin looks so soft. She's staring off into the middle distance like a blind person. She must have had a mugshot too, probably many of them, enough to have a whole other gallery show.

"The sheriff only held us for a few hours to teach us naughty girls a lesson, and then escorted us back to the bus station. On the ride home some women wanted to know: aside from humiliating ourselves, what did we achieve? We didn't save Willie McGee from execution. But I argued that we spoke the truth, and who knows what the ripple effects of that might be.

"Soon after we came back, your grandfather introduced me to his friend Carl, whom I married. I didn't need Lydia in the same way. We grew apart and at some point she stopped coming around entirely. Carl and I moved to Tennessee for his job and then I didn't see Lydia until many years later at your grandfather's trial."

The trial. The trial Mom never talks about.

"When the prosecution called her to the stand, I didn't recognize her. Her hair was dyed black, or maybe this had been its real color all along. Her posture was different. She didn't wear glasses. She said such awful things, ugly things, and had no problem looking at us as she said them. Lydia Van Horn wasn't even her real name.

"I tried to understand why she'd betray us. Some said money—she'd been in debt and it turns out that she had a sick son to support—but she was so ruthless on the stand I think it must've been ideological. This is mere speculation because really I didn't know her. She'd been mirroring me back to myself and I'd been too caught up in everything to notice.

"The charges against your grandfather were sedition, inciting a riot, being a Communist spy because he had been using his name to buy properties in white neighborhoods and then transferring the deeds to black families. The jury wouldn't have known the difference between 'communism' and 'rheumatism' if it bit them. Such fear-mongering garbage, spearheaded by my very own Lydia-the-FBI-mole."

Mom never told me any of this.

"Three months into the trial, your grandfather's heart gave out. It was too much for him."

"That's how he died?" I ask.

"Yes. He was sensitive, but he was also staunch. He could have run. You know, your father offered to set him and your mother up in Canada, but Jackson wouldn't hear of it. Jackson said his sweat and blood were in that town and the only way he was leaving was in a coffin. Which is what he did."

"Because of Lydia?"

"I think in part."

"What happened to her?"

"A few years ago, I decided to write her a letter. I don't know if she needed my forgiveness, but I needed to give it to her. It took a lot out of me to write her, so you can imagine how I felt when the envelope was returned, unopened."

"She sent it back to you?"

"She died."

The woman stops talking. She looks down into my face. I would not have forgiven her.

"Do you think my grandfather should have run away?" If he had run maybe he'd still be alive, and then maybe Mom wouldn't be in the hospital.

"No." She shrugs. "Most of the time in life there are no 'should-haves.' You do what you can do."

I sit up, grazing someone's damp winter coat.

"Listen," she says. "You have a lot to be angry about, and that's certainly your prerogative. But anger is a sap on your resources. You feel angry because you feel helpless. But you're not helpless. What is it that you want?"

"I want my mother," I say. "I want to go home."

"So go," she says. "Go tonight if you have to. Pass me my purse."

I pass her the fringed leather bag at her feet.

"Here," she empties her wallet without counting it. "Take some money for the bus fare."

I'm surprised. She folds my fingers over the stack of bills.

"Go. Tell your mother… send your mother my love. I heard she was in the hospital again. If my daughter were doing better, I would try to visit. Speaking of which, I should get back to Franny. Help me up. Thank you."

She limps out of the coatroom. The door swings shut behind her.

# PART II

# Chapter 5

Date: April 14, 1997

**Identifying data:**
Name: Marianne Louise McLean
Race: Caucasian
Gender: Female
Age: 45 y.o.
Height: 5'5
Weight: 105lbs
Hair: Black
Eyes: Gray
Physical Description: Long ~~elegant~~ fingers. ~~Feline movements.~~
Marital Status: Divorced
Occupation: poet (?)/mother/ none

**Chief Complaint:**
Patient was brought in via Chalmers Hospital following a suicide
attempt (asphyxiation). Patient is in unstable condition. She is
being held indefinitely, as per the request of Doreen Williams,
her legal guardian.

## History of Illness:

Patient was hospitalized once previously, 12 years ago. Severe post-partum depression and psychosis suspected. Bipolar Disorder and Borderline Personality Disorder seems likely diagnosis based on her dissociative spells, unstable sense of self, splitting with regards to feelings toward ex-husband, and the hypomanic and depressive states.

Her father's death= formative trauma. Her father was a "saint," a "hero," her "only champion." In short, a sacred cow that the patient is not comfortable analyzing or discussing critically. Even the slightest probing from the therapist was met with disproportionate hostility.

The other loci of trauma at the center of patient's suicidal ideation seem to be: her failed marriage, her failure as a mother, and perhaps her failure (?) as an artist.

~~Delusions of grandeur. Believes series of best-selling novels were written about her.~~ [This has been confirmed to be true. Surprisingly, though, she doesn't consider this a great honor, and rather, finds the role of "muse" oppressive.]

As for her own work, she is dismissive of it. She said that her husband had encouraged her to be dependent on him for artistic validation, which he was "generous with but only because there was no threat in [her] ever overshadowing him, or of being particularly good or bad." I believe it's important for a person of her artistic temperament to have a creative outlet for self-expression. We have discussed this, but she remains ~~difficult~~ non-compliant and refuses to participate in arts & crafts activities.


## Treatment:

Daily talk therapy. Also, have put her on 5mg BID of haloperidol. When she began treatment, there were several strange incidents that we think were potential side effects. Twice during a therapy session her eyes became glazed and unfocused as though she were in a trance. Her pulse, when measured, was very fast, a heart rate of 120 bpm, and yet she was flat in her affect, pale and withdrawn, with shaking hands. Both times when it happened she fell asleep immediately afterward, as one would following a seizure. When she awoke she was hesitant to discuss what had happened, but she seemed confused and thought she was in New York City. It is possible she was experiencing visual and auditory hallucinations. For this reason we are in the process of adjusting the dosage, and adding 25mg of olanzapine.

Quite an interesting ~~woman~~ case.

## Marianne McLean's Journal

[1985]

they make me fill out idiotic worksheets here. i wonder about my head. the feeling of cotton in my head. (I think of daddy, a cotton ball sticking out of his nose, out of his ear. oh! how he was prone to infections).

they say, not to worry! the cotton feeling is because of the coma. to give it a few days & it will dissipate. i think, no, as usual, i have not made myself clear: i want <u>more</u> cotton. i want to be taxidermied. but they don't do that at this hospital.

the therapist is an idiot. i told him about the tree stump—

about how i took the girls to the woods near where my house used to be (daddy's art studio flattened under a parking lot for a piggly-fucking-wiggly—there is no dignity, there is no justice...). we were walking even though I had not meant to get out of the car. we were walking & then i was hitting a rotten tree stump with a stick. it would make this thump when i hit it, a dull sound & i don't know why, but that sound excited me very much. i could feel it in my heart. the girls were like little monkeys. they found their own sticks & they were digging in the ground with them. mae had a wet cough. it gave me the feeling that her insides were the rotten stump & it was her i had been hitting. it's terrible. it's terrible to always have to keep track of the edges of things as they slide away from you.

of course, the therapist didn't know what to make of the story. it's okay to express anger, he said. hit something! that's an idea! holding out his palms for me to punch.

the worst part is that dennis is the only one left who has any idea what i'm talking about. how infuriating to have him as a screen always between me & the world. my translator! my apollo!

"what's it like to be married to a man who understands women so keenly?" people have asked me.

it's unbearable. unbearable. he is a thief. he steals from me constantly, though <u>what</u> exactly i can't say. & he's a liar. & <u>what</u> it is exactly he lies about i can't say either. but you see, this doesn't make it any less true.

& that i, at 16, could have foreseen it—i was the one, after all, who chose the name cassandra. apollo spits in my mouth & now nobody believes me. those thick alligator teardrops sliding down his cheeks as he suffocates me. for my own good! as he squeezes me from the bottom up.

*literally*? that's what doreen wants to know.

literally, not literally, what's the difference? his breath is on my face even when he isn't here.

## EDITH (1997)

The apartment feels like an insect husk. Empty and strange. Charlie left to go borrow a car. Dennis and Mae are still at the party. Everyone was busy holding hands and singing when I finally emerged from the coatroom, the thick wad of cash in the waistband of my pants. I extracted the keys from Dennis's pocket when he was mid-toast, pantomimed a headache, pointed to the door. I whispered in Mae's ear that I was leaving for good and she didn't even try to mask the joy. Something oily was sliding around behind those eyes, giving them a greasy sparkle.

I dig my duffel bag out of the closet and begin filling it with clothes from the dresser. Fine, Mae. You have your wish. You've always been slippery and now you're free of me. But be careful. Freedom isn't good for people like you. Who'll keep you tethered while I'm gone? Don't you get scared that you'll float off? Dennis has no idea what to do with you. Mom said he liked his birds with their wings broken, but she was wrong. It's his wings that are broken. I can see that now because the rage has scrubbed me clean. It passed through me and got everything out and now I see things for what they are. The woman in the coatroom, my fairy godmother, she was right. I'm not helpless.

I've packed all my clothes except the sweater. It's soft and green, made of cashmere, a present from Aunt Rose on one of her early visits. I won't need it. I'll leave it for Mae.

Her sheets are rumpled, the blanket balled up. A peach pit in a glass, wedged between the mattress and the wall. Black specks, flies, hover by the rim. There's a faint sweet smell that makes my skin crawl. A sex smell. But when I sniff again, it's gone. Maybe I imagined it. I lay the sweater out on her bed like it's a person.

A knock on the window. I jump. The glowing tip of Charlie's cigarette. He's ready. I gesture "one minute" at my own reflection in the glass. I throw my shoes in the bag and start to zip it. Do I have everything? I go into the living room and check under the couch, then into the kitchen and look under the table. I go into Dennis's room, though what could I have forgotten here?

There's his typewriter. Should I leave him a note? I unlatch the cover, slip in a blank page.

*Dear Dennis,*

I begin, the keys clanging like motherfuckers.

*This is my first letter to you, at least the first one you'll get to see, and I'm writing to tell you that I'm going home.*

I pull the lever and it slides back to the left side with a ding.

*I'm sure it's no surprise, since I've been talking about leaving since I got here. I know, I know, "Mom isn't well." Your refrain. And all I can say to that is: Duh. Of course she isn't. That's why I need to go home and take care of her.*

All these years, whenever I've thought about Dennis, I pictured him all-powerful and heartless, but now I see that there's no wizard behind the curtain, there probably isn't even a curtain. I have an impulse to say something kind, so I type:

*Anyway, I know you've tried to make up for the lost time, and though of course, you failed, still it was better than nothing, DAD. There, I said it. That's the most you'll get out of me.*

*Please take care of Mae.*

And then on a lighter note, a quick sign off.

*What is it you guys loved to sign your letters with? Keep On Keepin'*
*On? God Bless? Mahalo? Ta-Ta? Peace, Peace and Chicken Grease?*

*Over and Out?*

I type out my name quickly, before they come back home and find me here.

*Edith.*

I open the window and pass Charlie my duffel bag, catch Cronus before he attempts a great escape, nuzzle him briefly.

"Bye, cat," I say and shut the window.

Charlie drops his cigarette and the embers spark out on the asphalt seven stories below. Through the slats of the fire escape, I see the idling pickup truck.

Our feet thump on the metal stairs. We pass the drawn curtains and blinds of the other neighbors, 5C, 4C, 3C, 2C. The night air, the night city air. Thank you, Ms. Ann Carter. From the alley below, Dennis's windows look very small.

Charlie tosses my bags into the bed of the truck.

"G-g-g-good to go?" he asks. I nod.

Inside the cab, it smells like a campfire. He swings an arm over the seat and throws the truck in reverse. It stalls. He starts it again, and we lurch out into the street.

My substitute-teaching job ended and the film student lost interest in our project. I'd been spending a lot of time alone in the apartment, so I was glad when Edie appeared at my window. She told me she wanted to use my woodshop. I showed her a few things—how to use the table saw and the sander. She came by a couple days in a row. I started looking forward to it. The day of the party we smoked a joint on the fire escape and I felt happy for the first time in a while.

I arrived at the gallery early but I didn't want to appear too eager, so I went for a walk around the neighborhood to kill time. When I finally got up the nerve to go inside, I was almost too late. I caught Edie as she was leaving for Port Authority. I remember being seized with that feeling you get right before you jump and I offered to drive her all the way to Louisiana. Why not? I needed to get out of the city. I loved New York, but I needed a break from it. I borrowed a truck from a friend. He was backpacking through Europe so he wouldn't even know it was gone.

Something about Edie put me at ease. My speech impediment can make me shy. People look away from me like I'm an invalid, but not Edie. She looked at my face openly the way children do. I don't mean to say she seemed like a child. I didn't at any point think: I am pouring my heart out to a child. As we drove, I told her everything. I told her about how when I crawled through abandoned subway tunnels or climbed up the beams of the Williamsburg Bridge, I would see the city as a big pulsing thing that was mine and that I could love, even if the people in it had found a way of disappointing me. As I was jumping from roof to roof in Chinatown, I wasn't thinking about my dying grandmother, or my emotionally distant brother. I'd sit at the top of the scaffolding on St. John the Divine and look at the lights in people's apartments go on and off to a rhythm that the people themselves weren't even aware of. They were all simply cells in this big, beautiful organism, and they had no idea. The city had loved me and always been kind to me even when the individual pieces had not.

"I'll be kind to you," Edie had said then. She had her knees up, her cheek resting on them, looking at me. It took a lot not to just drive off the road. It was like in *Yesterday's Bonfires*, when Cassandra and Gregor are in the tent together in her father's backyard, connecting without touching. I kept driving and driving, trying to cover the sound of my pounding heart.

## MAE

We stayed at the party until it was just me, Dad, and the gallery assistant closing the place out. Dad was, in retrospect, pretty drunk, though I didn't pick up on this at the time. I was 14 and not very worldly. The gallery assistant put on a Sam Cooke record and danced for him, but when Dad saw me leaning against the gallery wall, watching, he gestured for me to join in. "Bring It on Home to Me" was playing and Dad and I danced, a swaying, clutching sort of thing. The song was already dripping with nostalgia, but more so under the watchful eyes of those beautiful mugshots. He was singing, so I sang too. I have an excellent singing voice and this surprised him because he had never heard me sing before.

The gallery girl tried to join us several times, but Dad ignored her, and for a while she danced next to us alone, until finally she got the hint. Then she turned on all the lights and started sweeping, and when that side of the record was over she switched it off and swept us out the door.

On the cab ride back it was only the two of us, no more Edie, no more Amanda. We didn't talk. Dad sat there like a sad bear, humming and looking out the window. Whatever had been set in motion was beginning to feel real. I held his hand. I knew that Edie would not be there when we came home, but I said nothing.

When we got to the apartment and Dad found her gone he was devastated. It's dumb, I know, but I'd expected him to be as pleased as I was. He picked up the phone and hung it up several times, not knowing who to call. He asked me for the name of the boy she was always talking to. Markus, I told him. Last name? Conti. Dad called information, had them repeat the number three times, squinting with one eye at what he'd written down.

"Shit. Shit. Shit. I'm drunk," he said after he hung up. He wiped his mouth on his shoulder, stood up, and went to the kitchen sink to put his head under the tap. He came back with water streaming down his face and beard, onto his shirt. It was very late, and of course when he called Markus's family, he woke them all up. Dad got a little tangled in his words, but managed finally to ask them to call if they heard anything.

He paced for a while, then stopped and looked at me with his wet face.

"Did you know about this?" he asked.

I said that I didn't, but he could tell I was lying.

"Would she have taken the bus?" he asked.

I nodded, averting my eyes.

"Go to bed," he said and left to go look for her at Port Authority. I spent the night worrying that he would find her and bring her back and was relieved when the next morning, I found him alone, awake and bleary eyed, sitting at the kitchen table.

There was a knock on the door and he shot up, probably hoping it was Edie, but instead it was the little old woman from the party and her large middle-aged daughter. The daughter was tall and swollen-looking. Something about her didn't seem quite right.

Dad hugged them both, offered them some coffee, apologized for his state. He explained that Edie was missing.

"I know," the old woman said, taking a sip of her coffee. "I'm the one who gave her money for the ticket."

Dad was furious. They argued. Her daughter stood up and shuffled over to wait by the door.

"Ma, we gotta go," the daughter said, jiggling the handle, but the old woman acted like she hadn't heard her.

"Really, Dennis," the old woman said. "I'm sure you were going all over the country when you were her age, and don't give me that garbage about how much safer it was. You know that's not true. Marianne was only a year older than Edith when she married you."

"I mean it, Ma. I can't take one more second," the daughter said, baring her little, yellow teeth.

The woman got up. "Frances, calm down. Take a breath. We're leaving," she said and hugged Dad's waist.

He was furious. After they left, unkind words sputtered out of him all afternoon: "...Ann Carter handing out parenting advice, that's rich... Poor Franny, covered in track marks and looking like an overfed tick... Who knows what could have been prevented..."

Despite his anger, I could tell his resolve to bring Edie back was crumbling. He was accepting that she was gone and that he had no right to care now when he had been absent all those years.

That night I lay awake, listening to Dad in the other room, getting drunker, knocking over glasses. Eventually, I drifted off and woke up a while later to him standing over me in the dark. Because I slept on the top bunk, his face was not much higher than mine. I could feel his breath. It was warm and smelled like alcohol, almost citrusy. He stroked my face and my hair. I pretended to be asleep because I didn't want him to stop. He must have remembered that at least he had me.

## FRED

My friendship with Dennis came apart gradually.

It started with his relationship with Marianne. There's a long, rich historical tradition of men marrying younger women: fine. And, it was the era of free love: fine. But if Jackson McLean had lived, no way would Marianne and Dennis have gotten together! Marianne was a kid. Dennis made a show of nurturing her but really he plundered her for his own work. The same way he had used me and the Civil Rights struggle, and I don't think his work was good enough to justify this exploitation of pain.

It was after Marianne came to New York that Dennis began writing in earnest. The more he wrote the more dazed and uncertain she seemed. He was an emotional vampire. He needed her to be in a certain state to be his muse.

I'd given up the idea of a literary career quickly. I'm a much better critic, and that's where my interest lies. It wasn't jealousy that drove a wedge between us. It was *Yesterday's Bonfires*.

He brought over the stack of pages, straight from the typewriter. He and Marianne waited for me in the living room while I sat at the kitchen table, reading. Somewhere in the middle of the book, it got dark outside and Diane came in and turned the light on. I think it was Diane. It could have been Marianne. I'd barely noticed that I'd been trying to read in the dark, nose pressed to the page, hands shaking. The panic I was feeling was giving me tunnel vision. All I could do was keep reading.

There, in the manuscript, was a thinly veiled and very unflattering portrait of me: *Robert*. So this is how he sees me! I thought. A naïve buffoon, his entrée into the world he wanted to write about. Things, private things, I had told him in confidence, were laid out bare, typed neatly paragraph after paragraph. It was incredibly hurtful. He wrote about my affair with Diane's friend, an organizer in Tennessee, something Diane hadn't known about. He quoted me saying unflattering things about our friends and colleagues in the heat of the moment, questioning certain people's commitment to the cause unfairly. But there were also things that wouldn't even seem like secrets to most people that felt like as much of a violation—like when he described me tasting a plum for the very first time. I was a freshman in college and Dennis had given me my first plum and it had brought me joy. That he would include this simple moment, distort it to fit his narrative—the plum an obvious symbol for my sexual awakening—oh, I know it sounds silly, but it still makes me furious! Yes, when I got to the last page of the manuscript I was just in shock.

After that book came out, his version of the movement became gospel. He became famous. Everyone assumed I'd be grateful to have my name in the acknowledgements. Oh, thank you, Dennis, for saving me a spot on your raft of immortality! Don't get me wrong. I still followed his career from afar, invited him to guest lecture at the university. I used him like he used me. He was a talented motherfucker but those books were as limited and brutal as he was and it was Marianne's blood in those pages.

## Amanda

Everything I've gotten in my life has been acquired through persistence, hard work, and determination. My relationship with Dennis was no different. I am the kind of person who could have been an astronaut if I'd wanted to.

The motel I was staying in was near Times Square. It housed divorced dads and prostitutes—the kind of people who paid by the week. I got a doctor's note from a disreputable osteopath that said I was suffering from distress and complications related to my lost pregnancy and this allowed me to go on leave from the university without losing my stipend.

I did not mope around. I busied myself by setting up interviews and meetings with Dennis's friends, ostensibly for my dissertation. I developed a relationship with his sister, Rose. She seemed like she'd been waiting for a long time for someone to ask her opinions about the various events in his life.

I wanted to know everything, but most of all, I wanted to know what he looked for in a woman. I was sure that I could embody all those qualities. I knew already that he found me physically attractive, so that wouldn't be a problem. We hadn't slept together because of my surgery but we had been intimate.

After long days of interviewing people and visiting Dennis's childhood haunts I would often be exhausted but unable to sleep. I wasn't used to the noise of the city—the motel in particular had an active nightlife because of the prostitutes—and because I was so focused, wound so tight during the day, at night I found it difficult to relax. I would ride the subway or pace the motel hallways to try to lull myself to sleep. Sometimes the prostitutes had pot and they'd share it with me and that was nice because it helped me sleep.

The stipend I was getting from the university was not going very far in New York City and I had to charge the motel room to Barry's credit card. Eventually Barry said that he wouldn't keep paying for the motel unless I let him come visit. So he came over a long weekend, and I dutifully went with him to the opera and the Met and we "made love," as he called it, and afterward I held him as he sobbed. That visit showed me that I was not much different from the other inhabitants of the motel. When he got in the cab to go to the airport, I waved to him from the sidewalk, so happy to finally be free of him. A week later my uncle died and left me a small inheritance, and after that I cut off all contact with Barry. I could've moved to a better motel, or even an apartment, but it didn't seem necessary.

## EDITH (1997)

The trees are thick on both sides of the highway. They pop out, illuminated by the headlights, then flatten, slip into darkness. For long stretches we are the only ones on the road.

Charlie is telling me about a woman he met in an abandoned subway tunnel.

"She had a whole apartment under there. A c-c-couch. A bed. A fridge. A bookshelf. She had more furniture than I do, and she was tapped into the p-p-power grid. It was basically an apartment underneath 7th Avenue."

I turn away from the window and look at him.

"Was she beautiful?" I ask. An underground mermaid. Dirt in her long hair. My mother.

"The h-h-homeless woman?" He looks at me.

Was that a strange thing to ask?

"You just said she wasn't homeless, that she had an apartment inside the tunnel."

He nods. Then after a while he says: "No, she wasn't b-b-beautiful."

"I was just trying to picture her," I say under my breath, and flip the radio on to cover my embarrassment. I turn the dial through the stations, backwards and forwards, but I don't find anything. I leave it on static and turn it down until it's very quiet, then lean back in the seat.

He smiles. "You like static?"

"Yeah."

"Why?"

"I don't know… It reminds me of being a little kid." I look at his profile. "My mom would put Mae and me in front of the broken TV set."

"White n-n-noise is very soothing. Sounds like the inside of a womb."

"No."

"N-n-n-no?"

"No. I mean, maybe it's soothing, but that's not why she did it."

"Why then?" He yawns with his mouth closed. His nostrils flare.

"She'd make us watch the snow on the screen and tell her what we saw."

"Like a g-game?"

"Yes." It was. Mae would say it wasn't. I guess there were times when it hadn't felt entirely playful. I haven't told Charlie yet about the mental hospital. I'd just said "hospital." If he knew would he still call it a game?

"So, what kind of things d-did you see?"

"I didn't see anything. I saw snow. But I made things up, described scenes from shows I'd seen at other people's houses." I could tell Mom wanted something and I was trying to give it to her. Trying and failing. "My sister would see things, though."

"What kinds of things?"

"Visions. Strange stuff."

"How do you know she wasn't m-m-m-making them up too?"

"I don't. But she would go into a trance. You could pinch her and she wouldn't even notice. Also, the kind of stuff she saw wasn't anything exciting. A snake slithering up a tree. A boy rowing a boat. Like if she were to make them up wouldn't they be more dramatic? *A man with a knife!* That kind of thing. Why make up a boy in a boat?"

"She would stare at the TV set and s-s-see those things?"

"Yeah. Does that sound crazy?" I'm not sure what I want him to say. Yes, but if he were to say "yes," I wouldn't like it. She'd certainly been acting crazy in New York, but not like externally, not in a way I could explain to anybody else. It was the kind of thing where if I tried I'd be the one who sounded crazy.

He shrugs. "It sounds c-creative. My parents never invented games. If our TV broke they would fix it. They wouldn't see it as an opportunity to nurture my c-c-creativity. They had no sense of h-humor. They weren't unhappy, just very practical."

I guess that's what she'd been doing, nurturing our creativity. I yawn. The clock on the dashboard says 3:52 a.m. It's been a very long day.

"It's like those M-Magic Eye books," he continues.

"What?" I ball up a jacket and use it as a pillow.

"You know. Those p-p-p-picture books that look like abstract art, but if you stare at them and unfocus your eyes, or actually more like f-f-f-focus on some point in the distance, a 3-D picture emerges. A l-l-lion's head, or a house, or w-w-whatever. You've never seen a Magic Eye book?"

I close my eyes. "No, I've never heard of them."

"Yeah, I l-l-like that," he says after a while, out loud but to himself.

I'm drifting off. My body is heavier but my brain is lighter.

"That s-seems like something your mom would do," I hear him say through the haze of sleep.

I'm standing in the middle of the kitchen, water is overflowing from the sink. How would Charlie know what my mom would or would not do? I'm asleep. The whistle of the teakettle wakes me up. It's dark out. I am alone. A train is going by outside the truck. We are parked on the edge of an empty field. Charlie is not in the driver's side. He abandoned me here. The train is very close, maybe he jumped on one of the cars. Hadn't that been one of the stories he told me? He rode the rails out to Ohio after his mom died. I roll down my window and squint through the darkness hanging over the field. The air feels very still and wet. I turn and look back and there he is: stretched out in the bed of the truck, asleep.

## Mae

I'd hoped that Edie's departure would bring Dad and me closer, but it didn't. Not at first. He was distant and his mind was often elsewhere.

It was hard not to take it personally, but there were probably other things at play that had little to do with me or Edie. He was under a lot of pressure to produce his next book. I followed him to a meeting with his editor at an Upper East Side restaurant and when he caught me, he let me tag along, maybe because he hoped I would serve as a distraction. The editor was an older gentleman with a gray mustache who questioned me about my hobbies and interests through the drinks and appetizers, but once the entrees were brought out, he shifted into business mode and told Dad in no uncertain terms that if they had to push back the delivery date on the manuscript one more time, the deal would be null and void and Dad would have to return the advance.

Dad was silent on the walk back from the restaurant. It was unseasonably warm so we cut through Central Park, which was crowded with people rollerblading and walking their dogs. I couldn't stand seeing him upset. I begged him to return the advance if that's what he wanted. I told him that I'd be happy living in Central Park under a rock as long as it was with him.

Who was that Mothball to tell us what to do? We didn't need that stupid Old Mustache's money. Dad smiled wanly and rumpled my hair and bought us both fudgsicles from a cart. The truth was that we *did* need the Mothball's money because, among other things, it was paying for Mom's hospital bills. I hadn't realized until then that Dad had been supporting us financially in Louisiana. Mom had never mentioned it and I had never given much thought to where our money came from.

Soon after that meeting, Dad began writing. He wrote all day, and often into the night. The typewriter he used was very loud. At night I'd lie in bed, listening to him pound on it. I'd try to decipher what he was typing by the sounds.

He never left pages in the typewriter. In the mornings when he was still sleeping, I'd slip into his room and check. Sometimes I'd lie down next to him and stare at his face. If I unfocused my eyes a certain way and the light was dim enough I could see the man from the mugshot. There were traces of this buried face around the corners of the mouth, the cheekbones. When I'd get tired of that game, I would tickle his nose with the tip of my braid until he woke up, then I'd make us coffee and sit with him at the kitchen table, waiting for him to say something nice to me, to acknowledge and love me.

## Rivka

I was in my back room, looking at a delivery from a new artist, a deaf mute who paints magnificent landscapes of food. The show was about The Bottomless Hunger, something that exists inside each of us. I was lost in thought, watching my assistant unwrap the canvases, and so I was startled to find a strange woman standing next to me.

"You are not allowed in here," I told her.

"Rivka Procházková," she'd said. "I was hoping we could talk."

I froze. Her voice, its intensity—I still remember the feeling it gave me. Ice inside the heart. I thought: here is the moment I've been dreading. My daughter has found me. I had only been a teenager when I left her in the Prague orphanage.

For a long time I thought I wanted my daughter to appear so that it would be over and done with. So that any time a woman of a certain age looked at me, I wouldn't feel faint. Eventually I came to realize that I wanted my daughter to appear for other, more sentimental, reasons. And then finally, I started thinking about it so often that I decided to track her down, and this became a very sad story. But it has nothing to do with the woman in the gallery. That woman was not my daughter. She was writing some kind of book about Dennis. I think she said she was a student or was it a journalist? I was still catching my breath as she explained.

Her questions about Dennis were personal. I don't know why I answered her so obediently. I must have felt like I owed her something, carried over from the misunderstanding. She asked how Dennis and I had met, and I told her we had shared a table at an awards dinner. She asked if I had pursued him, and I said that I had. She asked how he had been as a lover, and I said he'd been good, very good. I'd had many lovers, but he'd been particularly memorable.

"Why is that?" she asked.

I told her that most people think being a good lover means relief, however temporary, from The Bottomless Hunger, but Dennis understood that it was quite the opposite, that we had to become the Hunger. She didn't like this answer. It was too abstract. She wanted to know what his sexual preferences were. I told her she'd have to ask him. Did I crawl to him on my knees? She wanted to know. Did he piss on my face? Her persistence took me aback. I told her that I had nothing else to say. My assistant escorted her out, then locked the door and led me into the back room where he fucked me on the floor among the newly arrived canvases. He is a man who enjoys hearing me talk about my relations with other men.

## MAE

I'd be bored out of my mind, listening to Dad type and crumple pages all day and night. I'd play with the cat, choreograph a dance to the rhythm of the typewriter, open up a book and start reading from the middle. None of these distractions could really hold my attention because I was so completely focused on him—I couldn't concentrate on anything else.

The highlights of my day would be the mealtimes, when he'd come out of his room. For lunch he'd take me to either the Thai restaurant around the corner or the Greek Gyro place across the street. Often, though, he'd be lost in a haze, and it hurt my feelings that he preferred the alternate reality of his book to spending time with me. He had not acted this way when Edie was around.

It was at the Thai restaurant, after an entire meal had gone by without him saying a word, that I finally couldn't contain myself any longer. "You love her more than me," I said as he stared off into space, our empty plates between us.

"Who?" he'd asked, blinking several times, momentarily brought back to me.

I had meant Edie but I could see then that he was thinking about someone else.

I was upset. I pouted and gave him the silent treatment all

afternoon but I don't think he even noticed. When he'd pass me in the hallway on his way to the bathroom or to the kitchen, he'd look at me without really seeing me. Maybe this is how Mom had felt when she'd been with him. I understood how it could drive a person mad. I'd do stupid things to get his attention. I'd cut myself on purpose while slicing vegetables for our salad. He'd bandaged me up, but so what? The tug of whatever was in his mind was much stronger than the scenes I was making. It's like he was in an underwater cave, and I was splashing in the bathtub. If I wanted to be with him, I would also have to descend into that cave. And eventually that is what I did.

## Edith (1997)

I wake up and we're driving through the mountains. They're beautiful. God, I feel good. I feel like yesterday was a cocoon and today I've emerged from it as my true self. I must have been asleep for a long time, because the light coming in through the windshield is yellow. Afternoon light. The best kind, according to Mom. Mom, I will be seeing you in a matter of hours.

I watch Charlie drive, his mouth hanging slightly open, hair falling over his forehead, eyelashes glowing in the sunlight like little halos. He looks so normal when he's not stuttering, so handsome. I think about the way his lips and chin tremble when he talks. Mae's right, it's repulsive, but it's also kind of fascinating. I picture his trembling mouth on top of mine. His tongue seizing up against my tongue.

"Good m-morning," he says. He's noticed me watching him.

I yawn and stretch. Yawn again. He's squinting at the road, so I reach over and lower the sun visor on the driver's side, and he looks at me like it's the kindest thing anybody has ever done for him. I take a sip of lukewarm coffee from his paper cup. The clock on the dashboard reads 5:47 p.m.

"Where are we?" I ask.

"West Virginia. Are you h-h-hungry?"

The billboards along the side of the highway interrupt the

view of the mountains. They are counting down to a diner that serves breakfast all day. The eggs glisten, the sausage glistens, the pancakes look like you could take a nap in them face down. We decide to go there. I feel giddy. Giddyup.

In the parking lot, the air is warm. It smells so nice. I grab Charlie by the sleeve of his plaid flannel.

"Do you feel that?" I ask him, lifting my face up to the sky, into the wind.

"W-w-what?" We left spring and entered summer.

"The air. It's already Southern."

He laughs. "You s-s-smell that you're closer to home. Like that dog who always f-f-f-finds its way back."

"Are you calling me a dog?" I ask, shaking him by the sleeve, laughing. "Are you calling me a fucking dog?"

Our laughter follows us into the diner, invades the hum of the fluorescent lights and the scraping silverware. I ask for the scenic booth facing the mountain, and let go of his sleeve only when we sit down.

"It smells like a swimming pool," I say.

"They j-just mopped the floor." Charlie points to a bucket and mop, left out and leaning, in the corner of the room.

The fat waitress brings us water. The skinny one argues with someone in the kitchen through the little window.

"What are you getting?" I ask, unsticking the laminated pages of the menu. There are photos of all the dishes.

Charlie points to a picture of a Jell-O salad and I laugh at this familiar game—find the grossest thing on the menu. "The l-l-l-local delicacy," he reads.

I flip through to the entrees and point to a picture of a gray slab of meat on a bed of spaghetti. The washed-out colors of the print job make it look particularly gruesome. "I'm gonna go with the crime scene photo," I say.

He cracks up. We laugh longer than we probably should because it's not that funny. I look at the picture again and laugh harder. No, it's pretty funny. Charlie pulls the menu off the table so we can't look at it anymore. He catches his breath, takes a sip of water, chews on the ice, grins.

And then, we're just staring across the table at each other, smiling and not saying anything. Several minutes go by like this, or maybe much longer. I look away. Something in his face looks so open that it makes me embarrassed. A feeling drills through me, down my throat and between my legs. Our ice water in the plastic octagonal glasses casts long shadows on the tabletop. Little black-and-white oceans.

"W-w-what are you thinking about?" He breaks the silence first.

"I guess… that I'm happy," I say, looking up at his face, but not his eyes.

He nods. "Happiness was like a bull and they were trying to hold on," he whispers weirdly.

"What?"

"It's a l-l-line from your dad's book," he says. "S-sorry, I thought you knew it."

"Oh, no," I say. "I've never actually read him."

Whose happiness had Dennis been writing about? His and Mom's? The Happiness Rodeo. I'd say he and Mom did not manage to hold on very well. They both fell off and what? Happiness trampled them? *C'est la vie!* What a weird metaphor. I wonder how you say *bull* in French? *Vache?* No. That's *cow.* Happiness is like a cow. The waitress is like a cow. Her belly, bisected by that apron, looks like an udder. She licks the tip of her pencil and takes our order. Neither of us get what we said we would.

When she leaves, Charlie lights a cigarette. I gesture for him to pass it to me.

He hesitates. "I d-d-didn't know you smoked."

My hand brushes against his fingers as I take it.

"I don't," I say, and let the cigarette hang out of the corner of my mouth without breathing in.

I try to do a smoke ring. My mom taught me how once, but I start coughing.

"You al-l-l right?" he asks, taking the cigarette back, and pushing my water towards me.

I nod but can't stop coughing. An old couple in a booth across the restaurant is watching us. The woman has tubes coming out of her nose, connected to an oxygen tank. I wave and cough, wave and cough. Take a sip of the water, a deep breath.

"That was embarrassing," I finally say after I've stopped coughing. He must think I'm a real idiot.

"It's probably better not to start anyway," he says with the cigarette in his mouth. The cigarette changes his face. It's sexy. A little bit tough.

The waitress sets down a monster stack of pancakes in front of me. "Anything else?" she asks Charlie.

I watch him pour hot sauce over his eggs and dip the wheat toast in the yolk. We chew for a while in silence, staring out at the mountain. Unlike the ranges in the distance that look blue or even purple, this mountain is covered in light green grass. It looks like a very difficult golf course.

"So," I say after I swallow several mouthfuls of pancake. "What about you? What are you thinking about?"

That you're also happy? That you think I'm wonderful despite my making an ass of myself with the cigarette?

He finishes chewing, swallows, then carefully puts the cigarette in his mouth before answering. "Mountain top removal," he says.

What?

He keeps the cigarette in his mouth as he talks. "See the grass up there?" He points with his fork, the tines gluey with yolk. "It's not supposed to look like that. A coal company, probably Massey, blew the top off that mountain to get to the coal, turned the surface of it into a fucking moonscape, polluted the water and air with chemicals. There's a big toxic lake in there with the runoff, called a slurry pond. People around here, children, are 30 times as likely to get cancer, asthma, all kinds of nasty stuff. Then the coal company 'beautified' the whole mess by planting that bullshit grass..."

That's what it is! He hasn't stuttered. It must be having a cigarette in his mouth. Maybe that's why he smokes. Or, maybe it's because he's ranting about the mountain. Like if he talks about something he cares about he overcomes it or something.

"What?" he asks.

I shrug.

"You're l-l-looking at me funny." The stutter is back. He puts the cigarette out and reaches for my hand across the table. "So, do you want to go?"

"Where?"

"To a s-s-slurry pond. A little adventure."

"Okay."

His hand is warm and callused. I want him to touch my face and body with his big, strange hands and kiss my mouth. He'll taste like hot sauce, cigarettes, and coffee. He's so much more substantial than Markus ever was. The whole thing with Markus was ridiculous. I can't believe that I was at all broken up over it.

Charlie lets go of my hand and reaches for his wallet when the waitress sets the check down. I offer to pay but he doesn't let me.

And then he stands as if nothing has just passed between us. He walks ahead, not noticing that I am hesitating, that I hadn't wanted the moment to end quite yet.

I stop next to a table of church ladies. Will he look back and notice I have fallen behind? Turn around and look at me, Charlie. Am I testing him? Maybe. He keeps walking. Am I being immature? Probably.

One of the church ladies, wearing a teal straw hat, puts

down the salt shaker emphatically and says to the other: "Nancy Douglas is a bitch." When Charlie gets to the door he turns around and waits for me to catch up. I run across the restaurant and almost into his arms. Into his truck, anyway.

## MAE

After a while, the pounding of Dad's typewriter slowed and slowed and stopped. Dad would be sitting in his room, and when he saw me looking at him from the couch he'd get up and close the door. Occasionally, I would hear a few taps but nothing like the racket I'd become accustomed to.

Once I heard him literally banging his head against the desk. The noise woke me up and I knew exactly what it was. Don't ask me how, I just recognized the sound, and sure enough, the next day he had a purple welt on his cheekbone, a big bruise, and when I tried to touch it, he swatted my hand away, no acknowledgement at all that this hand was connected to someone he cared about.

Rose would call in the mornings and try to make plans with us, but Dad would come up with excuses not to see her. He didn't tell her that Edie ran away. He must have felt ashamed.

I remember eavesdropping on their conversation while Dad and I had breakfast.

"It's not healthy," I heard Rose's tinny voice coming from the receiver. "They should be in school. They need to be around people their age. You have a responsibility."

I hated people my age. They'd been nothing but cruel to me,

or at best indifferent. I pinched Dad's arm and looked at him pleadingly, my mouth full of unchewed cereal. Sending me away to school would have been a huge betrayal.

He must have felt sorry for me, because he lowered his voice as if I couldn't hear him, and said: "Of course, Rose. But it's a delicate situation. You understand. They'll start in the fall."

Rose was easily disarmed if Dad bothered with it. "Well, an evening class at a university, at least," she said.

"A university class. That's an idea!" Dad said and winked at me. I looked down at my bowl of milk and shrugged, trying to appear neutral and agreeable, though I wasn't keen on him getting rid of me, even for a few evenings a week.

I'd hoped the whole idea of school would be forgotten, but later when he came out of his room for dinner after another tortured afternoon of not writing, he asked me what I'd like to study.

"Nothing," was the honest answer, but I said, "Photography." I'd chosen it pretty much at random. Once, when we were still going on our walks, Dad had taken Edie and me to The Strand (18 miles of books!) and bought me a monograph of Garry Winogrand's zoo photographs.

Dad seemed pleased with my answer. He beckoned me into his room. I hadn't been allowed in there for days. It was a mess. Tangled typewriter ribbons. Overflowing ashtrays. Crumpled and torn pages on the floor. A sour smell. I sat on his bed and watched him dig through the boxes in his closet until he found what he'd been looking for: Grandpa Jackson's old camera—a 35mm Leica, which I still use to this day.

Dad showed me how to adjust the light meter but when I tried to photograph him, he grew irritated, said I was distracting him, and sent me out into the living room to photograph the cat.

## Edith (1997)

Charlie gets out a map and traces something with his finger before he starts the engine. I listen to my breath as I watch him concentrating, like he's full of electric sparks.

"There's a path to a slurry p-p-pond," he says, "not too far from here. A b-b-buddy took me once."

I picture a sludgy swamp, the kind we have back home, hidden somewhere inside that grassy golf-course mountaintop. I picture Charlie and me holding hands and sinking into it, slowly, slowly. Warm toxic mud rising up our legs. That's how fossils are made.

We drive for a while up a narrow road under big industrial metal chutes. They look like broken amusement park rides, metal slides or deconstructed roller coasters. The road has gone from paved to gravel to dirt. By the time we drive off the road and park between two pine trees, the air outside is shadowy and blue. A sound like maracas. Crickets or tree frogs?

"Won't it be too dark to see anything?" I ask.

Charlie shakes his head and passes me a flashlight. "It's better in the d-dark."

I click it on, but he covers the light with his hand. "Not yet," he says.

We climb over a chain link fence and walk along a dirt path.

We walk in silence in the thin gray light, with him several steps ahead of me. At one point the path curves and the trees thin out and we have a view of the highway below, the last bits of sunset reflected off the windshields of the passing pickup trucks.

We keep walking. There is another fence, this one has barbed wire at the top. Maybe we should turn back if someone doesn't want us here this much. Charlie doesn't hesitate, though, and I don't say anything. He climbs the fence in a couple quick movements, drapes his Carhartt coat over the barbed wire and holds it there so I don't cut myself. Once I'm over, he carefully pulls the coat free without even ripping it. His movements are so swift, precise, and controlled—why doesn't this extend to his mouth?

It's dark already when we get to a small clearing with the parked cranes and tractors. Their outlines look like dinosaurs. We zigzag between them, then continue on the dirt road into the woods. We see the headlights of a car in the distance, coming downhill, and Charlie pulls me in behind a big rock.

"What are they going—" I start to ask him, but he shakes his head quickly and puts his hand over my mouth for good measure. What are they going to do to us? Is he scared at all?

He breathes against my cheek, and I think he is going to kiss me but he doesn't. As soon as the car passes, he gets up and we keep going. Even though it's dark now, he still doesn't want to use the flashlights. We almost trip when we get to the third fence. It's waist-high and wooden. The wood is old and mossy, rotten. It must have been put up a long time ago and forgotten.

## LETTER FROM
## JACKSON McLEAN TO DENNIS LOMACK

January 4, 1969

Dear Dennis,

I hope you're well and that your studies are progressing at Columbia. Things here have heated up. I'm sure you've heard from Ann about the charges against me. I've tried to shield Marianne from this as much as possible, but there's only so much I can do. And on top of all this, my health is failing.

As for the trial—I didn't really expect to stomp on the face of "everything we hold sacred" and get away with it. It was inevitable that there would be a backlash. If you push in one direction, the pendulum will swing back with equal force, and here I am, standing in its path. I wish I could say that I share Ann's stubborn optimism, but I don't. If the trial won't kill me, my illness will.

This is a difficult letter for me to write because I admire you as a man a great deal. I consider you a friend and a decent human being. However, I think you understand why I asked you not to come. The truth is—and you can deny it all you want, but why lie to a dying man?—I have watched something growing between you and my daughter for quite some time.

I am not writing this to hurt you. You deserve happiness, but not with my Marianne. She is sensitive and I know you well enough by now to say that you will harm her. I don't care if it's not intentional. I don't care if it's by accident. You will hurt her and I don't want you near her. Do you understand? I should have never encouraged your correspondence. She is a child. She looks up to you and sleeps with your letters under her pillow and probably thinks that she is in love with you, but what does she know? What she feels will change. In two years you will be a distant memory.

Please, stop writing her those letters, those awful letters, flirtatious but never overtly so. Why do you do that? So you can deny it when I catch you? Am I supposed to believe that your interest is pure? That I'm misinterpreting? Who do you take me for, Dennis?!

Consider this a dying man's wish.


Yours,
Jackson McLean

## EDITH (1997)

Charlie and I crawl across the grassy knoll until we reach the drop-off. From here we can see the tarry black lake glistening in the dark below us. On its oily sheen, a yellow smudge—the reflection of the moon. Charlie pulls his shirt over his nose and mouth and gestures for me to do the same. The smell makes me dizzy, permanent markers and dead animals, the guts and bowels of the earth. My mouth tastes metallic.

Charlie grabs my hand and squeezes it. I can't see much of his face in the dark, just his profile as he looks down below. He whispers through his shirt: "Eight hundred and fifty million gallons of carcinogenic runoff."

He lists more facts, but they don't matter to me. The lake is beautiful. It's something from a fairytale nightmare. It's the embodiment of everything mean and awful and wrong, contained and glittering.

We don't stay long because the fumes are so toxic. On our walk back to the truck I keep thinking of Mom, of the pond inside her, of the broken dam and the sludge contaminating her, pouring out into her veins. If Mae were here, what would she think of all this?

I know what she would say. She would say that I don't understand anything, that it was she who'd been Mom's slurry pond.

"Are you okay?" Charlie's voice comes from many steps ahead. "We need to keep walking."

# Chapter 6

The night air is warm and wet. I roll my window down all the way and let the breeze blow through my matted hair. I'm home. I'm finally home. This air is enough to make my bones feel like they've turned to cartilage.

"Turn off at the next exit," I say, patting Charlie's shoulder. He clicks on the blinker. It's been a long day on the road. Every once in a while he bulges out his eyes as if he's being strangled, a technique, I think, for keeping himself awake. He's been doing all the driving because I don't know how to drive stick. He tried to show me in a dark parking lot after we stopped for gas but it didn't go well.

"Are w-w-we going to your house?" His question turns into a yawn.

"To the hospital."

I know it's late and that the hospital will probably be closed to visitors but I want to feel like I'm near her for a moment. It seems cold to drive all the way down here and not go straight there.

I watch Charlie's face as we pull up to the building past the sign: St. Vincent's. There's no flicker of recognition or judgment. I haven't told him that it's a mental hospital, so maybe he doesn't know. Nothing about the building gives it away as such.

Southern Louisiana has a lot of old haunted-looking places, but this isn't one of them. It's a newer construction, nondescript, seven stories tall with a fenced-in garden. I'd driven by it a million times and assumed it was an office park or a community college.

The parking lot is mostly empty except for a few cars in a gated section that must belong to the doctors and nurses.

"The lights are on," I say hopefully, as Charlie pulls up to the front entrance.

"Hospitals always l-l-leave the lights on," he says.

I get out while Charlie waits in the car. The front doors are locked. There is an empty room, a waiting room maybe, couches, tables, a front desk where a nurse or somebody usually sits. At the end of the room is an open door leading to a long, well-lit corridor. A security guard sits halfway down the hall, reading a newspaper. I knock and wave, but the glass is so thick it barely makes a sound. The guard doesn't look up.

I walk along the side of the building until I get to a hedge growing around a tall wrought iron fence. I think about all the fences we climbed in West Virginia, but I don't try to climb this one.

The fence goes around the residential wing of the hospital. The windows are square, ten on each floor. They're the kind office towers have, the kind that don't open. Of course they don't open. Duh. It's a mental hospital. In the rooms where the blinds are up there's nothing to see—ceiling tiles and fluorescent lights.

Which of these rooms is Mom's? Is she even on this side of the building? I try to concentrate on each window. Do any of them give me a "Mom" feeling?

This is stupid. Something Mae would do. If she were here she'd point to a window and be like, "That one! I just know!" like she has some kind of homing device in her brain that I don't. But really, Mae, and obviously I never said this to her, but if you're so "in tune" and always know everything, then why the fuck were you upstairs while Mom was in the kitchen, tying our old jump rope around her neck?

A hand on my shoulder. Jesus. It's Charlie. I hadn't heard him get out of the car.

"Are you all right?" he says. "I d-d-didn't mean to scare you."

Have I been here long?

"An orderly told me that they start taking visitors at 10 a.m. tomorrow. I caught him on his s-s-s-smoke break."

I don't want to leave yet. Charlie stands there and looks at me. I smile. I smile so that he'll stop looking so closely.

A thump. The sound of a bird flying into glass. And then again. The sound is coming from the top floor. A woman's face slams into the window, over and over. I feel the smile quivering on my mouth as Charlie pulls me away from the hedge. Two nurses inside rush to the woman, lower the blinds.

For a second, I thought that woman was Mom. But it wasn't. It wasn't Mom at all. Just some crazy person. Charlie is guiding me back to the truck, but I'm walking sideways because I can't stop looking at the wall of windows.

On the fifth floor, I think I see the blinds shift, a shadow move. I stop.

Charlie lets go of my elbow.

"W-w-what?" he says, turns around and squints at where I'm looking.

It's her. I'm sure of it somehow.

"Nothing," I say, and get into the truck.

"We'll c-c-come back in the morning," he says and starts the engine.

## MAE

One evening, Dad was late picking me up from my photography class. I waited and waited outside the building. When he finally showed, there was something about his face that scared me. It looked literally darker. His skin, his eyes, even his beard, had a gloom to them I'd never seen before.

He said that the deadline was approaching and he had nothing to give his publisher. What he'd written was utter shit. A photocopy of a photocopy of a photocopy of his first book. The critics wouldn't even bother tearing it apart. It wouldn't be worth the newsprint. He was giving up.

He'd never talked to me about his writing before, and it was thrilling that he was confiding in me about his fears.

"Fuck the critics," I said, feeling rather bold, but he didn't seem to hear me.

He could never ask me to do what I was about to do, but I knew that he needed me to do it.

I swung my camera over my shoulder and said, in a voice not my own: *I don't want to go home yet, take me somewhere else.* It was not a question. It was a command.

The street lamps had been switched on, though it was not dark yet. The sun was beginning to set somewhere on the other side of the buildings. Dad looked at me oddly. I wasn't going to wait for the hesitation, the hedging. I took his hand and walked a few paces ahead of him.

Was this intentional? I don't know. I don't think I was conscious of it. I don't think I was thinking: from behind, with my hair falling down my back and my new walk, borrowed much like my voice, I would transform into the spitting image of my mother.

I led us downtown, past the East Village tenements. How had I known which building to go to? How had I known which was the one he'd lived in with her? Which rooftop had been the site of their first kiss? How had I known there would be paper jammed into the lock, so that it would open and we would be able to walk up the stairs, six flights, and then another, until we were standing on the tar paper roof under an orange sky?

I just knew.

A skeptic might say that he'd been guiding me, despite my walking ahead of him, that I was no different from a shopping cart or a baby carriage. That dogs can't count, that I was responding subconsciously to his slight movements, to the tensing and twitching of his warm hand. But I don't think this is true. I think, I really do, that my mother was sitting in her hospital room, melding her mind into mine. I was there, but someone else was there too, someone who knew exactly where to go and what to do.

Up on the roof, Dad and I stood facing each other. I pushed his hair back with my wrist the way Mom would have. He stared at me with his cloudy, miserable eyes. The sun was a bloody orb hanging in the sky behind us.

It's possible that up until that point I'd been playing a part, but on the roof, I can say with certainty that what happened was not in my control. The words coming out of me were not my own.

"Marianne," Dad said, grabbing me by the wrist. And as he

said it, the lunacy of the situation must have dawned on him because he shuddered. He dropped my hand and backed away from me as if I was some kind of black hole that was pulling him in. His own daughter. When I tried to put my arms around his neck, he pushed me, hard enough that I fell and skinned my knee.

He left me on the roof, and I became myself again. I was too ashamed to move. I thought: he's finally seen how sick and disgusting I am. This was Mom's way of punishing me for choosing him over her.

It was dark when I finally came down and found Dad sitting in a taxicab with the meter running. I got in and we rode home in silence. I was humiliated. I couldn't look at him. I went straight to bed without saying a word. I lay there stiffly, fully clothed, thinking I'd ruined my one chance at happiness.

And then, I heard him begin to type. There had never been a more beautiful sound than the typewriter that night, pounding through the wall into the morning.

The next day, Dad was sweet and considerate and we acted as if nothing out of the ordinary had happened, as if things were back to how they were before Edie left. He even took me to the Film Forum to see a Fellini film, and I put my head on his shoulder and everything was fine.

I'd bring Rose lunch at her dingy law firm in Queens. Her clients were court appointed—rapists, gang bangers, small-time drug dealers. The waiting room was crowded and smelled like cat piss. Rose's default expression was sour and pinched, but when she'd see me her demeanor would change completely. Once her face relaxed, there was even a familial resemblance to her brother. She loved talking about Dennis. As a boy, she said that he'd been sickly and imaginative, an inveterate liar, who, despite being the youngest, would always tell the most engrossing bedtime stories. She invited me to her place on Long Island where, she told me, she had various Dennis-related artifacts. I took the train out to her large Victorian on the grounds of Montauk Academy, an elite boarding school where her husband was the headmaster. Rose served me coffee and took me into a room that had been arranged like a museum exhibit.

There, on display, was Dennis's very first book, which he'd written at the age of eight and illustrated himself. It was an adventure story about a man who becomes a ghost and then haunts the woman he loves—thematically in keeping with his later work. And next to it on the shelf, forgotten and gathering dust, the slim volume of his fairytale translations. The text was rare. I had only seen Prof. Jones' photocopy. And, it had a sentimental dimension for me, since it was my entry point into Dennis's life. I'd banked on it being an obscure enough choice of study to pique his interest and differentiate me from the throng of other graduate students who wanted to talk to him about *Yesterday's Bonfires*.

Rose saw that I was lingering with the book so she offered to lend it to me. She wanted my full attention as she complained about Dennis's ex-wife. She had not approved of his marriage to Marianne and didn't shy away from saying so.

She showed me a photograph of Dennis and Marianne in New York, standing on the steps of a courthouse. It took me a moment to realize that it was their wedding, since it was such a casual snapshot—no white gown, no tuxedo. Marianne was wearing some sort of Indian hippie caftan, and he was wearing jeans and a tweed jacket. The only thing that indicated it was a wedding photo was the blurred bouquet of flowers Marianne was getting ready to throw toward the camera.

I much prefer the solid, adult Dennis to that beardless creature, the expression on his face so bare, so disgustingly earnest, that I felt embarrassed for him. The way he was looking at Marianne in the photo made my hands shake and I spilled coffee down the front of my dress.

My jealousy only increased, when on my train ride home, I discovered what must have been Marianne's notes in the margins of the book. The handwriting was feminine—tight and neat:

*the witch & i lay by the river.*
*i held her by her hair so she wouldn't fly away.*

*i whispered:*
*"i have done everything you've asked. have i not done everything you've asked? why have you always,*
*why have you always hated me?*
*i have loved nothing & nobody but you.*

*the smallest grain of sand that you've given me,*
*i've carved into a castle.*
*the smallest feather,*
*i've turned into a flock of birds.*
*the smallest glance,*
*i've turned into a child.*
*i have given you all of these things."*

*"but i did not want any of those things," said the witch.*

The text continued on the next page:

*"what is it that you want?" i asked. "i'll give you anything you want."*

*the witch turned into a termite & crawled into my ear. she chewed tunnels through my brain & down my throat, through my guts & into my cock. she chewed through every organ & blood vessel. the last thing she ate was my heart.*

*"now we're even," she said in her tiny termite voice.*

Her assertion that she had hollowed out Dennis infuriated me. I would have given anything to be "held down" by him. And her choice to write these "poems" from Dennis's point of view was irritating—meek and presumptuous at the same time.

That evening, as I scrubbed the coffee stain from my dress in the motel sink, I considered abandoning my project. I've always been a jealous person, so prying into Dennis's love life was unpleasant. However, I decided it was crucial to be fully informed and prepared because I knew that I would probably only have one more opportunity to be with him and I couldn't blow it.

## Edith (1997)

I take Charlie on a night tour of my empty town.

"It's all on the way," I lie as I direct him to Old Metairie Rd. I make him slow down as we pass my high school. I point out the adjacent field where people go to dry hump, watch his face as I say the words "dry hump," but he just yawns. I make him drive past my favorite record store, which is closed, of course, the metal grate down, covering the windows. I make him drive to the abandoned house by Lake Pontchartrain, where you can jump right off the splintery dock into the water.

"Want to go for a dip?" I ask. We can swim naked in the cold lake, have our first kiss in the moonlight while treading water.

"No, Edie. I'm t-t-t-tired. Let's go home." He holds my hand as he shifts the truck into gear. It's sweet the way he said "home," not "your house." He hasn't realized yet that this is it. This is really our last night together. There'll be no place for us out here. He won't fit in with my life, with caring for Mom, and once he sees how I am with my friends he'll realize that I've only been pretending to be someone interesting and grown up.

He drives down Crescent Blvd. We're getting closer and closer to the end of all this, whatever "this" is. We turn onto my street. It looks the same. The Lewises are watching TV in their upstairs bedroom. I can tell by the flickering blue light. The other houses are dark. This isn't New Orleans. People turn into pumpkins at midnight.

I don't point my house out to him, let him drive past it. I can't go back yet. I just can't. I'm not ready. Dennis had been in such a hurry to get us out that who knows what kind of mess we left in there. A bowl of rotting fruit on the kitchen table, the bread knife on the floor where I dropped it next to a puddle of piss. No. I want to have one last night that's my own. Is that horrible? Tomorrow, I'll come home and deal with everything. But tonight I'm not going to be weighed down by that stuff.

I make a production of looking for my key. "I'm sorry, I guess I forgot it," I say and give him directions to a motel by the hospital.

"Really? You d-don't have a spare h-hidden?" He seems a little put out by these drives, these loops, but that's all he says. I pretend I didn't hear him, stick my head out the window and close my eyes, let the warm wind hit my face.

## LETTER FROM
## DENNIS LOMACK TO MARIANNE LOUISE MCLEAN

[1985]

Dear M—

The keys are on the counter. Doreen says they're releasing you tomorrow. I promised her I'd be gone by the time you came home. I don't want to go but I see myself draining you of everything good and I don't know if it will ever come back. Edie is so tiny and worried. Mae cries inconsolably because your misery is poisoning your milk. She literally chokes on your unhappiness. (What if it had been the girls who found you and not Doreen? Do you not think about these things? You don't. Of course you don't.)

And all these dramatics because of what, exactly? That stupid letter?

First of all: I loved you more than anything, anything. Second of all: I would have tried to stay away, probably, but, if you remember, it was you who came to me. YOU on MY doorstep, not the other way around. Standing there, wet. Walked all the way from Port Authority in the rain. And I still remember your hair matted to your neck and that stupid tiny suitcase. What can a person even fit into a suitcase that small? Thirdly: What did he know? That's what I had thought. What did your father really know? You always magnified him into a seer-god-saint-prophet. But, really, what could he know about our happiness?

I loved you, Marianne. I still do. You've accused me of loving not you, but rather, of loving how you make me feel. What an absurd distinction. And not even accurate. You make me feel terrible most of the time! But I can't imagine feeling anything without you. I can't imagine being away from you. But I don't have to imagine it, I suppose, because I'm leaving. You're right, I don't know how to be with you without wanting to take everything, without wanting to kill you and devour you and then bring you back to life, and then write about you and do it all again. Isn't that love?

But so is this: You're free of me. I promise you. Completely free. I will not call. I will not write. I won't come near you. You say that is what it takes for you to be better, it's done. I'm gone.

I love you.
Dennis

## Mae

That spring, Dad was the only thing that existed for me. I wanted very much to please him. I wanted his attention constantly. If his attention was on Mom, and it always seemed to be, well then I would *become* Marianne. I would defy logic, physics, the time-space continuum, whatever it took to get and hold his attention.

After the incident on the roof, he would let me sit with him as he worked. He would talk to me sometimes, deep in thought, and I would answer him as Mom. I would come and light his cigarette and sit on his lap until he began typing again, and then I'd disappear for him, existing only in the sound of the keys. When Dad wasn't looking at me or thinking about me I felt as though I wasn't there all the way.

We hadn't been leaving the apartment much, so when one afternoon he took me to a horse track in Yonkers, I knew it was an important outing. He never asked me to become Marianne, instead, as we sat on the bleachers, he removed a black velvet pouch from his pocket and handed it to me. Inside was a pair of gold-plated binoculars. I can still imagine their weight in my hands, and that feeling as I held them, of me shrinking and Mom expanding inside of me.

Dad barely looked at the track. He was watching me watch the horses through the binoculars. I've never liked horses but this didn't matter because I was watching the races through Mom's eyes and not my own, and thus I was able to find the horses beautiful and the races thrilling. I could feel Mom inside of me, guiding me to a small dappled horse named Eagle's Dream. Even his name seemed like something out of one of her poems. When, despite the 20:1 odds, Eagle's Dream leapt ahead to the finish line, Dad and I jumped up and down, clutching each other, flushed with excitement. I won $200. It was such a thrill being with Dad out in public on this invisible stage, with all the cigar-smoking men and the ticket-selling women as unwitting extras in our performance. I think Dad saw the win as a sign, divine permission for what he was asking me to do. We began to go on other outings like this.

I knew when I was channeling Mom well because there'd be a tremor in his face or in his hands that would've been imperceptible to anybody else. He missed her terribly, and having her back, even in these fleeting moments, meant a lot to him and to his work. After these scenes we would come home and he would type through the evening and into the night and I would scrub my face and change into pajamas and exhausted, be returned into my role as "Mae."

I had an incredible talent for being Dad's muse. It was easy to convince myself that as Mom's understudy his feelings for her were meant for me.

## Edith (1997)

The motel I take Charlie to is called The Aquarius. Markus and I once saw our physics teacher drive up here with the school secretary. We'd joked about getting a room for ourselves, but of course we didn't. I didn't have a fake ID and Markus is a coward.

The room Charlie gets us is on the second floor. It looks just like in the movies—a dark green bedspread, wicker furniture, a glass ashtray on top of the television set. I get undressed and climb under the covers. Charlie pretends he isn't looking at me. He slowly unlaces his boots and stares at the painting hanging over the bed.

"How's the b-b-bed," he asks me only once I'm fully under the sheet.

"Fine." I stretch out like a starfish. "Comfortable." I bounce a little and the springs creek.

"You tired?" I say.

"Mhhm," Charlie says. He angles his body away from me as he gets undressed down to his boxer shorts. His back is pale and muscular. I want to tell him that he looks like a marble statue. He does—so white and hairless—but I'm too shy to say it out loud.

He clicks the light off with the switch on his bedside table. The room goes dark, but then my eyes adjust to the greenish light coming in from the parking lot—from the streetlamps and the motel's neon sign. Charlie is lying on his back as far away from me as possible.

He turns to face me, hand under his cheek.

"I'm sorry we couldn't get separate beds," he whispers.

I shrug. I'm not.

"Are you all right?" he whispers. He doesn't stutter when he whispers.

I shrug again. He reaches his hand out to me but then puts it back down. "Goodnight," he says.

I'm not ready for "goodnight." I watch him shift and close his eyes and my heart starts racing. This can't be it. I stand up on the bed, take a couple wobbly steps in his direction so my legs are towering over his head. I inspect the painting he'd been looking at earlier, run my fingers over the bumpy surface of the canvas. Even in the dark I can tell that it's a sailboat on an ocean. At home, in Mom's room, we have a big oceanscape that my grandfather painted. It's funny to think that I hadn't seen the real ocean until I visited Dennis.

I glance down at Charlie's face. Is he asleep? No, but his eyes are closed. I poke his shoulder with my big toe.

"What?" he whispers. I poke him again. "What?" He smiles, but keeps his eyes closed, wraps his hand around my foot.

"Uh… Have you ever been sailing?" I ask. I can't think of anything else, and I don't want him to go to sleep. He doesn't let go of my foot. He's stroking the bottom of it with his thumb. I hold my breath and hope that he won't stop.

"Mmhm," he finally says, "I have." And then when I can't think of anything else to say, he says: "We should get some sleep."

Disappointment swells in my throat. Does he really mean it? I keep standing there in the dark. I won't move until he touches me again. 1…2…3…4…5…6. He shifts and looks up. The whites of his eyes glint like a knife. I put my foot on his neck, feel his pulse against my arch. Is it fast? Will he touch me? I feel him swallow. We're both very still, the feeling between us that has been building over the long car ride... Or am I just imagining this? No. He wraps his hand around my ankle and slides it up my leg.

A weird croak comes out of me, not mine exactly. Maybe I should be embarrassed but I'm not. His hand stops mid-thigh, I step harder onto his throat. He licks his lips. Reach your hand farther, I want to say, but he stays very still, then suddenly he arches his back and grabs my hips, pulling me down onto his face. He kisses me through my underwear. He kisses hard, with his teeth, and sucks through the fabric. He slips his hand under the elastic, puts a finger inside of me. I lean my forehead against the wicker headboard. It feels so good what he's doing, hot breath between my legs, a finger swirling in a circle, wider and wider. Nobody's ever gone down on me before, not for real, not like this.

Charlie pushes me onto the bed and gets on top. His mouth, a minty ashtray and also something else. Me? It makes me feel like a cannibal, knowing what I taste like.

"Are you sure—" Charlie starts to say.

"Yes," I interrupt and jam my tongue in his mouth before he has a chance to change his mind. I reach down and wrap my hand around his dick. It surprises me. From the way it felt against my leg I hadn't expected it to be so big. Thick and heavy. Markus was always kind of half-mast wobbly. This thing is a cudgel. I squeeze it and watch his face. He closes his eyes, but not all the way, there's a flutter of white eyeball. It feels powerful, holding him there, like he's on a leash. So this is what it's like with a man. I remember that part in Dennis's book, the part Mae read to me.

His eyes go wide. "Not so hard," he says. No trace of the stutter. His face looks different in the dark. I don't know him at all. It's a stranger who's pulling off my soggy underwear. Charlie is locked in the bathroom and this is his double, nudging the tip of his dick against me, pushing it in. He gasps, transformed again, another unfamiliar mask, eyes rolled back, jaw clenched. I feel myself stretching and his dick creeping deeper into me, inch by inch. It's impaling me, I think, as it finally hits against something. A lung? This is how I'd like to die, death by dick, mind totally blank. He puts his hands over my breasts. His hands are rough, like gloves. I don't like this at all, but as I try to move them, he pinches my nipples harder than I thought would feel good. The pain shoots through me and transforms into something else. Why has nobody done this to me before? I hear a moan. He pulls out a little.

"No, don't take it away," I try to say but my mouth trembles in a silent stutter. Is this an orgasm? Pinpricks in my face, like it's fallen asleep. I try to catch my breath but he stuffs his fingers in my mouth, pushes them towards my throat, and thrusts. Our bones slam. And again. I'm choking and contracting. Nothing exists.

He takes his hand out of my mouth, wipes the strands of saliva on his chest, wipes my stomach with the corner of the sheet. I can't move. I'm limp, but he's efficient, like he's clearing the table. Feeling comes back to my face slowly. He gets up to get the ashtray and his cigarettes from the pocket of his pants, lies back next to me, and pulls me into his chest. My cheek is resting against my own spit. I hear the click of the lighter, the inhale.

"Happiness is like a bull," he says as he exhales.

I look up at him, and he blows the smoke out the side of his mouth.

"You're happy?" I ask.

"Yes." He kisses the top of my head.

I want to ask him if that's why he's not stuttering, but I don't really want to bring it up. Maybe I've cured him. Or maybe he's been faking the whole time. This bunny on crutches is actually a wolf.

"What?"

"What?"

"You were smiling."

I nod. I feel light, like if not for his arm, I could float up, up, up.

He stubs the cigarette out and sets the ashtray on the bedside table. I look at his hand, the same hand that had just been in my mouth, and the muscles inside of me tremble. The aftershock.

"Goodnight," he says. He closes his eyes and slides down into his pillow.

I might as well tell him now about my mother, while he's too tired to ask me questions.

"St. Vincent's is a mental hospital," I say quietly, in case he's already asleep.

He doesn't respond. A light whistle in his breath.

There are 127 ceiling tiles. Seven of them are stained. I count again, 129. I start to count a third time but lose interest. I'm not going to be able to fall asleep.

I get up and put on his flannel shirt, stand by the window. The street is empty and the air is wet. The fog is making a halo of green light over the neon sign. I think if I squint, I can see the street the hospital is on. What if Mom is different when I see her tomorrow? What if she has become a stranger? That's stupid. She will never be a stranger. She will be so happy to see me. So relieved. There are cigarette holes in the hem of the curtain. Someone before must have been standing here, just like me, looking out this window.

"I know," I hear Charlie say. It takes me a moment to realize he is saying that he knows about St. Vincent's. I don't know if he is awake or asleep, but he sits up and reaches for me and so I get back into bed and lie for a long time in the pocket of warmth he created under the sheet. I finally fall asleep as it's starting to get light out.

## CHARLIE

I often feel betrayed by my body because of my stutter but when I was with Edie I felt in control. The sensation of being choked by my own tongue would disappear. I felt powerful being able to give her what she needed.

Women my own age usually fuss over me like I'm their sick poodle. That kind of thing drives me crazy. All my resentment gets funneled into fucking them, which is what they secretly want, I think, to be fucked like that because they think it's "passionate." But it's not. It's just rough. Passion is what Edie and I had.

The morning after our first night together, I waited for her at the diner down the street while she went to visit her mother. I ordered a breakfast so big that it took the waitress several trips to bring it all to my table. I was in a very good mood. There was a couple sitting at a nearby booth. Nurses or doctors, I don't know, clearly just off a shift. They were still in their scrubs, and they looked tired, but also happy. They were feeding each other pie, and I thought, that could be Edie and me one day. Why not?

I still wonder why not, sometimes, though of course I know the answer to this question. For me, Edie will forever exist as she was at 16, feet on the dashboard of that truck, the wind whipping through her hair.

## ROSE

Denny kept me waiting in front of the Guggenheim for almost an hour. We'd made plans to see the Balthus exhibit and he was usually very punctual. I tried not to worry at first, maybe he took the train and it got stuck underground, it's not uncommon. But when he showed up looking as he did, disheveled and unkempt, with only one of his daughters in tow, I knew something was wrong.

*Where was Edie? What happened?* I was on him immediately. He told me very calmly that she'd left.

*Left where?* It seemed incongruous that he could be so calm. *Left when?*

He told me that she wanted to go back to Louisiana, so she left.

*And you just let her go?*

Denny bristled at this. He said it would have been hypocritical for him to try to stop her. Most of the people on the Freedom Rides weren't much older than she, and when he was her age he'd run off to Montreal for a while.

His attitude struck me as cruel. I rarely fight with Denny but I couldn't look at him then. I got ahead of them in the exhibit and cried for a while in front of a painting of a young girl playing with a cat. Denny's job was to protect his daughters! Childhood is precious and there are no do-overs. Denny had missed out on the girls' childhoods and by extension I had too. I could never get that back. Nor could I get back the chance to have my own children.

Eventually I saw Denny and Mae coming up the ramp—the Guggenheim is designed in such a way that there aren't nooks or crannies to hide in, only that one long circling ramp. I had to regain my composure and quickly, because I'd be no use to anyone if I was falling apart. I've always been the one who did the things that needed to be done: I took care of Mother when she was dying; I took care of Denny after his divorce. I needed to be someone Denny and his daughters could rely on.

Once Denny and Mae joined me I tried to act like everything was normal, but I was disturbed by how much Mae looked like the girls in the paintings. Even her clothes—knee-high socks and some sort of plaid jumper—they were the kind of thing normal girls her age wouldn't have been caught dead in.

When I asked her what she thought of the artwork, she hesitated and then recited an answer that was clearly parroting whatever opinion Denny had just expressed to her. She was holding onto Denny's hand with both of hers like she was a little kid. It seemed regressive. They were in their own world, talking only to each other as I trailed after them through the remainder of the exhibit.

Afterward, we got lunch at the museum café. I avoided mentioning Edie again because I didn't want to fight, but I had trouble thinking of other things to say. I told him about Amanda, what a pleasant time I'd been having with her, and he jumped down my throat, told me not to meddle in his affairs. I told him Marianne must've really done a number on him if he thought that if a woman was interested in him there had to be something wrong with her.

After this, most of the meal went by in silence. Mae didn't let go of his hand even as they ate. She watched him like he was the only thing in the room. Finally, he apologized for snapping at me. He explained that he had started writing again and that the publisher was breathing down his neck. It had been so long since Denny had written anything that I'd forgotten how crazy he got when he was in the throes of his creative process.

I offered to have Mae come stay with us on Long Island while he wrote to free him up from any distractions. When I said this, Mae shrank from me as though I was offering to throw acid on her face.

"No, no," he told her reassuringly. "I couldn't. I need her. She's helping me."

There was something in their behavior that I found disturbing even at the time, but I told myself that I'm not a parent, that I don't really know what it's like to reunite with a long-lost child. I thought that if I could arrange for Amanda to be there, this might be enough. She had seemed so competent and down to earth, and I hoped that she would be able to keep things from going off the rails. I should have insisted on taking Mae. Of course I blame myself for not doing that.

## LETTER FROM
## MARIANNE LOUISE MCLEAN TO DENNIS LOMACK

Aug 8, 1968

Dear Mr. Dennis,

I just came home from the lake. I've been practicing my back-stroke the way you taught me. Remember when you showed me how to float? How did you hold me up with just two fingers—under the skull? The water was so warm that day it felt like I was the lake. I was hoping you would kiss me and then you could have become the lake too...

Do you know that there is a sea called the Dead Sea where the water is denser because it's full of salt, so everybody floats? Sometimes the liquids inside of me feel denser and other times like vapor. When I get your letters for instance... vapor! vapor! vapor!

I read the book you sent. I liked it. The poor cockroach man. I don't think the world is so cruel. Anyway, must go help my father stretch some canvases.

Yours, forever and ever, until the cows come home (assuming that they never do.) m

## EDITH (1997)

The nurse said Mom was in a session—with a psychiatrist, I'm assuming, but she didn't specify. There's a man waiting too. I guess we're the only ones because it's a weekday morning. The man has a gray beard over a fat red face and he looks very sad. He's reading a magazine with a photograph of a cake on the cover. The magazines are all things I've never heard of: *Cancer Today*, *Fat Free Digest*, *Cat Lovers*. They're warped with pages stuck together, like someone spilled water on them. Is this a sign of the kind of place this is—they can't even get fresh magazines? Or maybe it just means the hospital is so efficient they don't usually keep visitors waiting? How am I supposed to believe that a place with a soggy cat magazine in the waiting room could be the kind of place where Mom will get better?

I come up to the nurse's desk. She scratches her shiny forehead with a pencil. I can see the corner of the crossword she's working on. "Just a few more minutes," she says. I don't want to sit back down, so I pace.

I'll have to figure out what paperwork I need to file in order to get her out of here. Doreen probably knows. Then I'll go to the house and make sure it's in order, ready for her. What does that mean? Lock up the steak knives? Watch her all the time. And what about school? I'll start in the fall. By then everything will be back to normal. Maybe Charlie can help. No, that's crazy. I'm sure he'll want to leave soon. This was just a ride. Could that really be it? It wasn't complicated the way it always felt with Markus, like everything was a negotiation, tit-for-tat with a measuring cup. I feel like he reached into my mouth and dislodged some sad, heavy stone. How is it possible for someone to make you feel that way and not really know you? It isn't. So he must know me. I want him to do it again, to rip me out of my body...

Distant screaming, muffled but terrifying. The nurse looks up from her crossword puzzle, and as though this was the cue, she says:

"Ms. McLean is ready to see you now. Fifth floor."

She points me down a hall to the elevator. I shouldn't be thinking about Charlie right now. What is wrong with me. The elevator stops on the second floor. There is the source: an old woman. She is screaming and her face looks like a hole. She's being restrained but two orderlies. They're not gentle. Her shirt is riding up and her belly is covered in scars. The smell is terrible. Like shit but worse. Hell. Literally, hell. I feel woozy. The spins. A male doctor steps into the elevator and the doors close behind him.

"You all right?" the doctor says and steadies me by the elbow.

"I'm fine. I'm fine." I straighten up. I need to stop being stupid, how embarrassing. I don't look at him and he lets go.

When the doors open on the fifth floor, I'm scared that I'll step out into a similar scene, but it's quiet. The smell is regular, like a hospital, like cleaning products. A nurse is by the elevator banks, waiting for me.

"You must be Ms. McLean's daughter!"

I follow her down the linoleum hallway. Her ponytail bounces with each step. She can't possibly be one of the mean ones Mom wrote about, the ones who tortured her with cold baths.

The nurse stops suddenly before turning down a new hallway and says: "I'll come fetch you in 10 minutes. Dr. Gordon says that's as much as she's allowed right now." I start to protest but she interrupts me. "Also, don't be alarmed, we're still adjusting her medication." Alarmed how? Her shaking hands in the letters. What else? What else have they done to her?

The nurse leads me to an open door at the end of the hallway. "Your visitor is here, Ms. McLean," she says in a voice that's too loud, the way you'd talk to someone who's stupid and deaf. It makes me want to rip that ponytail right off her bitch head. I shove past her into the room.

There, sitting on the edge of a metal bed, is Mom. She's wearing the flowery pajamas I sent her and a weird silk scarf. They've cut her hair short, which is enough to make me tear up. That type of bowl cut you only see on retarded people.

"I'll be back," the nurse says.

It takes a moment for Mom's eyes to find mine. She's trembling. She reaches her arms out towards me.

I feel a prickly fear that goes away as soon as I even recognize it, and it's replaced with shame. I hug her. Hard. Harder to make up for not completely wanting to. Her hair was recently washed and it smells like fabric softener or a baby blanket. It's a sweet smell that reeks of humiliation. I breathe through my mouth.

"Nice scarf." I force a smile and finger the silk fabric. It slips slightly and I see why she's wearing it. The rope burns on her neck. They must have gotten infected, because they look scaly and red and glisten with some sort of cream. She reaches for her scarf self-consciously and won't look at me.

I start to talk, to talk like everything is normal, to fill the space between us with my words. I tell her that I've missed her, of course. And that I am so glad to see her. That I drove through West Virginia and saw some mountains. And I tell her about New York. But you know, postcard stuff. As soon as I say anything the least bit critical I can sense that I'm losing her, that her mind is drifting. So, I don't complain. I don't talk about Dennis. I just talk about museums and parks. She nods and nods, in this palsied way.

She finally interrupts me. "Where's Mae?" she says.

Of course that would be the first thing she asks me. I lie, say Mae got strep throat. She'll be fine, but she can't travel.

"You were supposed to be taking care of her," Mom says.

Really? That's all she has to say to me? Not that she missed me, not that she's been thinking of me, not that she's glad I drove all the way here to see her? There's a stack of my letters on her table. She hasn't even opened them. I look away because if I look at her, I might lose it. I look out the window at the garden below, then over at the other side of the room, an identical bed and desk—

Jesus. There's a woman. Has she been here this whole time? She must have been. A small woman, sitting like a statue at the desk at the opposite end of the room. She's wearing a green bathrobe and staring straight into the wall behind me.

"Who is that?" I whisper to Mom.

Mom ignores me. She's playing with a string that has come loose on the sleeve of her pajamas.

"Can we go take a walk in the garden?" I ask in a lowered voice, not wanting that creepy woman to hear any more of what I have to say.

Mom shakes her head. Her ugly bowl cut swishes around her face. "I'm not allowed."

"Why not?"

She doesn't say, keeps looking at the string.

"I'm going to get you out of here," I whisper and hug her again.

She pushes my hand away and says, "You kept me alive, well, you got your wish. Here I am. Go back to New York."

I was Marianne's roommate at St. Vincent's. I had been in and out of there for two years, mostly in. I retired from being an architect, and then the lack of structure, the loss of identity, I don't know what it was, but I spiraled into a depression. I was diagnosed as bipolar. At first I was relieved that there was a name for what was wrong with me, but I've come to see these labels as pretty crude. Anyone with suicidal tendencies who wasn't wearing an aluminum foil hat was bipolar at St. Vincent's. Marianne was bipolar too. And she also had a personality disorder. If the diagnosis of Female Hysteria were still available at St. Vincent's they probably would have used that on her as well.

I'm not saying there wasn't a reason we were all in there. Clearly we all had some things to work out, but the categories the doctors used didn't mean all that much. And when you didn't respond to their treatment they took it personally. They kept upping Marianne's dosages, even though it was clear the meds weren't helping her. Some people would try to starve themselves until they disappeared. Marianne did that by talking less and less, until there was less of her there after a while.

When Marianne had first moved in with me, we would talk. We'd lie in our beds and tell each other about our lives before, our marriages and childhoods and so on. She talked about having children. She said it was the point when her husband finally succeeded in invading her. He deformed her—not just her body, but something at the very center of her was stretched out and defiled. I don't have children of my own—but I could imagine feeling as she did. Even so, I was dismayed when her daughter visited and I saw how Marianne treated the poor girl. No kindness. I was pretty numb at the hospital, but that girl's voice tore into me in a way I didn't expect. I remember being disgusted with Marianne then, feeling like I had misjudged her. My mother had also been a very cold woman.

Now, what her daughter probably didn't realize, what she'd probably never know, is that after she left, Marianne cried and cried, quietly so as not to arouse the nurse's interest. And that's when I finally understood Marianne's behavior—a primal instinct to get her daughter away from herself and to safety, even if it meant breaking the girl's heart.

# *Chapter 7*

**Edith:** Hello?

**Mae:** Edie?

**Edith:** Yeah. Can you hear me?

**Mae:** Yeah. It's not a great connection though.

**Edith:** I'm at a pay phone. Outside the mental hospital.

**Mae:** Oh.

**Edith:** Well?

**Mae:** Well, what?

**Edith:** Aren't you going to ask me about Mom.

**Mae:** No. I know about Mom.

**Edith:** Do you? Well, it's worse than in the letters. Much worse. She doesn't seem like herself anymore. And they cut her hair.

**Mae:** Her hair?

**Edith:** Yeah. It looks horrible. And that's not all they did to her... But you probably know about that since you're such a genius.

**Mae:** I have to go.

**Edith:** She asked about you, of course. It was the only thing she asked. Certainly didn't ask me how *I* was doing.

**Mae:** Dad's waiting downstairs. I have to go.

## MAE

One time, when Dad took me on a picnic by the duck pond in Central Park, I decided that I would have him to myself and I wouldn't share him with Mom. Sitting on the plaid, moth-eaten blanket, I let Dad feed me dried figs and dates, and olives stuffed with almonds. I found the textures of these foods revolting, but I ate them and smiled my Mom smile, swallowing them quickly, so they barely even grazed my tongue. After I had sampled everything in the picnic basket, Dad looked at me with quivering anticipation as though this was my cue. Cue for what exactly, I wasn't sure. He must have felt that something was amiss.

I sat like Mom, stared out at the pond like Mom, touched my hair as she would have, hummed a song I'd heard her hum before, but none of it was right. He was restless. He could sense that I was an imposter. He was waiting for me to do something, but as myself, I didn't know what it was. I sighed. I stretched. I lay back down and sat back up. None of this was what he wanted from me.

His mouth was pursed in frustration. I was doing the same thing I had been doing, how did he know that I wasn't her? My eagerness to please only irritated him. Finally, he said very quietly, almost inaudibly under his breath: *tell me that you don't love me, that I'm a bore, a mistake, that you should have never come.*

I did not want to say or even think these things. I felt humiliated. My love must have meant very little if he was willing to contaminate it with Mom's cruelty. But I couldn't say no to him. I'd do whatever it was he needed and so, I let Mom's tentacles tighten around my throat and force those words out of me: *I don't love you, you're a bore, a mistake, I never should have come.*

He wanted me to hurt him, so I did. I said all that he told me to and more, and with each terrible thing that came out of me I felt myself inflating bigger and bigger, until I was the size of a float in a parade and he was cowering in front of me. I had never before felt this kind of excitement. I was both omnipotent and completely out of control. My skin was on fire. I couldn't breathe.

## AMANDA

I was on my way to visit Dennis's old high school when, by pure luck, I spotted him and Mae, spreading out a blanket by the edge of the pond in Central Park. I rented a paddleboat and tried to float by them casually, but they were so engrossed in each other that they didn't see me waving. I made several loops around the pond, but each time I passed, they didn't look up. I could have called to them, but I knew that I needed to tread lightly. There are only so many times you can plausibly run into a person. I turned around and began to head back to the boathouse when I heard shouting. Their idyllic picnic had, in an instant, transformed into a fight. His daughter looked wild, clawing and kicking him while he tried to fend her off. I jumped from my boat and ran to them through the shallow water. Dennis's face was bleeding. They both seemed dazed when I pulled her off of him and then she took off running. Dennis looked at me, but I don't think my presence even registered. He staggered after her, leaving behind all their belongings. I called out to him but he didn't turn around.

Later that evening I came over with Rose to return the picnic basket. The house was in disarray. I remember the cat's litter box had overflowed and those dusty pebbles were scattered through the living room. It was pretty early, but Mae was asleep, snoring. I washed all the dishes while Rose and Dennis talked.

"She'll stay out of your way. She wants to help you write your book," I heard Rose say. And when Dennis tried to protest, she wouldn't hear of it. "Stop being so selfish. Stop it. You owe that girl a home. Look at this place."

He promised he'd hire a housecleaner, but Rose wouldn't budge. Dear Rose, sweet Rose. I don't know what would have happened without her intervention.

## NEW YORK TIMES BOOK REVIEW

[September 7, 1980]
Cassandra Speaks;
By Dennis Lomack;
p395.

By this point, our culture has become inured to the mating rituals of hippies, but Lomack has found a new way to make his readers squirm. In his latest effort, *Cassandra Speaks*, Gregor, a cuckolded revolutionary is tortured by his young wife, Cassandra. We're back in the South from *Bonfires* but two decades later. As the naïf transforms into a vamp, Gregor transforms into a ghost, literally, of the man he once was. The mixture of fantastical and prosaic has certainly been done before (ahem, Kafka), but not quite like this.

In one scene, Gregor watches as Cassandra picks up a "malcontent with a ravaged face" in a bar. Gregor follows them to the man's apartment inside a seedy house on stilts, a flood zone equivalent of the Baba Yaga's hut atop chicken feet, and watches through the window as the ugly stranger makes love to his wife. The apartment has no furniture, only an enormous red paper umbrella, "the kind of thing you would find in a tropical drink or in a bordello," hanging upside down from the ceiling lamp and casting a pink glow on the copulating bodies. Yet, it is the scene that immediately follows this, of Cassandra and Gregor walking home together, that's even more unsettling. The tenderness between the two of them has its own violence. It is this very tenderness that prompts Gregor's transformation into a ghost.

Once a ghost, Gregor gives up his own earthly pleasure in order to possess his wife's body and force her to have relations with others so as to experience these infidelities with her. Gregor's possession of his wife seems a clear metaphor to the writing process itself, where Lomack inhabits the minds of each of his characters and is forced to experience life through them, possess them. Maybe the act of writing forces empathy but it does little to mollify his deep rage...

# Therapy notes for
# Marianne McLean

May 4, 1997

Third session in a row in which Marianne refuses to speak.

I asked: how are you feeling? Is there anything you would like to discuss? Silence.

The new medication has side effects (bloated face, waxy and gray skin, unpleasant twitching). Between that and what she did to her hair (chewed it off with her teeth, according to the nurses), her stay here is negatively impacting her appearance.

However, this doesn't mean she isn't getting better. Improvement is rarely linear.

I read to her from a transcript of an earlier session, one in which she was more forthcoming:

> My father never talked about my mother. It made him too sad. She'd died so suddenly: a defect in her heart. I never asked him because I didn't want to hurt his feelings. I didn't want him to think that he hadn't been enough for me because he had. He had been enough. Dennis had this idea that having children would replace the void left by my father's death. But, of course, it just dug two more holes.

I asked her if she would care to expand on this. She shook her head.

Maybe she could write a poem about it? I offered her a pen and paper but she didn't move.

We sat the rest of the hour in silence. When our time was up, I told her that if she wanted to get better she'd have to start working harder.

Then, finally, she speaks!

She said she did not want to get better. And, that if she wanted to be dead, she should have the right.

I cleared her of this misconception. She does not have the right. Not in the state of Louisiana.

## MAE

Then, one day, Amanda was back. She would take care of me, Dad said. Can you imagine? That lank-haired ghoul ministering to my needs.

I tried to protest, but Dad wouldn't hear of it. He was getting to a point in his novel that required his full attention, and Amanda had offered "very generously" to make sure "everything else" ran smoothly. "Everything else," being me. She made herself indispensable. She made him lunch from recipes Rose gave her and left it by his door, cleaned and fixed things around the house, and took me to my photography class. Most importantly, she made herself scarce when Dad needed me to be "Marianne." They must have had some sort of understanding.

Otherwise, Amanda was always in the apartment, making me feel self-conscious as I sat on the floor outside Dad's room, waiting for him to open the door. "Mae" had begun to feel as much of a performance as "Marianne." I sat there, the embodiment of sweetness and innocence, posed in a patch of sunlight, playing with the cat. When Dad came out to use the bathroom or put his empty lunch tray on the counter, he would pat my head or say a few kind words, but he only really noticed me when I was "Marianne."

Though I was expected to keep "Mae" and "Marianne"

separate, after the picnic, certain things from "Marianne" began to bleed into me in ways I couldn't control. I kept returning to that moment of Dad, down on his knees. I would find myself thinking about the look on his face, which now I recognize to be a combination of arousal and despair. At the time I couldn't have articulated this, but thinking about it made me slightly nauseous and excited. My heart would start racing and I'd find myself doing things that I didn't understand to relieve the strange pressure building inside me. I'd press myself against the doorknob or the lip of the dresser and rock back and forth. I had no frame of reference for what I was doing. I was so sexually innocent, I'd never even kissed a boy. And yet, when Amanda caught me humping the dresser, I knew to feel ashamed. I'd blushed and pretended I had been dancing.

In the evenings, Amanda would go back to whatever hole she'd crawled out of. Dad would sit in his room, typing, and I would lie in bed, feeling Mom's lust descending on me like dread. I began to have dreams in which I was Mom, and Dad was doing the things to me that he did to her in his books. In these dreams he was a blurred hybrid of himself as I knew him and himself from the old photographs I'd seen.

So much of my art is about this subject, and yet I still find honesty difficult. I said dreams, but that's not really what they were. I was awake. I said dreams because it felt so much outside of my control. Just like if I say that this lust belonged to Mom and if I think of it as hers, as this external force, it wouldn't have been mine.

## Edith (1997)

It's strange seeing my old neighborhood from the window of the truck. I watch in a daze as we drive past a couple kids running through a sprinkler. One slips and falls, starts to cry, the other keeps playing like nothing happened.

How can Mae be so calm when Mom is rotting in there? Literally, rotting. Even if you can't smell it, you feel it. The line from Mom's letter about the molecules from the hospital becoming part of her. That woman screaming on the second floor is in me. And Mom's roommate, her dead skin cells and spit cells, they're in me too. Can Charlie tell that I've been contaminated?

Charlie breaks the silence. "So, how w-w-was she?" he finally asks.

"Not good." As soon as I say it, I feel like I've betrayed her. Why am I telling him anything? He will probably just leave me. Why would he stick around. "But not bad either. She's definitely not crazy, not like the other people in there. She can just be selfish sometimes."

He nods. Why is he nodding?

"Not selfish, that's not what I meant," I say.

"Well, k-k-killing yourself is a selfish thing to do."

What is he talking about? I move my hand away from his.

He's acting like he knows us, but he doesn't. He doesn't know anything. And, she didn't kill herself. If she had killed herself, she would be dead.

"I'd rather you didn't talk about my mother," I say.

He apologizes and tries to put his hand back, but I don't let it near me. It's so rough. I can't believe I was just touching it. I can't believe yesterday those freckled, boney fingers were inside of me. They twitch now in his lap. How vile.

"You can let me out here." I open the door before he stops all the way.

Someone's car is parked by the side door. An old black Honda. Strange. It must be the DuPres's. The dad is a mechanic and they have a constant rotation of cars they need to park off the street.

"Is that yours?" I hear Charlie's voice behind me.

"No. A neighbor's."

I'm about to get the spare key, but something catches in the corner of my eye. Rope. Rope hanging from a branch in the oak tree. And attached to the rope... a tire. A swing. What's wrong with me, panicking like that at the sight of a swing? But where did it come from? It's not ours. Who put it there? Also the DuPres? They have two boys, but why wouldn't they put it in their own damn tree?

"What are you d-doing?" Charlie asks. He's holding my bags, standing by the side door.

"Nothing." I let go of the tire, go get the spare key hidden behind a rock under the back porch. I don't bother to explain why I had lied about the spare key last night, and he doesn't ask.

I can't tell at first what's wrong. The smell inside the house makes me uneasy. It smells like Vicks VapoRub and fish. What could we have left out to make it smell this way? Charlie follows me up the side steps into the kitchen.

Our things are there. But they've been rearranged.

"What the fuck." The big glass jars on the counter where I kept beans and rice now have... I don't even know what. Dried mushrooms?

"W-what?" Charlie says. "W-w-what's wrong?"

I open the cabinets and they're full of packaged food. Not our food. The writing on them is in Greek or something.

"This isn't our stuff," I say.

Did I go into the wrong house? The houses on our street are similar. Are we on the wrong street? A parallel street? Of course not. That's ridiculous.

I go into the living room.

The green couch is out of place and there's a baby pen. A baby lives here now? The carpet still holds the dents from where the couch legs used to be. The room feels off balance. It's more than just the couch. What is it?

A little boy appears at the bottom of the stairs.

I shriek in surprise, and this scares him because he shrieks too.

"Who are you? Why are you in my house?" I ask him.

"D-d-d-don't yell at him," Charlie says uneasily. I wasn't yelling.

A woman, wide eyed, comes down the stairs. Yanks her son away from us. She shouts upstairs at someone in a phlegmy language I don't recognize. A man comes down, buttoning his shirt.

"Why are you here?" I ask them. "This is my house."

"My house," the man says.

"This is my house," I repeat.

"We have lease," he says.

The woman hesitates, then comes to me. She's holding the cordless phone in her hand like it's a gun. I don't understand what is going on at all. She tries to talk to me, but the only word I understand is "hospital." She keeps saying Du rin. Du-rin. Doreen. Of course, Doreen is behind this. Giving my house away to strangers.

"Give me the phone." I grab the cordless out of her hands and call Doreen's house.

Doreen picks up on the fifth ring.

"Doreen. What the fuck?!"

"Excuse me," she says. She sounds like I woke her up.

"It's Edith. I'm at my house. But it seems you've given it away."

"You're what?"

"I'm. In. My. House."

"Jesus, Edith. Who told you to do that? Get out of there!"

"It's my house!" Why does this even need to be said?

"Not right now it's not! I rented it out. How do you think your momma's paying for the hospital? You get out!"

I turn my back away from Charlie and that stupid family.

"Doreen, I swear to God—"

"*You* swear to God??!! *I* swear to God! I told you not to come. They can sue you now. It's the last thing we need. Get over here this instant."

I hang up.

The squatters look at each other. "Leave or we call police," the man says again. I hand him the phone and turn back to stare at my living room.

It's the gourds. That's what's missing. The shelf with the gourds that hold my grandfather's ashes. What did these people do with them?

"What did you do with the gourds?" I ask them. I point to the place on the wall where they used to be and gesture a gourd shape with my hands. If they threw them out or damaged them in any way, I will break everything in this room… The woman looks confused. The man is on the phone, presumably with the police.

Then I spot a cardboard box in the corner, my grandfather piled carelessly in there. I grab it and elbow my way past the couple, out the front door.

Charlie starts the car and I inspect each gourd to make sure none of them were damaged. When I was little, Mom used to stand in front of them and talk to my grandfather, sing to him. I shake one to make sure the ashes are still in there and a small gray cloud escapes from the little hole drilled at the top. A few specks settle on my lips and shirt.

"W-w-what's that?" Charlie asks. He looks a little too exhilarated, like this is another of his adventures and not my busted life.

## DOREEN

Do you know the story with those damn gourds? After her divorce, Marianne got all giddy, dumped her children on me, and took off to Honduras with some little man with a unibrow. She said he was Trotsky's grandson or some shit. Anyone with half a brain could tell he'd be bad news—shifty, dirty, not much to look at, I don't care whose grandson he was. I remember he fainted a lot too, which Marianne, of course, found *fascinating*. Anyway, he was a visiting scholar or something at Tulane, which impressed Marianne, and the two of them took off for Central America without giving a thought to how it would affect anyone around them.

Edith was terrified of being abandoned. When Marianne dropped them off at my house, Edith sat on Marianne's foot to try to keep her from leaving. She broke Marianne's toe, but that didn't stop Marianne. Nope. Marianne hobbled off with her broken toe and ugly boyfriend and one-way ticket to Honduras.

A couple weeks went by and I finally got a call from her. That guy disappeared. She was rambling about some sort of international conspiracy, though it was pretty obvious to me that he just got sick of her and left. Took her money too. All she had was a hotel room full of those stupid gourds, lord knows where she got them. She was telling me she was going to use them to build a monument to her father, or to open up a little store where she'd sell gourds and poems. Big ideas. Cuckoo stuff. I paid for her return ticket myself.

I was having a hard time with my husband and I had enough to worry about. Edith wet her bed and Mae was always watching me. It got on my nerves. There was nowhere to put them other than in my son's room, and then he was forced to sleep on the floor of my room in a sleeping bag. It was disruptive. Of course, none of this was their fault, and I probably could have been kinder to them. If my mother had been alive, she would have been disappointed in me.

The girls only stayed a few weeks. Marianne came home, still limping, her suitcases full of gourds, looking happier than she had any right to be, talking about all of her plans and making a whole lot of empty promises.

And then, déjà vu, Edith shows up at my house with those damn gourds again. I could have smashed each one of them. I'd told her on the phone: stay in New York. But she's a stubborn girl, always was. When she got something in her head, good luck getting it out. She didn't give one thought to the fact that my brother was staying with me—he had stage-three pancreatic cancer and I was working extra shifts to help him pay for treatment. No, it didn't occur to her that I had bigger problems than Marianne.

Instead of being with Dad, I had to waste most of my days going on dopey errands with Amanda. Before leaving the house, she would brush my hair with unnecessary roughness. I was too old to have my hair brushed, and yet, I sat there and let her. Oh, how I hated her. The feeling was mutual. When we were out of sight of Rose or Dad she wouldn't bother to pretend.

I remember once at the grocery store she bought me children's cookies. They had garish faces on them—vanilla on one side, chocolate on the other, and a crème filling that came out through the eyeholes. I remember feeling deeply insulted. It didn't even occur to me that it could be a peace offering, because it wasn't. It was her way of saying that I was a stupid, insignificant child.

I tried to get back at her by taking pictures of her. In my photography class, I would print the least flattering ones in triplicate. At home, I would spread them out on the floor and hack them up with scissors, presumably for a collage that I never bothered to assemble. She'd sit nearby, watching me with that impassive face of hers.

She never said anything about the re-enactments. I had naively assumed that it was a secret, but she must have known. She must have been dying with jealousy when she went to the antique stores to pick up the objects that Dad and I would use. With Amanda it was a game, I see now, I couldn't possibly win. I was just a child.

## EDITH (1997)

Doreen heats up a half-eaten rotisserie chicken from the store and some canned peas. Charlie stutters for a long time through his name. She shakes his hand but looks over his shoulder at me while she's doing it.

"Where'd you find him?" she says.

"He's my neighbor in New York."

"How old are you?" she asks him. Like it's any of her business!

"25."

"Doreen," I say before she can sidetrack us with more of this nonsense. "How long are those Greek people going to be staying in my house?"

"They're not Greek, they're Ukrainian. And they signed a two-year lease. He's working at the hospital. We're lucky to have found them."

"And where is Mom supposed to go when she gets better?"

Charlie's gaze darts back and forth between Doreen and me. Why is he still here?

"We'll cross that bridge when we come to it, Edith," Doreen says, and there's the edge back in her voice, the edge she gets whenever she has to deal with our family's shit. You don't want to deal with it? Don't deal with it! You aren't doing me any favors.

"I had to pull a lot of strings to get her into St. Vincent's,"

Doreen is saying. "If anyone can help her, it's them, but they can only do so much. And... Well, you visited her. You saw how she is."

My bottom lip starts to quiver, so I bite down on it hard. Doreen is one of those people who think they're being honest, when really they're just being mean.

"I don't think you ever understood her," I say. That's as far as I dare take it with Doreen.

She just snorts and clears our dishes off the counter. She and my mother have always seemed more like sisters than friends. When I was little, Mom would have her over for coffee and I remember feeling embarrassed because Mom was always holding onto Doreen's hand, begging her not to leave so quickly, and Doreen was always pulling her hand away and looking at it, as if Mom had left a goopy stain on it. How dare she. It's Doreen that should've been embarrassed for being such a bitch.

"Well, where am I supposed to stay? Since you stole my house?" I say it.

As soon as it comes out I regret it. Doreen lets whatever she's washing clatter into the sink. She turns around and I brace myself because she's about to slap me with her soapy hand. It wouldn't be the first time.

But she doesn't slap me. Instead she pulls me into her chest and holds me there. Her boobs are so big she gets all her bras from special catalogues, and I can't help it, I cry into them like they're pillows.

"Shh," she says. "Shh... baby. Poor baby."

I hate how comforting it feels. I hate that Charlie is watching all of this. Gaping at me. Why hasn't he left already? I pull away and wipe my eyes on my sleeve. I've left a big wet spot over Doreen's heart.

"Does your daddy know you're here?" she asks.

"He doesn't have a say in the matter," I tell her.

Doreen shrugs, already growing distant, like that hug has used up her quota of warmth for the week.

"Well, you can stay here for a couple days, but that's all. And don't even think you'll get to share a room with your boyfriend," she says as she's already walking away, heading up the stairs.

Charlie's not my boyfriend. He opens his mouth like he's about to say something "comforting" to me. His pity is about the last thing I can handle.

"I'll see you later," I say and quickly squeeze past him. Markus's house is a 45-minute walk from here. I need to be around someone who actually knows me.

I don't turn around but I know Charlie is following me. What's his problem? I break into a jog, cutting through people's yards. When I get to Beaux Artes Ave. I look back and he's not there. I feel disappointed. No, that's stupid. I feel mostly relieved.

## WALTER

I ran into Dennis Lomack and the girl at the Turkish Baths on E. 10th St. I recognized him immediately, though he had no idea who I was. My wife was his therapist when he first moved back to New York. She's a genius at unblocking creatives but she counted Lomack among her few failures.

My wife never discussed her clients but her practice was on the ground floor of our brownstone and the vents carried sound. I was curious about the author at first. I'd expected him to be more interesting, based on his books—a man of action. Instead, he would cry and carry on about his ex-wife. It was practically all he could talk about. That, and sometimes about how badly he felt leaving his daughters. But tell me, what kind of man abandons his children in the first place? Particularly with a woman who, by his own account, was so unstable? Rather than cry to my wife about his creative blockages, why didn't he *do* something?

So, all those years later, when I saw him in the swimming pool with his daughter, I thought, how nice, maybe in the end he came through for someone. The girl was a teenager, but she looked young. I remember she was wearing an old-fashioned-looking bathing cap. She was on her back and he was holding her, pulling her back and forth through the water. He seemed completely focused on her.

At first their display touched me. He was a gruff guy, so it was sweet to see him doting on this girl. But then as I swam closer, I began to feel unsettled. The girl's eyes were shut tightly as he pulled her through the water. They were murmuring to each other, and though I couldn't make out what they were saying I could sense the intensity. I remembered the abrupt way he'd ended the sessions with my wife, how for weeks she would cry in the bathroom, where she thought I couldn't hear her, and pick fights with me over nothing. His books would be disturbed on our bookshelves so I know she'd been reading them. He'd talked about himself as a toxic force in other people's lives despite all his best intentions, and maybe this was true. He certainly didn't do my marriage any favors.

I got out of the pool, went to one of the sauna rooms, had a massage, the kind where they beat you with birch sticks, came back to the pool for one last dip, and found Dennis and his daughter in the same exact place, in the same positions.

I hadn't thought much of the odd encounter until I saw his daughter's piece in the Whitney Biennial. It made me ill to know that I had probably witnessed one of their rituals.

## MAE

I didn't know that this would be the last scene Dad and I ever staged. Dad watched me from his window as I walked back and forth in front of his building in the rain, holding a small battered suitcase that Amanda had bought a week earlier to his specifications. I don't know what was in it because it was locked, but it was heavy despite its size and covered in old travel stickers. That morning Dad had laid out my clothes for me—a pale yellow blouse with cloth buttons and a navy skirt that smelled like mothballs.

I walked in circles up and down 7th Ave., around the block and down the alley. I felt disoriented, as though I was seeing the city for the first time. When the rain got stronger the rats scurried out from under the dumpsters and ran for higher ground. Rain came down in gusts, tearing through the drainpipes. My soaked blouse turned see-through and the wool skirt smelled like a wet dog. Each time I passed the front entrance to the apartment building, the doorman would try to run after me and give me an umbrella, but I studiously ignored him until eventually he gave up. I don't know for sure if Dad was watching me or not. Several times I glanced up at his window, but I couldn't tell.

Maybe the idea of me out there was enough for him, or maybe he was walking from room to room, from window to window, tracking my every movement.

Time went by. The rain eventually eased up into a drizzle and then I came inside. The doorman avoided eye contact as I waited for the elevator. He mopped up the puddles I'd made without looking up.

When I got to Dad's apartment, I pressed my forehead against the front door, clutching the suitcase to my chest and shivering. I remember thinking: something is about to happen. I was thinking it both as Mom and as myself. I was thinking: my life is about to change.

## CHARLIE

Doreen was kind, but also suspicious of me, which was good, I think. What normal person wouldn't have been in that situation? After Edie left, Doreen talked to me like I knew a whole lot more about the situation than I did. I played along. She said that after Marianne's dad died Marianne lost it and never got it back.

I asked her what she meant by "it." Her sanity?

Doreen said, no, not quite. Or, yes, but that there were so many ways to be insane, it wasn't really saying all that much. All she knew was that Jackson's death broke something in Marianne—her decency, maybe.

Then Doreen sighed and said that she didn't know anymore what the right thing to do was, that maybe if Marianne wanted to die, she should die. Then Doreen put her head on the table and we sat like that for a while in silence.

I didn't know Marianne yet, but I felt like I did because I'd read Dennis Lomack's novels. In those books Marianne had seemed like the most fascinating and enchanting woman, but maybe Doreen was right, maybe she wasn't particularly "decent." I hadn't really thought about it in those terms. Decency is something you value more as you get older. It makes sense that these were the terms Doreen saw things in, since Doreen was the kind of woman gravity held down to earth with a stronger grip than most.

When she sat up, her face looked completely calm. I thought maybe she'd been crying, but no, she hadn't been. She said she needed to leave for a half-shift at the hospital and told me to make myself comfortable on the couch, gave me a remote for the TV.

After she left, I sat there for a while. I wasn't sure if I should go look for Edie since she had run out, or if I should give her space. Something between us had changed—I could sense that, though I was hoping it was temporary. I tried to watch the TV but it had been years since I'd watched one, and I found all the shows difficult to follow. The actors had very similar faces and teeth and voices and I had trouble telling them apart. Eventually, I turned it off and sat in Doreen's house in silence.

After some time passed, I became aware of sounds coming from upstairs. I thought it was the wind at first, or maybe some kind of animal. When I climbed to the second floor though, I realized it was a person moaning behind one of the closed doors. I stood for a while, listening, before I entered the room.

A man was inside, lying on a hospital bed. He looked ancient but he probably wasn't even old, just withered from illness. His eyes were open, but I don't think he could see me. His pupils were the size of quarters. He was moving his mouth and sounds were coming out, but they weren't words.

"What d-d-do you want?" I kept asking him. I lit a cigarette and offered it to him, but he didn't seem to want it. He was agitated, so I sat on the edge of the bed and took his hand. I hadn't noticed the smell downstairs because of all the chemical air fresheners, but upstairs, after I finished my cigarette, I had to breathe through my mouth. I don't know if he was aware of my hand in his or not, but he eventually settled down and I fell asleep. When I woke up, Doreen was standing in the doorway. I could tell she didn't like me being in there, so I left.

I became an adventurer after my mother died. When you're forced to acknowledge mortality you stop wasting time. Modesty, restraint, self-respect—all that is garbage. It's all ego. I don't have time for it. Nobody does. Even little children who have more time than anyone else, even *they* know better. I knew all this, but over the previous few months I'd lost track of it. Being with that dying man clarified things for me: I might've just met Edie, but I loved her and I'd do what I could to help her.

I felt very alive. I got in the truck and drove to the mental hospital. I'd been so determined and had moved so swiftly that it hadn't occurred to me to get nervous until I was in the elevator. My reflection, distorted in the metal doors, made me look deranged, like I belonged there as a patient.

I knocked. Dad opened the door. He opened it right away so he must have been waiting for me on the other side. We both stood completely still, the strange force field between us humming like an electric fence.

"Marianne," he finally said. He needed to say that to frame what could happen next, to give me permission to be her and not "Mae."

And then, I pulled his face towards mine and kissed him. He tasted like ash, an erupted volcano. His tongue was soft and warm. It was my first kiss. I don't know how long it lasted. It could have been minutes or hours. I lost all sense of time.

## Markus

Edie's departure had brought a certain amount of relief. I was deep in the closet and having her around made me feel like I needed to prove my heterosexuality to everybody, including myself. I was able to have sex with her and even enjoy it on some level, but it made me feel empty and sad afterward. At the time, I blamed it on my Catholic guilt, but now I think it was because I could sense something about me was not right, but I just wasn't ready to deal with it.

I remember that sinking feeling I got when Edie showed up on my front steps out of breath and raggedy. And I also remember feeling embarrassed for her. It was the same way I felt when I would go over to her house and her mother wasn't feeling well, and the house was dirty, and her mom was dirty, and her sister was round-eyed and silent. I remember one time when we got there and all their things were in the front yard and her mom was sitting in the middle of the kitchen floor, and Edie made me help carry her mom up the stairs and bring all their things back inside. I remember thinking it was strange that Edie wasn't more embarrassed. If it were me, I would have died. But that was the wonderful thing about Edie, she was loyal. My parents were completely normal, boring, but anytime my mom said anything to me in public, I would turn beet red. I was so self-conscious, always thinking that people were looking at me and judging me, and then there was Edie—her mother was a mess on the floor in a pile of cereal, and it didn't even occur to her that I would be petty enough to think less of her.

My parents felt so sorry for Edie that they were going to offer her to stay with us while we finished out high school. They believed in doing good works, and I think my mom sensed my gayness and hoped that a live-in girlfriend would help stem the tide. The idea of Edie there for the rest of junior and senior year, I could not even handle it. I got into a big fight with my parents about it, and they were very taken aback because they thought I would want her to stay. I lied to them, said that Edie was happy in New York with her father, despite the constant despondent messages she would leave on my family's answering machine. When it became clear that I would have to do better than that to discourage my parents, I told them that Edie was addicted to heroin and that I didn't feel safe with her drug dealer friends. My parents are typical New Orleanians, they were all "Let the Bon Temps Rouler!" and our backhouse was frequently full of underage drunk kids, but they've always been terrified of me using drugs, so that was what it took.

I feel guilty now, but it had been an issue of survival. I was doing what I felt I had to.

## EDITH (1997)

I have the spins. I hold on to Markus's elbow, but he is walking fast. He is walking ahead of me. He doesn't turn his head towards me as I'm talking to him.

Markus, I say. Markus, have you missed me? These last two months, these last two months have been shit.

I am looking at his ear as I talk to him because he doesn't turn around to look at me.

Markus, I say. I say, Markus. The hedge of the nearby house scratches my arm. I lose my balance.

My knee is bleeding.

*Ew, Edie, God. Why did you get so drunk? Sober up. You're going to get everyone in trouble. Stop pulling on me.*

His face is in my face. He is going to kiss me.

He is not going to kiss me.

He pulls me up and I am on the ground again. It's so quiet. I just realized how quiet it is out here after New York. All I hear is the blood beating in my ears. No cars or people.

*Edie, get up.*

I close my eyes, but that makes the spinning worse. I open them. I am very scared. I am suddenly very scared. My mother's face was there when I closed my eyes. Her pupils are so black that they are holes. You look in them and you see the emptiness inside. I think, my mother. I think, my mother needs to come back. I think, she is gone. I think, she is not coming back, she is gone. I saw today. She's not going to come back. I thought I could make her, but I couldn't. I didn't save the part of her that mattered. That part was already gone. It was already gone because otherwise she wouldn't have done it. It wasn't an accident. I saw today that I am nothing. I am nothing because she is gone already, has been gone.

I say, Markus. I try to say, Markus, I am very scared. But the words aren't coming out. My throat is tightening and my chest too. I can't breathe. I can't. What is happening to me? My mother's neck. The scabs. This is how she must have felt, hanging there, no air in her throat, dizzy. Dizzy. Markus's face is spinning and receding. He pulls loose and I fall.

I don't know what just happened. I can't see off to the side. Grass on my face. The sidewalk. It smells bad under me, and then the swell again in the chest. It burns my throat and splashes. Markus is far away, walking back to his house.

Markus, I try to call again, but then everything contracts again. It contracts and it's so hot in my mouth. Hot pineapple juice barf. My nose is running.

I crawl away from the mess I made. But the mess follows me because I am the mess. I sit up, slump forward, sit up. My face hits the grass. I sit up.

I am empty and cold. Everything hot inside of me has come out. The sound, I realize now, is my teeth. They are chattering. It's not fair of Mae to have left me here like this. Why is she so slippery? And Markus too. He wants nothing to do with me. He did not look at me the way he used to. Maybe he was upset because I talked about Charlie. I tried to make him jealous. I will get up in a minute. Apologize to Markus. My mother is receding already in my head, though I don't dare close my eyes again. I keep them open. Don't blink. Mae and I would play that game, stare and stare until the tears rolled down our cheeks. Mae always won. If she decides not to blink, she won't blink until her eyes shrivel up and fall out.

Did Mae know? Did Mae know I would see what I saw? Is that why she didn't come?

I don't realize that I am staring at a truck until the window rolls down.

*Edie.*

Charlie comes out and pulls me up. I am steadier on my feet than I thought I would be, but tired and embarrassed.

I'm sorry, I say so quietly that he doesn't hear me. He is drying me off with a towel. I lift my arms and he pulls my vomit-spattered shirt over my head. I am not wearing a bra. I pull off my pants and throw them into the bed of the truck. I am standing naked in the street. Charlie tries to cover me in a towel, but it falls and I don't pick it up. He is the only one who is nice to me. Why have I been pushing him away?

I'm sorry. I'm so sorry, I say. And then I see a shadow, something, move inside the truck.

# Chapter 8

I was prepared for complications. I would have bound and gagged a security guard in the stairwell if the occasion called for it, but it didn't. This was a hospital, not a jail. I got past the nurses and orderlies and doctors without a problem. As an urban explorer, I have a lot of experience going into places I don't belong. The key is moving with confidence, having a neutral facial expression and avoiding eye contact. The last part is particularly important for me, as my stutter makes it difficult to pass unnoticed if I need to start conversing.

I took the elevator to the top floor and worked my way down. There were no doors on the rooms, or if there were, they were all propped open. It didn't take me long to find Marianne. She was sitting on the edge of her bed. I recognized her from Edie's description—recognized the silk scarf on her neck and the hairstyle Edie had been so distressed about. I didn't linger in the doorway, as this is the sort of thing that draws attention to itself. Instead, I came in, reached out my hand to her, and she took it. She followed me without questions or hesitation. Her roommate called after us, but quietly. Marianne seemed to be moving as though in a dream. I don't know if she fully understood who or where she was.

She climbed into the truck, sat primly. She seemed zonked. I began to introduce myself, but my words clung to each other in my mouth. She didn't turn to look at me, but hit the dashboard with her palm as if to say: "Drive!" So, I did.

The character of Cassandra was the basis of all my early sexual fantasies, but more than that, she had created the very framework for my sexual desire. Gregor and Cassandra had a romance for the ages, even in the later books, even when it was clear that things would end badly for everybody. Rather than being expansive, their love seemed to condense further and further inward—a circle, then a spiral, then a point, ratcheting the whole thing tighter and tighter, until the spring popped and Marianne went flying halfway across the universe.

What was it like to meet the woman who was the basis of all my sexual fantasies? I don't know. I never met her. Cassandra had existed for such a short moment on the pages of Dennis's books—burning fast and bright. The woman in my truck was the pile of ash left over.

As we kissed, I had the sensation that I was breaking apart. Dad's tongue slipped into a place inside of me that was already cracked and pried it open.

I understand why in fairytales a kiss has the power to transform a frog into a person and bring the comatose to life. I would have stood there kissing him forever until I died, until I was nothing but a cloud of atoms. He was the one who pulled away. I remember his face. Eyes bulged, lips in a rictus and wet with spit. It was going too far for him. I was not who he wanted. I had never been her. I was a prop. No different from the golden binoculars or the little suitcase. The kiss must have reminded him of this.

"Go change out of those wet clothes," he said. His face was neutral. A little sad. When I reached for him he took a step back. For a moment, he had been mine and now, he wasn't.

My body was still buzzing as he walked into his room and shut the door. I couldn't bring myself to move. He began to type, fast and hard. It sounded like a firing squad and I could feel every letter lodging inside of me like a bullet. I'm not sure what happened after that.

After I kissed my father, I lost my mind.

## Edith (1997)

Mom and I are lying in the front room of the shotgun on a nest I made from my laundry and a couple of blankets. The room is dark except for the streetlight coming in through the broken shutters on the front window. In this light, Mom looks like herself. Her eyes are closed and they don't bulge, and her face doesn't look fat or yellow. It barely even looks puffy and that'll go down. Whatever pills they were giving her that made her this way, that made her eyes swim, they will be out of her system soon. I'm so happy. I don't know how Charlie got her out, how he convinced her to leave. I don't care. He could have stabbed all the orderlies and doctors in that hospital and I'd still be grateful. Whatever he did, it worked. Mom is curled up on me, asleep with my hand pressed to her mouth. Her lips are chapped. I have some lip balm in my bag, but I'm worried that if I move I might wake her and then something could change. She could wake up and go back to how she was being in the hospital. So I stay still. I keep my eyes open as wide as they go because when I close them everything starts spinning. I'm still drunk, I guess, though I don't feel drunk.

Charlie smiles at me from the kitchen doorway. There are three rooms between us, but I can smell the kielbasa he's frying. We bought it at a gas station. What does Mom think of Charlie?

She must have liked him enough to leave with him. She didn't like Markus. She never said that, but the way she said his name sometimes I could tell. Mmmmmarkus. Like the lash of a whip. God, he'd been such a dick. Each time I tried to talk to him he had taken a step back from me as if I was going to give him a disease. It makes me wish I had a disease just so that I *could* give it to him. Preferably something with lesions. Why had I even gone to him when I had Charlie? It seems incomprehensible. My Charlie. I watch him lean away from the stove and flip what's in the pan.

When it's ready, Charlie brings me a plate of sausage. He sits next to me on our pile of blankets. An indoor picnic. I'm nauseous, but hungry. I adjust my seat, careful not to wake Mom. Outside it has started to rain. Charlie set up a metal bucket under a leak in the kitchen. We listen to the drops ping softly like a milk pail. The house belongs to the uncle of someone he knows in New York. We can stay here in the Marigny until it sells but we have to clear our stuff out every morning when the real estate agent shows the place.

"Did you know," Charlie says, taking a slice of sausage off the plate, "that these houses are called shotguns because if you sh-shoot a sh-sh-shotgun through the front door, the bullet goes straight through the house and out the back."

"I don't think that's true," I say. "Have you ever shot a shotgun? The shot scatters." I belch into my hand.

He grins at me.

How did he do it? I want to know. How did he get her out?

He wipes something off my chin with his thumb and answers me before I even ask.

"I just went in there and got her," he whispers.

"Just like that?" I whisper back.

"More or less."

"But what about the doctors and nurses and all that?"

He shrugs, looks down at my mother in my lap. Her eyes move under her eyelids back and forth like she's reading. "They were busy."

"And she just went with you?"

He nods.

I take the last bite of sausage. "She's getting better already." I hope that's true. I'll make it true. Charlie pulls my head towards his, presses our foreheads together. My outlaw.

He finishes chewing and swallows. Kisses me on the nose. The rain outside is getting stronger, lashing at the window, trickling into the bucket. Inside we are warm and dry. Charlie and I are like the parents and my mom is our baby. Together we will nurse her back to health.

## MAE

It was irresponsible of Dad to encourage me as he did, but he didn't know, he couldn't have known, what it would lead to. My mind cracked. Between the kiss and the fire I remember only strange shards. Jumbled bits. I was running a low-grade fever for days. I wasn't eating or sleeping. I was unwell. My mom took up most of the room in my chest, and what was left of me was squeezed in the edges around her. It was like always being in a room with a very low ceiling. A coffin.

I remember lying on the floor, my cheek pressed to the cool wood, eye to eye with the cat as Amanda swept around me. Do animals sense madness? Does it scare them? My arms were torn up with scratch marks as I tried to lure Cronus out from under the dresser but even he wanted nothing to do with me.

When Rose came over to dinner, Amanda tried to hide me away, bury me in blankets on the bottom bunk, but I crawled out to the table and joined them. Eating was incomprehensible. I watched what the others did and imitated them. It felt like I was chewing clumps of dirt. The food hurt my stomach. Dad didn't stop talking. I couldn't follow anymore what he was saying. He was at the other end of the table but he was receding farther and farther away from me. I remember Amanda's face as she brayed at something he said. Rose laughed too. *I'm losing him*, I realized, and started to choke. *He's not coming back to me ever again. He's so far away.* Amanda hit me on the back, and a laugh, shriveled and tight, fell out of my mouth.

After dinner, Amanda played the piano. She rolled her sleeves up with a flourish. Oh, how insufferable she was. I tried to climb onto Dad's lap on the couch, but he didn't let me. He shoved me off without even looking and asked Amanda to play another.

The piano playing went on and on. I was the only one who noticed that her shoulder blades were jumping under the fabric of her shirt. Wing humps. She didn't turn around, but if she did, I knew that I would see her true face.

After each song, Rose and Dad clapped. It was as though I didn't exist. I was beginning to wonder if maybe I didn't, if I was only a character inside one of Dad's books, but then I spotted the button from my yellow blouse glinting under the piano bench. I was still wearing that blouse, who knows how many days later. Amanda had tried to take it off of me but I had bitten her. Seeing that button on the floor felt like proof. If I could lose a button, I must exist.

## EDITH (1997)

I wake up with a splitting headache. Mom is gone. Where is she? She is already up. She and Charlie are sitting on milk crates in the backyard under the plantain tree, passing a cigarette back and forth. I watch them from the kitchen window as I rinse my mouth out in the tap. I come outside and Mom stops talking and looks up at me like I'm interrupting. The morning sunlight is too much. A sharp pain pierces the inner corner of my eye. I rub it with one hand and my forehead with the other.

"Good morning," Mom says.

I bury my head in her neck the way I did when I was little. She tenses for a moment, then strokes my hair. "You smell like a distillery," she says. "If I lit a match you'd burst into flames." Her voice is odd, words over-articulated.

"I drank too much," I say. I start to tell her about a dream I had where a doctor was ramming an icepick into my eye, torturing me, but why? He was giving me a lobotomy. I trail off once I remember these details.

Mom keeps stroking my hair, mechanically. She's not listening, or at least she doesn't acknowledge anything I've said. "I was just telling Charlie about your grandfather. We'd come into the city for the Krewe du Vieux. He'd help build the floats." Going to that parade with Mom was always my favorite part of

Mardi Gras, my favorite part of the year. The fact that she hadn't done anything for it this year, that she hadn't even gone to watch the parade, I should have taken it as a sign.

Charlie comes up and crouches next to me.

"You f-f-feeling okay?" he asks me.

I manage to sit up. "Sure." I shield my eyes from the light. "Let's go for a walk."

Charlie goes to get me some sunglasses out of the truck.

When he's out of earshot, Mom says: "Ribbit, you need to take better care of yourself."

The irony of this isn't lost on me. "I'm fine."

"If I'm not around, I need to know that you're okay. That you aren't doing stupid stuff."

"But you are around. So I can be as stupid as I want." I put my hands on her shoulders and stare into her eyes. It's a game we used to play when Mae and I were little. Mom looks away. She's watching Charlie and the truck. I keep staring though, so finally she stares back.

This is the game: we read each other's thoughts. Mae was better at it, but she hated playing.

"Okay," Mom says. "Fine."

"I'll go first..." I concentrate hard on her eyes, try to see what's there. "You want coffee," I begin.

She smiles because she always wants coffee.

"You're happy to be out of the hospital, with me. You're thinking that you are feeling much better, and that maybe, what we need is to go on a trip." Something flickers in her eyes at this word, *trip*. "And, you're thinking about Mae, probably, because you're always thinking about Mae."

Mom rolls her eyes. "You're too old to get jealous of your sister. Of course I think about her. She's not like you. She's more..."

"Whatever," I cut her off. I don't want to talk about Mae. "Your turn."

Mom looks into my eyes and I feel like she is reaching her long fingers into my brain and squeezing my thoughts, checking each of them for ripeness. My ears are ringing so I try to think my thoughts loudly so she can hear each one above the din.

"You're thinking that you're having a nice time with your boyfriend. Your head hurts. You're thinking you shouldn't have drank so much last night. Shouldn't have drank at all! You're only 16."

She's not even trying. I'm disappointed.

"Do it for real," I say. "Like you used to." Climb into my head. I grip her shoulders harder and stare at her more intensely. I can feel my eyes bulging with effort.

"Hey," she says to Charlie, trying to shake me off. "You ready to go for a walk?"

Without looking away from her, I say: "Charlie, can we have a minute?" In my peripheral vision he takes a step back.

"What am I thinking, Mom?" I say again. How can she not hear?

I'm thinking: Thank God you're back. I'm thinking: Don't go anywhere again. I'm thinking: Stay this way, you're fine right now, stay fine. I'm thinking: Love me without all the stuff you put up. Love me without distance.

"No," she says. "I'm done." She turns towards Charlie and smiles like a little bird, asks him for the rubber band around his wrist. She uses it to put her hair up, the way she wore it in the summers, off her neck, but the strands are too short and escape at weird angles. And she looks different than she used to. Her face droops like it's been stretched and then deflated.

God, I've been selfish. The game was too much for her. She's still fragile. I shouldn't have pushed her. Now she'll just withdraw even further.

She strokes my arm and says, "Let's go for a walk. An adventure." And the way she says it, there's nothing *wrong* with it, but it fills me with despair because the real her has burrowed away from me. This is all just scaffolding. I try not to show my disappointment. I need to be agreeable and then maybe she'll come back.

## MAE (2012)

Once, Mom and I were driving through the swamps near where her old house used to be. I was so tired. Nothing seemed real. The windows were down. The humid night surrounded us. We looked like two ghosts, our white nightgowns flapping in the breeze. Suddenly, she stopped the car. There, illuminated by our headlights, lay a dead raccoon in the middle of the road. We watched as three birds of prey descended on its body and eviscerated it. The sound of their wings was deafening. A beating and flapping that stayed in my ears for days.

This was the sound I was hearing as I watched Amanda and Dad on the couch, their knees touching. I couldn't make out what they were saying. Rose's face was in my face, obstructing my view. Her lips were moving. She was talking to me.

"Are you all right?" I finally heard her ask. People only ask this when they know you aren't.

"Fine, fine," I managed to say, but it wasn't convincing.

Dad came over and put his palm against my forehead. I was so grateful for his touch.

"She's still burning up," he said. The three of them talked about me like I wasn't in the room. Rose wanted to take me to a doctor. I knew that if I left with her to the hospital I would never come back. Dad finally extracted his hand from my grip and agreed to wait and see.

Rose brought me a chalky pill and a glass of water. She tilted it for me as I drank it. "She should lie down," she said. As Dad led me to bed, Amanda turned and there it was: her sharp hooked beak, her round, unblinking eyes and oily feathers. Nobody else seemed to see her for what she was. I tried to tell him but none of the words came out. He tucked the blanket around my feet and closed the door.

As I lay immobilized in Edie's bottom bunk, my fever gathering heat, I could hear the front door close behind Rose and then the sound of Amanda, flying heavily through the small rooms. She squawked as she descended on my father. I could hear the sound of her talons tearing open his belly, and the slippery sounds as she pulled out the wet ropes of his intestines with her beak. Through the wall I could hear him moaning. It took all of my strength to rise from the bed and crawl to them. I was ready to offer myself instead, but his door was locked. I was so weak. I know he must have carried me back to my room at some point in the night because I woke up in my bed to him patting my sweat-soaked head and giving me another chalky pill to bring down my fever.

He never loved Amanda. Even later, even after he married her, she was never anything more than a convenience.

## EDITH (1997)

The bars all have their doors propped open to air out from the night before. Stale smoke, booze, and vomit waft faintly as we pass. Or is that smell coming from me?

We stop outside the R Bar. I've been here once before on Mardi Gras, I think. Charlie goes in to get a drink and Mom and I lean against the building and watch a boy ride back and forth on a bicycle with a girl balanced on the handlebars. I'm facing them, but watching Mom out of the corner of my eye. She's humming something quietly, eyes on the kids. Charlie lent her his clothes—men's work pants, several sizes too big, and a shirt that used to belong to a gas station attendant named "Maury." They make her look like a stranger. I don't like it. When I was little she'd let me dress her. Well, not let, I'd *have* to dress her, I guess. But I didn't mind. She was like my big doll. I'd try to get Mae to help me pick the outfits but Mae never wanted anything to do with it. Mae was scared of Mom when Mom wasn't well. Mae was selfish like that. We can stop and get Mom some clothes in the Quarter. Or, no, maybe it's best just to leave it. If the hospital is looking for her, Charlie's clothes can be her disguise. She does look like someone else in them. A character from *Reality Bites* or something.

Charlie comes out with three Bloody Marys in to-go cups.

"Hair of the d-d-dog," Charlie says, handing me a cup, but Mom intercepts it.

"Hair of the dog my ass," she says and I laugh and Charlie smiles politely. I don't argue because I'm glad she's in a good mood, and anyway, the smell of the drink is enough to make me queasy again.

She takes a sip from both cups, then sets mine down next to the head of a drunk sleeping on the sidewalk. "Good morning," she says, shaking him by the arm.

"Angel," the man calls after us. And she does look sort of floaty. It's because the pants are too long on her and she has a light step. Mae would have things to say about it. I hear her voice in my head: *too* light, she says. But so what? And who asked her. I take the celery stick out of Charlie's Bloody Mary and crunch down on it. Hold it for him as he takes a bite too.

I realize after crossing the street that Mom isn't with us. She's standing on the edge of Jackson Square in front of a man playing the accordion. I watch her from the other side of the road as she sways to the music with her eyes closed. The man finishes the song, and she keeps swaying, not seeming to notice that the music has stopped.

"Is she..." Charlie starts, but trails off.

The accordion player starts the next song. A family pauses to listen, looks at Mom, then moves along. Should I cross back and get her? Mom finally stops swaying mid-song and opens her eyes. She looks startled when she sees us staring at her, as though she can't quite place us.

As soon as she crosses the street I take her hand. "Should we go up to the river?" I say quickly to change the subject and smooth things over so she doesn't have to be embarrassed.

Up on the levee, we find a place in the grass and take our shoes off to dangle our feet in the water. A barge full of orange shipping containers floats by. This is the spot Mom used to take us to when we were little, near the bend before the ferry terminal. The water level is high today, I guess because of all the snow melting up north. Last time I was here it was much lower. This part was all rocks.

"I've missed music," Mom says, scrunching her face for emphasis. "Oh, *music remembers it better.*"

"Remembers what?" I start to ask her, but she turns to Charlie and takes his hand.

"Thank you," she says to him.

He blushes a little and tries to say the word "Sure," but gives up. She watches his mouth as he does this and her mouth twitches silently along with his. For a moment I'm seeing her real, unguarded face, and she's showing it to him and not to me. Of course this makes me jealous. It's stupid but it does. Mom must sense something because she lets go of his hand and turns to me.

"Are you having a good day?" she asks.

I say, "Of course," because I *am*, really. It's stupid to be jealous. I'm happy just to be with her again. And then I say, "Really good," so that she'll know that I mean it.

"We c-can go see some music tonight," Charlie offers.

She nods, but she's not really there anymore. Her eyes close. Something is hurting her. Maybe my hangover is contagious. I massage her temples. She smiles like she's tolerating my touch.

"It's all right," she says. "It'll pass."

Charlie moves my hands out of the way and does these strange cupping gestures moving his fingers over her face without touching her.

"Is this h-helping?" he says. I can tell it isn't but she nods her head "yes."

"It's the medication they had me on. Missing a dose gives you headaches."

It makes me want to cry, the idea of them pumping this poison into her. Of course she's been acting a little strange, but who wouldn't be?

Charlie and I are both staring at her. She opens her eyes and puts her hands on each of our shoulders.

"I'm fine," she says, "I'm fine," and kisses our foreheads with her dry, chapped lips. Then she lies across our laps. I get her head and Charlie gets her legs. She really is our baby. I stroke her face and watch the boats float down the river. A fishing boat, a ferry, a cruise ship.

"Do you want to go s-s-swimming?" Charlie asks.

I shake my head. "You can't here." I rip a handful of grass and throw it in the water. He doesn't look convinced.

I'd say more but then the calliope starts playing in the steamboat. God. That sound. Joy itself.

"W-w-what is that?" Charlie asks, squinting at the steamboat.

"That," I say, "is the ghost ball. Remember the ghost ball?" I ask Mom, poking her in the shoulder. She smiles faintly but keeps her eyes closed.

That's what she'd told Mae and me when we were little. *Can't you see all the men and women in their fancy dresses, dancing on the river?* she'd said. *Look at them waltz,* and then her eyes had moved over the water like she was really seeing them. And for a second I would see them too. Pirates and outlaws and ladies with big powdered wigs.

Edie's mother was frankly a little repulsive to me and yet there was something hypnotic about her. Marianne would talk in this odd way, talk *at* me, making it clear I didn't matter at all as the subject, and then something would shift, and it would be electrifying—this moment of connection. I don't quite know how to describe it. It must have been part of the mental illness, the boundaries around things and people would shift, would be revealed briefly as being illusory. I understand why, if I were a person who made art, I would have found her compelling.

As it was, though, I found being around Edie's mother barely tolerable. She was always coming on to me. One night, I slept in the truck because she wouldn't stop fondling herself and me as Edie slept on the other side of the room. I didn't tell Edie that her mother was doing these things because it would have hurt her and she would have blamed me for it. Her mother could do no wrong in Edie's eyes.

Her mother's suffering was so huge it was like its own person: it needed to be constantly fed and tended to. I don't know what it would have done to me to grow up with a mother like that. My parents had always been so in control of all their faculties. Seeing Edie with her mother made me only love Edie more. To still be so protective and sweet.

## MAE

Dad finished the book and my fever finally broke, though I didn't get better. Still, to celebrate, Dad took me to Coney Island. What an odd place to take someone who is in the midst of a psychotic break, though of course he didn't know this was happening to me, didn't want to know.

I remember being on the Ferris wheel with him. The sun had just set and the lights of the fair glittered below. Amanda was in the gondola behind ours. She was always nearby. I could smell her even from that distance, the spongy smell of rotting meat.

The Ferris wheel stopped when we got to the top. Amanda waved at us. Dad waved back. He was trying to seem cheerful. I stood up and leaned over the edge. The ocean below looked like it was made of tar. The night felt like a swarm of insects. How had I ended up inside this nightmare?

"We could dive in the ocean and swim to the edge of the earth. Nobody would know who we are," I said. Maybe the voice was mine. Maybe it was Mom's. I couldn't tell anymore. "We could run away together."

Dad yanked me back into my seat by the hem of my shirt, hard enough to make the whole gondola swing under us.

"Stop it, Mae" he said. He said my name constantly now, as though it would be enough to remind me of who I was.

"I want to be with you," I said and started to cry.

He pressed me into his chest. "Poor Mae," he said. "You *are* with me."

"No," I wailed. "I'm not. Not really." I knew that he had stopped loving me. He was done with his book and done with me.

"I'm right here," he tried to soothe me.

"No," I cried. "You know that's not what I mean. I want to *be* with you." I bit his chest through his shirt. "I want to be your wife. I would do anything you wanted."

I was a wild animal and he was trapped with me a hundred feet up in the air. He had to restrain me finally, using his knees. It must have been horrible for him to create me and then lose control of the narrative in this way.

## AMANDA

Dennis told me he thought that book was his most potent work to date, and I don't doubt this. I saw the intensity of feeling that went into writing it, even if I never got to read the actual manuscript. What an enormous honor it was to be in the room when he finished it. I had just brought him his lunch and I got to watch him type the last word and take the sheet out of his typewriter. He seemed shocked. He let out a whoop. "I'm done!" He twirled me around, pulled me onto his lap.

Oh, how we celebrated! To finally possess him, to hold his life force inside of me... It was magnificent. I don't think we could have had such a meaningful physical relationship if I had not been given the opportunity to show him the depths of my devotion. Writing that novel seemed to have purged some darkness from him, and he was suddenly available to me in a way he never had been before.

I was so swept up in our newfound happiness that I'm afraid I was not clear-eyed enough about his daughter. I was too cautious because of what happened last time, when he'd sent me away. I tread too lightly and as a result I failed to manage her. She was determined to gain her father's attention at any cost. The histrionics! The dramatics on the Ferris wheel! She was jealous that her father was finally happy with a woman who loved him. I found it all very irritating, but it seemed like teenage girl stuff. I assured Dennis it was just a phase and we both wanted to believe that.

## EDITH (1997)

The three of us are inside the Spotted Cat on Frenchman. Onstage there's a man crouched on top of his white bass as he plays it, a girl on the fiddle, another on the washboard, the accordion man from earlier but now he has a painted-on mustache, and a fat man with breasts on a horn. Every time the fat man blows, his face turns deep red and his chest jiggles. Mom pulls Charlie and me onto the packed dance floor. Charlie is shy at first, but Mom starts spinning him and now he's spinning me, a cigarette dangling from the corner of his mouth.

Yes, yes, yes, yes, yes.

Everyone around me blurs into one ecstatic mass. Then Charlie spins Mom. You can see the dark sweat stains spreading as he lifts his arms, and Mom's hair has come loose from its little ponytail. She grabs him by the shoulders and shakes, shakes, shakes, sweat from her face flying onto his. I don't remember the last time I saw her dance like this. Sometimes in the kitchen with Mae and me when we were little and maybe at Doreen's. Her face looks so intense now. Like she is more alive than anybody else in the room.

*Aren't you glad,* I want to scream over the music, *aren't you glad to be alive?*

Of course she is. She grabs my waist and dips me. I'm taller than she is and I nearly topple over, but Charlie catches me, and spins me again like a top. I collide with an old man in a three-piece suit, dancing with an umbrella. He holds the umbrella over me even though we're indoors.

"All right, all right," he's shouting over the music. He does a two-step around me. We're in the center of a circle that's forming.

"Go, Uncle Lionel, go," people are shouting. He's ancient but he can dance. I try to keep up, but I can't quite. He makes a flirty face at me and I start laughing. He's probably a hundred years old. People clap. A woman closer to his age cuts in and they both hold on to the handle of the umbrella and circle around it. Is Mom seeing all this? Where did she go? I look around for her and try to catch my breath. It's so hot in here.

A tall woman stoops down to let a short guy light her cigarette and over her shoulder I spot Charlie leaning across the bar, ordering something from the bartender. And there's Mom draped over Charlie, her arms circling his chest. Is she all right? What's wrong with her? She buries her face in his back and he's talking to the bartender as if she's not even there. I watch her blow on the back of his neck. What has he done to her? I try to push my way towards the bar, but a drunk man with slicked back hair grabs onto me for balance.

"Get off me." I try to slip out from under him, but he leans his full weight against me.

"Wass your name?" he slurs over the music. His breath in my face makes me want to vomit.

I shove him and he topples onto someone else. I move past them, squeeze between two fat women dancing and almost collide with a guy with a goatee, standing on a bar stool, photographing everyone from above with a camera. By the time I get to the bar, it's just Charlie. Mom is gone.

"You w-w-want anything?" Charlie asks when he sees me. He must think I'm a real idiot.

"No, I don't 'w-w-want anything,'" I say back to him. "Where's my mom?"

He looks hurt about the stuttering but not as hurt as he would if he didn't deserve it.

"Edie, w-w-what's wrong?" He puts his hand under my chin.

"Really?" This is unreal. I jerk my head away and knock his drink over. Ice and vodka spill down his shirt and over the bar. "Where's my mom?" I repeat. He thinks he can take advantage of my mom? That I would let that happen? He thinks I would let him do that? She just came out of the hospital. That sick fuck. I can't look at his stupid quivering face. Everything is starting to darken around the edges with rage.

"Hey! Hey!" The bartender is on our side of the bar now, pulling me towards the door. "I don't need to see your ID. I know you're underage." Charlie is following us. I break free and run back to the bathroom. A black door with a picture of a pinup girl.

"Mom! Mom!" I shout. A woman comes out of the stall but she is not my mom. The door swings open and the bartender grabs me by the arm and yanks me back out.

"Don't touch me." I go dead weight, but he lifts me. I kick, kick whoever is in my way.

"I'm looking for my mom," I shout to him, but he doesn't care. He deposits me outside by the bouncer.

"I don't know how she got in," the bartender says. "But you need to do your job."

I try to slip back in again but this time the bouncer takes hold of my arm. "No, ma'am," he says.

"I'm looking for someone," I say. He acts like he didn't hear me. He cards a group of old women who giggle as they show their IDs. Charlie is hovering beside me but I ignore him. What if she's looking for me in there? I press my face to the window, but it's hard to see through the steam and it's so packed.

"Edie," Charlie's saying, "Edie, t-t-t-talk to me. N-nothing happened."

That's what he thinks I care about? I don't care. If she wanted him, he's all hers. If she chooses him over me, that's fine. "Where is she?" I finally say. "Where did she go?"

"I d-don't know," he says. "I thought she went to f-find you."

Did she? Is she in there looking for me? She'd forget Mae and me sometimes. At the mall you had to stay close. No. I don't know. I don't know. I feel something is... Something is wrong. I know something is wrong. It's how I felt when I opened the front door before I even saw her hanging from the rafter. I put my hands on my knees and double over. I try to catch my breath. Taking her out of that hospital was a mistake.

"You have n-n-nothing to be jealous of. I d-d-d-didn't do anything."

I bat Charlie's hand away. "I don't care," I say. "Go back and find her."

He disappears inside. I wait. The bouncer lights a cigarette and watches me pace back and forth.

"You aright?" the bouncer finally says.

I shrug. Of course not. I'm so stupid. On the dance floor the intensity on her face, that was not happiness. It was something else. I'm so, so, so stupid. It's like when Doreen's momma suddenly sat up and started talking to us and I thought it meant she was getting better but it didn't. She died right after.

Eventually, Charlie comes back out. "I c-c-couldn't find her," he says. I start to cry.

"Keep looking," I say even though I know she isn't in there. "Don't touch me." I stand upright.

"M-maybe she went back to the house?" he says. "I swear to God, Edie, n-n-nothing happened."

"Of course something happened!" I scream in his face. "She's gone."

## CANDICE VANCE

Yes, I remember them. A woman, a man, and a girl had started staying in the shotgun next door in late May. That house had been empty for a while, so I was glad to have them there. It gave me something to do, something to be curious about. You lose your curiosity and you might as well be dead, that's what I'd always tell my late husband. He was not curious. I can't get out much on account of the diabetes. It's hard because of my legs. On Sundays after church the gals come by, but otherwise, looking out the window and calling in to the radio is how I stay tied to the world.

I'd see the new neighbors and think, is this some kind of love nest? Are they bank robbers? They seemed like they were hiding something. I don't know if they were in the house legally or not, since the "For Sale" never went down, and I never saw a moving truck. They weren't there very long before I got a knock on my door, sometime after midnight. I was old then and now I'm ancient, but I still remember everything perfectly. It was the girl. I'd waved at her from the window and she'd waved back, but this was the first time we spoke. It was an odd time of night for her to come introduce herself, and she looked like she'd been crying.

She wanted to know if I'd seen her mother. I had not. I'd been sitting by the window all evening, hoping to see somebody, so I'd have noticed.

I asked the girl what was wrong, but she wouldn't say. She asked to use my phone. I set her up in the kitchen with a Yellow Pages. I didn't have long distance, so I insisted on dialing the numbers for her. The first number she had me call was a loony bin out in Metairie. The loony bin didn't have her. The woman had not seemed crazy to me, but who knows. My Aunt Ginny had seemed normal enough too until she stabbed everyone at the hat shop where she worked with her sewing scissors. The girl used my phone for a long time, had me call everyone in the phonebook it seemed like. All the hospitals and hotels.

I told her, why don't you wait. Your mother probably just went for a walk. It's a nice night. Through the open window I could tell it was a very nice night. I told her, her mother probably just needed to be alone. Why all the panic? Why the doom and gloom? She said she needed to call the police. Then I tried to take the phone away from her. I said, listen, why are you getting the police involved? What are they going to do? Arrest a woman who went for a walk? Sometimes mothers need their space too. She's an adult woman. That's when the girl got rude. She wasn't interested in my wisdom. She grabbed the phone away from me and called the police anyway. And what did they do? Just as I predicted. They told her there wasn't a thing they *could* do until the woman has been missing for three days.

Of course the police did eventually get involved. A nice officer, young, practically a schoolboy, came by. He said his people were from Plaquemines Parish, which is where my late husband was from. He asked me some questions. I wish I could have been of more help. I never saw that woman again. I saw the girl and the man a few more times from my window, but they didn't wave back and then they disappeared soon after and the house was bought by a very nice couple. Mr. and Mrs. Perez. He's of Spanish descent. Lovely people.

One afternoon, a few days after that trip to Coney Island, Dad and Amanda left me in the apartment by myself. I don't know where they went. They probably weren't gone long.

After Coney Island, Dad was never alone with me and never too close physically, Amanda made sure of this. It seemed impossible that a person could want something as much as I did and not get it, and yet here it was happening. I was pacing in the apartment, asking myself what I had done wrong.

My eyes weren't working properly and I kept running into things as I paced. When I opened a book to calm myself I found its pages incomprehensible. The words and letters had been replaced with scratch marks from Amanda's talons. Her stink was everywhere in the apartment. It made me retch. I knew that I would be sent away soon. Dad and Amanda were probably out arranging it at that very moment. I would rather die.

The only way I've been able to make sense of this period in my life is by making art about it. I use dolls and build sets and hire actors to read the voiceover. Some of the movies I make cleave closer to "fact" than others, but all of them are emotionally honest. Each film tries to recreate my subjective experience, to share what it was like to be consumed by this love for my dad.

My piece *Conflagration* sold to the Whitney in 2008. It was part of a triptych with two other films—one in which I recreate the experience of going to the horse track with my dad while pretending to be my mother. Another is a fantasy in which my dad and I finally consummate our relationship in the bird sanctuary in Central Park, and as a result, in an Escher loop twist, I am conceived. *Conflagration* is a recreation of the fire as I remember it:

*In the first shot, I am a doll, standing alone in the dollhouse apartment. It's quiet. I'm wearing a dirty yellow shirt. The light coming in through the kitchen windows is also yellow.*

*I run my hands over the Formica table and say—"goodbye."*

*The books stacked underneath—"goodbye."*

*The chairs—"goodbye."*

*The carved tea box —"goodbye."*

*The teapot—"goodbye."*

*With my doll-hand I trace the parallelogram of light on the countertop—"goodbye."*

*I move on to the living room.*

*I touch the couch—"goodbye."*

*The coffee table—"goodbye."*

*The cat made from actual cat hair—"goodbye."*

*The piano—"goodbye."*

*I drag over the piano bench so I can reach each shelf of the bookcase—"goodbye, goodbye, goodbye, goodbye."*

*My doll-fingertips are dusty. Cronus twitches his tail slowly as he watches me.*

*I open the hall closet and pass my hand over the coats, the scarves, the hats, all knit for this film—"goodbye."*

*I crouch down and touch the shoes—"goodbye, shoes."*

*I go into the bathroom.*

*I touch Dad's toothbrush. I touch Dad's comb. "Goodbye. Goodbye."*

*I try the handle to a locked bedroom. I try it again. Nothing. I stand for a moment, with my hand on the knob. My doll-lips moving. "Goodbye," they say soundlessly. My face is pale and damp. A strand of hair is stuck to my forehead. I take two steps back and slam my weight against the door. And again. And again. And again. Finally, a cracking sound. The door swings open.*

*The camera follows me as I stumble towards an empty bed and sit there for a long time, catching my breath. The window is open. A slight breeze rattles the blinds. I am so pale. Where is my dad? Why has he left me alone in this state?*

*The light outside is fading. Grayish blue. Now my doll-face is mostly shadow.*

*I run my hands over his pillow, over the nightstand and the empty bottle of whiskey. All these things are recreated precisely and painstakingly to scale. On his desk, next to the typewriter, an empty glass with a tiny, dried up wedge of lime. I reach under the cushion of his chair and take out the key. I open the drawers and touch everything in them.*

*"Goodbye," I say out loud to the little gold-plated binoculars.*

*"Goodbye," to his manuscript pages.*

*"Goodbye," to the photos of either Mom or me.*

*I arrange all these things neatly, in a circle on the little bed. The room is dark now. I'm just a silhouette as I take the tiny box of matches off the windowsill. Wooden matches. Strike Anywheres. Dad would light them off my zipper like a magic trick.*

*I climb onto his bed, into the nest I've made, and strike the match against the headboard. It sparks. A tiny leap of yellow. Slowly, I move my arm in a circle and the pages ignite.*

*I don't do this because I'm angry. Not at all. Do you know what Joss paper is? On one of our earlier walks, Dad showed Edie and me a store in Chinatown that sold paper objects. Paper cars and paper suits and paper jewels and paper cats and paper dogs and paper vases and so on. It's for Chinese funerals. People burn these things as offerings so that the deceased can have them in the afterlife.*

*That's why I burn Dad's book. It isn't spiteful. No, I just want company on the other side. I want him with me.*

*I lie down on my back, fold my arms over my chest. There is a crinkling* sound as the paper around me begins to burn. The flames are jumpy in the breeze from the open window. My face glows like I am lying on a birthday cake. Smoke rises off the duvet. The pages curl, turn to ash, drift into my doll mouth. They taste like our kiss. The mattress squeals when it heats up. My hair sparks and shrivels. My shirt catches like a curtain. My face. Look at it. Red and soft as it melts.

It's very loud, the sound of fire. And through it I can hear Mom's voice. Hush, hush, go to sleep, she says as she lowers her long braid down my throat until I choke.

## EDITH (1997)

I spent all night walking around the Quarter, retracing our steps, looking for Mom like she was something I dropped. But the whole time I was feeling the pull of the river, and finally, I let myself come here. Why have I been resisting it? This is where she went. I can feel it. I'll stumble on her, asleep on the riverbank. Her hair spread out over a rock like it's a pillow.

Someone far away is singing. I'm at the industrial canal. A thick fog hangs over the water as the sun is beginning to come up. I can't see more than a few feet in front of me. The air is slowly changing color from purple to gray.

The song sounds familiar.

*Because I, I've got a bulletproof heart*
*I've got a bulletproof heart*

"Mom?" I shout, even though I know it's not her voice. It sounds like a black woman. Which side of the river is she on? I can't tell if it's near or far. Is she on the river itself? I hear the water splash against the embankment.

"Mom, is that you?" I shout again.

The singing stops. I'm at the edge of the river.

"Don't believe that I am. No." The voice is feminine, but I think it belongs to a man. I hear the slap of a paddle on the water. The prow of a metal rowboat emerges from the fog a few feet away. The person on the boat has a crooked wig and a dress on, but also an Adam's apple and a stubbly chest.

"Sorry," I say. "I thought you were my mother."

"Interesting." The man in the wig says, this time in a deeper voice. "I haven't heard that one before."

"Have you seen a woman out here?" I picture her in the boat with him. He is taking her somewhere. Ferrying her across... to the afterlife. I'm being stupid. "She has black hair."

The man shakes his head. "Can't say that I have, child." Something about the way he says it feels off to me. He starts to push away with his oar, but I lean forward and grab the front of his boat.

"You sure you haven't seen her?" I say.

"Sure, I'm sure." Maybe I imagined it. His face looks completely blank now. His makeup is smeared on the side he must have slept on. I let go of his boat. "Good luck," he says and disappears into the fog.

## DOREEN

As soon as I heard Edith's voice on the phone, I knew there was trouble. *What now*, I thought. I'd just gotten home from working a double. My feet were swollen so bad I had trouble taking off my shoes. Edith asked me if Marianne was at my house. "What do you mean?" I didn't understand what she was talking about. Marianne was in the hospital. I wondered if Edith was beginning to lose it too. First, she appears out of nowhere, then she disappears without a word, runs off and doesn't even tell me.

"We found her clothes," she said. "In a pile by the river." The clothes she described were not Marianne's. I couldn't make sense of what she was saying until finally she told me the whole story. The story of her stupid albino boyfriend trying to be a hero and them thinking they could play house.

"What did you think was going to happen?" I kept asking her. She'd been the one to cut her mother down from the rafter. What did she think was going to happen this time around?

I said her boyfriend should be arrested for what he did. But then I thought about it. What good would that do? Marianne got what she wanted. And the Mississippi, it's not the worst way to go. The hospital administrators are the ones who should be arrested. They hadn't even notified me. Who knows how long they were hoping to keep this quiet.

Edith told me that she didn't think her mother had drowned. "Maybe she went for a swim," she said, like the river we were talking about was Denial, and not the Mississippi. You don't go for a swim in the Mississippi. Not down here. Not in June. Not with the riptides. Marianne knew that as much as anyone. People drowned in that river all the time and quick. Then Edith started talking about some drag queen in a boat and how Marianne hadn't left her shoes. I'd had about enough. "You think she got naked and hitchhiked on a boat with her sneakers on?"

"Maybe she went for a walk," Edith said. "Maybe she's in Alabama by now."

"Go back to New York," I said and hung up the phone. I didn't have anything else to say. She must've known as well as I did that her momma was dead. I knew the call would come about Marianne sooner or later and I was prepared for it. Well, as prepared as you can ever be for something like that.

When we were girls, Marianne told me a story about walking from my house to hers at night through the pasture. It's the Lakeview Plaza now, but then it was a pasture. And she said that she heard someone next to her, someone breathing.

It was probably a horse, I said. They left them out to graze at night sometimes.

No, she said. It wasn't a horse.

Well, who was it then? I was expecting her to say it was a boy from her class, or the town drunk. Someone a little dangerous, who might've tried to bother her.

Not *who*, she said. *What*. It was death.

Death? Well, then why aren't you dead?

Oh, she said, it just wanted to let me know that I'd been marked.

Everyone's been marked, I told her. All of us.

God, I thought she was dumb sometimes. It was just like her to think dying was special. Dying is not special. Everybody does it.

But then why does it always feel like such a surprise, no matter what, no matter how marked, no matter how much everybody's expecting it?

At least she's finally at peace.

I thought about organizing a second line. It would have pleased my momma, and I think Marianne would have liked that too, but then my brother died right after and I didn't have it in me to deal with arranging anything. It was also complicated by the fact that her body was never found. The current swept it out into the Gulf of Mexico.

# *Chapter 9*

I was in the hospital for a long time. I needed eight skin grafts. The nurses changed my bandages and bathed me in a special steel tub to clean out my wounds. This was a gruesome process and one medical student even fainted at the sight of me unsheathed. The burns were extensive, covering much of my face, arms, and chest, but they were mostly first and second degree, and I was on enough drugs that if I lay very still, it was bearable. It was the itching as my skin healed that was hard to take. Still, I didn't regret what I had done. I was faceless and bald, but I felt more like myself than I ever had before. I was a new person after the fire. I had performed an exorcism and Mom was gone.

When Dad came to visit me, I was surprised by how much smaller he was than I remembered. He wasn't a giant. He looked old. He came with Aunt Rose and cried while Amanda rubbed his shoulders. Tears streamed down his cheeks and got lost in his beard. I felt tenderly towards him, but he didn't really matter to me anymore.

"Don't cry," I told him. "There's nothing to cry about."

Rose fussed around the room, pretending to give us privacy, but when he took my bandaged hand and brought it to his lips, she was on us immediately, gently pulling his mouth away from my hand. That was the only indication I had that Rose knew about what had been going on between Dad and me. Amanda didn't say a word the entire time she was there, and I tried not to look at her.

I knew it was really over because Dad had brought all my things from the apartment, including my grandfather's Leica. My fingers had just healed enough for me to use it and I held that camera between us. I didn't even check if there was film in it—it was just a way for me to keep him at a distance. Our past and my madness was a sealed-up object now, scary but also beautiful. I wanted to hold it and look at it often, but it had nothing to do with me in the present.

After that visit, the camera and I became inseparable. When the hospital finally released me, I went to live with Rose on Long Island. I remember Dad standing across the street on the edge of the sidewalk, a few steps in front of Amanda, waving at us as the nurse helped me into the station wagon, and Rose and her husband loaded in my luggage and the crate with Cronus. I thought Dad must have felt relieved to see me go, though when I printed the pictures from that afternoon, he did not look relieved at all. The relief was all mine. I remember lying across the backseat, taking pictures of the sky blurring past the window and feeling blank, empty, and light.

## AMANDA

Mae was delusional. She's still delusional. The things she claimed her father made her do—utter lies. And that she has made a career out of this... out of humiliating us. She was so cowardly she had to wait until he could no longer defend himself. Well, I'll defend him. I was there! And it wasn't like that at all. Painters use live models all the time. Nobody accuses *them* of perversion. The creative process is delicate and geniuses are allowed their eccentricities.

I don't mean to sound unfeeling, but for me the tragedy of his burnt masterwork far surpassed what that girl did to her own face. Dennis blamed himself, unfairly, for the fire. He stopped writing. I offered to be his amanuensis, to help him reconstruct what he had lost, but he was not interested. For weeks afterward he'd wake up at night coughing, convinced he could smell smoke. Add to that the news of his ex-wife's death and he was not himself. It was good timing when Bard offered him a teaching position upstate.

I was glad to get away from the city and from his daughters, and even from Rose. I was grateful that she brought Dennis back to me, but after the fire she behaved strangely. It was noble of her to take in the girls, but she seemed to blame Dennis for what had happened to Mae. It was odd. This devastating tragedy had befallen him and his sister did not seem very supportive. When I said something about this, he was quick to snap at me so I let the matter drop. Their relationship is their business, and in some sense, the fewer other people he had to rely on the better for me, since it allowed for the construction of our own newfound closeness. It helped with our fresh start.

I told myself he would eventually return to writing, if not to the lost book then to something else, but after his stroke this no longer seems possible. It kills me to think of the beautiful novels his daughter has robbed from this world.

## EDITH (1997)

*"TICKETS!"*

A man dressed like a Civil War re-enactor in a blue wool suit and cap is standing over my seat.

"TICKETS, PLEASE!" he barks, then sucks on his nicotine-stained mustache as he waits for me to take the sleeve of Mom's coat out of my mouth and dig through all my pockets. I find the ticket in my shorts. I pass it to him and he hole-punches it, then tucks it above my head under the luggage bin.

"Tickets!" He continues down the aisle and into the next car. "Tickets, please!"

The only other person in this compartment is a woman reading an *US Weekly*. I wonder if Mom is riding on a train somewhere right now too. Naked, wet hair, reading a book. She doesn't read trashy magazines. Could I have been too hard on Dennis? Mom is definitely a difficult person to be with sometimes. Even she would agree with that. Why else run away from her own life?

And yes, she ran away. I don't give a shit what Doreen thinks. What does Doreen know? When has Doreen ever been right? If she's so smart, then why does her husband hate her? If she's so smart and knows everything, then why did she have my mother locked up in that shithole in the first place? All Doreen could talk to me about was funeral arrangements. She was so eager to finally be done with my mom, it didn't even matter to her that Mom wasn't dead, that they never found her body. Just hand Doreen a shovel and she would have buried my mom alive. Happily.

*If you see a suspicious package, please notify an agent. Thank you for riding the Long Island Rail Road.*

Doreen and Charlie. My two Judases. I think of Charlie telling me with his struggling fish lips that my B.O. smells like *P-pp-p-p-pears...* Ugh. How romantic. If I could just hook my fingers in his gills and pull until his eyes popped out.

*But iit wasn't his fff-ffffault!*

It was his fault *enough*! He did something, said something. He spooked her. What had I seen in him? Walking up and down the riverbank, pretending he was looking just so he could keep fucking me at night. This was him helping me search, you see.

*P-pp-ppp-ppppears*, I spit on the floor of the train. Rub the puddle in with my toe. I lean back in my seat and a tangle in my hair rubs unpleasantly against the headrest. I didn't bring a brush. I didn't bring anything. I got on the bus with nothing but Mom's coat. I try to comb the knot out with my fingers but it pulls too much on my scalp. I leave it. When I get to Rose's I'll cut it out with scissors.

When we were little, Mom's depression would lift suddenly, the door to her room would swing open, and there she'd be, looking like a broken arm that just had its cast removed. Stunned, she couldn't stop blinking as she tried to get the house and us back in order. She would spend the day cleaning, giving Mae and me baths. Mae's hair, she'd be able to brush out, but mine was finer, so the knots had to be cut with scissors. She would let me keep the balls of hair. I would line them up on the windowsill like they were dolls. No matter how long, or how dark the depression was, she always emerged—maybe not exactly the same as before, but close. Why would this time be any different?

*Amagansett. Thank you for riding the Long Island Rail Road.*

Oh, that's my stop. I look down at the back of my hand where I'd written it. Amagansett, yes.

I was expecting to see Mae waiting for me, but the platform is deserted. The air feels heavy and wet. I can smell the ocean. Then at the end of the platform, I see Rose waving. She's wearing flat shoes on her huge flat feet and a long floral skirt that whips around in the wind.

"Where's Mae?" I ask once I'm close enough for her to hear me over the wind.

"She's at the house." She hugs me. "I don't know how much you know about her… condition."

"What do you mean, 'condition'?" Dennis's girlfriend hadn't mentioned it over the phone and I haven't talked to Mae in weeks (or has it been months?).

Rose's face starts to twitch. "Well," she says, and starts walking to the car so she won't have to look at me. "Your sister is doing much better now. She was released from the hospital on Wednesday."

Prickling fear. We stop in front of Rose's old Saab.

"Where are your things?" she asks.

I shrug away the dumb question. Who cares about my things. What happened to Mae? She gestures for me to get in, but I don't.

"Something happened? She was hurt?"

Rose nods, avoiding my eyes.

"But she's okay?"

"No," Rose says, tapping her key against the car. "She's not okay. She set herself on fire. But, she's alive. Miraculously."

We drive down the main street in silence. I feel like I'm waking up from one nightmare into another one. If I fall asleep again will I be plunged into something even worse? Will it save Mae? Will it bring back Mom? What am I talking about?

"I have to stop and get some bread for dinner," Rose says,

pulling in front of a bakery with a striped green and white awning. Mae was almost burned alive and we are buying bread at a cute bakery. None of this makes sense.

My tongue feels dry and too big in my mouth. A fly got in through Rose's window and is buzzing around inside the car. Rose has left the keys in the ignition. I can see her through the plate glass talking to the baker. What if I just took the car and fled. But where? I have nowhere to go. And what would it change?

## CHARLIE

After her mother disappeared it all fell apart. She blamed me for what happened. Though it probably couldn't have lasted no matter what I'd done. Edie would have grown up, gone off to college, and become a different person. And yet, even now, thinking about her gives me an erection, as much for her as for youth, for freedom, for love.

I imagine what might have been if we'd kept driving across the country, across the Badlands, the desert, the Grand Canyon, down through Mexico and South America and then up to Alaska. We could have slept in the bed of the truck under the stars in Texas, or lived on a farm in the Pacific Northwest, or a houseboat in the Florida Keys. We could have found a stray dog along the way, an abandoned pit bull maybe. We could've built a house together by hand. I would've cooked her anything she wanted to eat over an open flame. I would've taken her anywhere she wanted to go. We could've had a kid. Edie would have been so beautiful pregnant, soft and round. I could have delivered the baby myself at home. We would've taken the kid with us everywhere as we rode the open rails or sailed the open sea. I would have fucked her into old age and I never would have gotten tired of it.

## Edith (1997)

We pull around a circular driveway to a green Victorian house. Rose's husband is sitting on the front porch, waiting for us with a pitcher of iced tea. He pecks Rose on the lips.

"Edith," he says, extending a hand. "Welcome. Welcome to the grounds of Montauk Academy. I'm your Uncle Stewart. It's good to finally meet you." His hand is weirdly soft.

"How was your trip?" he asks and pours me a glass of ice tea. "I assume long. Rose told me you took the bus and then the train."

I chug the tea, spilling some down my shirt. He passes me a napkin but I pour myself another glass. I drink it the same way. Not stopping for air.

"Thank you," I say breathlessly and set the empty glass on the wicker table.

"More?" he offers, but I shake my head.

"We were worried," Stewart says. "It's awful, everything that's happened."

"Uh huh," I say. I notice he's got a small piece of toilet paper stuck to his cheek. A rusty little splotch. He must have cut himself shaving. He should grow a beard—it would cover his pitted skin. I wonder why Rose never bothered to tell him this.

"Did you give Mae the pills I set out?" Rose asks him.

"I did."

"Is she awake?"

"She was 10 minutes ago."

"You want to go see her now?" Rose asks me. "It's up the stairs, second door on the left."

It takes a moment for my eyes to adjust to the dark foyer. I'm glad Rose hasn't followed me in. The house is quiet like it's holding its breath. Each step creaks.

"Mae!" I call from the bottom of the stairs. "I'm here!"

No response.

Along the banister are framed photos. Rose in a white dress next to pockmarked Stewart. A blond boy in a sailor suit, it must be Dennis. Oh, weird. There's one of Mae and me, from when we were very little. Mae is a baby and I'm holding her. Dennis and Mom's legs are in the shot also. Mom is barefoot. She has such beautiful feet. Why would Rose put this up in her house? What other people have photos of me hanging on their walls?

"Mae," I say, once I'm outside her room. Through the closed door I can smell something strange.

"Mae," I say again. "It's Edie."

"Edie," I finally hear her repeat.

When I open the door the smell is overpowering. Greasy and medicinal. It makes my eyes water. It takes me a moment to find Mae in the room—lying on the bed, propped up with pillows, wrapped in gauze. She's holding a gun. No, of course not. Why would I think that? It's the barrel of the camera.

Click. Click. She takes my picture. I cover my face with my hands. "Oh, God," I say. "Wait at least till I've showered." I try to act like I'm covering my face from the camera and not from her. I don't want it on film, that moment of horror before I was able to hide it.

"You look like a mummy," I say when she finally tilts the camera down. I force my voice to sound light. She doesn't look away or blink, so I try not to either. Her pupils are huge and black.

"Can I sit?"

She nods, a tiny movement of her head.

I sit on the edge of the bed. I try to breathe through my mouth so I don't have to smell the ointment.

"Does it hurt?" I ask.

She shrugs, her gauzed shoulders barely lifting.

I can see in the small slots around her eyes and mouth that her skin is pink, shiny, and raw. "It must hurt."

"I don't mind it. I don't know."

I take a bit of gauze that hangs loosely from her wrist and rub it between my fingers.

"Why would you do something like this?" I ask her, staring at the gauze in my hand.

"I had to," Mae says dreamily. Her voice sounds different and odd. I squint at her lips. It's hard to tell what they look like under the blistering. She barely moves her mouth as she talks.

"But it was an accident," I say. Even though of course it wasn't. She looks at me in response with those big, unblinking eyes. Can she even blink anymore? Does she still have eyelids?

I wipe my nose with the back of my hand and watch her pick the camera back up. She aims it at the middle of the room. It takes me a moment to see what she's looking at—a speck of dust suspended in a shaft of light. She follows its slow descent through the air down to the corner of the hooked rug on the floor. We sit for a while in silence.

"Why are you wearing that coat?" she finally asks.

"I took it. Did they tell you about Mom?" I ask.

Mae doesn't seem to have heard me. She's looking down at her camera, fiddling with one of the knobs. It must be hard with her fingers bandaged like they are.

"She disappeared," I say. "She'll turn up though. You know how she is."

A knock on the open door. Rose. Mae aims the camera at her. Rose pulls her lips over her teeth and grimaces. I guess that's supposed to be a smile?

"Why don't you help me make some lunch," Rose says through that bizarre grin, "and we'll let Mae rest a bit." I've never seen a person so uncomfortable in front of a camera.

I stand and the bed creaks under me. I reach to hug Mae, but I can feel her tense. Her entire body is one raw wound. Rose beckons from the doorway.

"All right, then," I say, bringing my hands back down to my sides. "I'll see you in a bit."

And then, as the door is shut almost all the way, I hear Mae say very quietly:

"She's gone this time. I can feel it. She's dead."

Heat shoots through my face. I put my palm on the door and try to push it open. "She's not! You have no idea what you're talking about. You weren't even there."

Rose pulls me away from the door. "Edie, why are you yelling at her? What is wrong with you? She's high out of her mind on morphine."

"My mom's not dead," I say to Rose. I might as well be a duck in a children's book. I feel so stupid. I hate that I'm crying.

"Yeah, okay, I heard you," Rose says. She opens a door to another one of the rooms. Mine. She stands behind me with her hands on my shoulders as I face away from her, crying. The flowers on the wallpaper blur and melt.

"I don't care if you don't believe me," I say.

"I don't 'not believe you,' Edith. But your mom isn't here, we can agree on that. Dead or not, she isn't here."

This makes me sob harder. Because I know she's right. Mom doesn't want to be found. Mom doesn't want me. And if I had been looking after my sister like I was supposed to be…

Rose lays me down on the brass bed, dries my cheeks and neck with the corner of the crocheted blanket until I finally calm down. I hiccup. The exhaustion of the last few months descends on me. There's the gray ocean outside the window. Rose's cool fingers linger on my face. She's humming a lullaby.

"Why did Mae do that?" I ask her.

"I don't know." She shakes her head.

"Where's Dennis?" I ask her. "Why isn't he the one taking care of her?"

A glimpse of something that she immediately tries to cover. "I'm better at taking care of people, I guess."

"What did he do?"

"What could he have possibly done? He didn't do anything."

I know she doesn't believe what she's saying. I give her a shove and she falls off the bed, lands on her hands and knees on the floor like a dog. I turn to face the wall, the red flowers and vines.

Before the fire I had assumed Mom and I would always be a closed system. We were like a hall of mirrors—her-creating-me-creating-her, and so on. Which one of us was real? Which one was the reflection? But then with the fire, that was all over. When I burned her face off of my face, I killed her in myself. And so it made sense to me that I killed her outside of myself, too. When Edie tried to tell me Mom was still alive, I knew she was lying. Mom was gone.

I blamed myself for her death. I suppose I still do, and I've coped with this and everything else by retreating into my camera. The world through the viewfinder was contained and manageable. My Leica became an extension of my new body. I slept with it pressed to my belly, so it was always warm.

When Uncle Stewart noticed my interest in photography, he set up a darkroom in one of the many spare bathrooms, and as soon as I was well enough, I began spending many hours a day in there. Aside from this, Uncle Stewart and I rarely crossed paths. They took very good care of me, my aunt and uncle. Rose took a leave of absence from work so she could nurse me back to health. Whatever her true feelings about me were—she was dutiful; she was consistent; she cleaned out my wounds, administered my medications, and drove me to endless doctor appointments. She didn't seem to want anything from me emotionally, for which I was grateful.

Unlike poor Edie, whose need for me was bottomless. I'd see her shadow under my door, just standing there, and instead of being kind and asking her to come in, I would pretend to be asleep. She tried so hard. She decorated my room with cutouts from *National Geographic* when I wasn't yet allowed to leave the house. Iconic photographs of mountains and glaciers, reminders of the wide world outside. Probably reminders she needed more than I did. It's easy to say now that I wish I'd been kinder to my sister, but at the time I don't think I was capable of it. Our father had just broken my heart, our mother had just killed herself, and I had just set myself on fire. I couldn't afford to be generous.

# ROSE

Stewart and I tried to have children when we first got married, but I wasn't able to conceive. After the girls moved in with us, when Stewart and I would be lying in bed about to go to sleep, I'd ask him: "Stewart, do you regret it—not having any children of our own?"

And he'd say, "Rose, what's the sense of regretting something we can't have?"

"But we could've adopted," I'd say. "We still can." I imagined my own babies, little Russian, Chinese, and Ethiopian girls. One for each empty bedroom of our huge house. And Stewart, because he didn't like to argue with me, would nod in agreement and go on reading whatever it was he was reading. But we never did adopt.

The closest I ever came was Edie. Sometimes, I'd pretend she was my own. I'd walk through town with her, and take her on errands to show her off, even though Montauk is a small place and our neighbors knew that we didn't have children. It was easy to see myself in Edie, not just in her looks but in her personal qualities. She was fiercely loyal and independent, but also vulnerable. She was a typical teenager of course, so slightly surly, not always very good at containing her anger. There were rough patches, but she came out all right. More than all right. I'm very proud of her. It was nice for me to pass on some of myself, family recipes and traditions, this sort of thing. It was nice to not feel for once like the broken branch on our family tree.

I never experienced these maternal feelings toward her sister. Mae was just so odd. Stewart reads a lot of biographies, and he says that all great artists have something awful or empty at their core that they need in order to fuel their work—Dalí and Picasso and Emily Dickinson. I don't know if I believe that entirely. Denny was never that way, but I guess it applied for Mae. She was intense and inaccessible, and she made sure you knew not to get too close.

Marianne had no doubt done a number on the girl. I've seen Mae's films, but I don't believe Denny was capable of doing those things to her. Of course not. Whatever kindness he gave her she must have misconstrued. But Mae was a sick and sensitive girl and he should have taken more care with her. She grew up with that madwoman, of course she learned to think that left was right and up was down. It's very sad.

I came to her once the movies were at the Whitney and begged her to take them down. I said: "I have done so much for you—I have put you through Montauk Academy and then art school. I have taken care of you. I've never asked you before for anything. But this, what you are doing, it's not right. It's not just hurting Denny, it's hurting his family."

I begged her. But she didn't care. There was something about her that had always been impenetrable. That didn't change. She'd never been a person you could reason with. I understand completely why Amanda had started that libel suit, but I was very much against it. I knew all it would do was get Mae's work more attention. And it did. Denny's books ended up getting banned in school libraries in Indiana, and you couldn't go into a hair salon without seeing Mae on the cover of half a dozen magazines—her face covered by a balaclava, her eyes staring out at you in a way that should have made me angry, but instead only made me feel sorry for her.

## EDITH (1997)

I took one of Mae's pills this morning. It was robin's-egg blue. I hope it was morphine and not an antibiotic. There were so many pills, who's going to notice one gone?

I'm watching Rose chop a carrot with the grace of an architect. Mae is on a special high-calorie diet for the burns—lots of meat. Meat makes meat. In the kitchen, there's nothing gooey limbed or foolish about Rose. Her movements are quick and confident. She sweeps the chopped carrots off the cutting board and into the gumbo pot.

The lightness hits me all at once. Like I'm floating over the black and white tile floor of the kitchen. I should watch my head on the hanging pots. The clanging! The clatter! Don't fall into the cauldron! Meat, meet Meat!

"What's so funny?" Rose says, smiling, ready to agree and be in on the joke. I shrug, shake my head, nod. I'm not making any sense, so I bend over to tie and untie my shoelaces with the concentration of a stroke victim. When I sit up, the floaty feeling dissipates a little. Rose is still talking. She has asked me a question.

"Sure," I say. I stick a stray tip of a carrot in my mouth, busy myself with chewing it. If I keep letting her talk, I'll figure out eventually what I agreed to.

"Back to school shopping..."

This has probably been a fantasy of hers for a long time. Us gals going shopping! Matching outfits! That poor woman.

"Do you want me to peel some garlic?" I offer. She passes me three cloves and watches me struggle to get the edge going.

"It's easier this way." She rolls the garlic with a glass bottle, then passes it back. I did all the cooking growing up, so no one taught me any tricks. The papery shell slips off like magic. Beneath, the clove is shiny and smooth. A little green shoot peeks out from the tip. I feel the pill gently purring in my stomach.

"Mince it..." Rose is saying to me.

She trails off. Is she looking at my pupils? Are they giving me away? No. Not that. I follow her gaze.

Mae is standing behind me in the doorway. Mae doesn't lean anymore. She stands stiff and straight. She looks like some Greek mythological creature—bare human legs, but gauze from the waist up. And always the camera.

"How are you feeling?" Rose says to her. "Lunch will be ready in half an hour. I heard back from Dr. Stern. He said he'd squeeze us in tomorrow. He's a parent of one of the boys at the academy, that's the only way I was able to get us that appointment. He's the best reconstructive specialist in New York, probably in the world. We're very lucky."

Mae nods.

Rose pauses with her knife. "I noticed one of your morphine pills was missing. It's not something to mess around with, Mae. It's highly addictive. You can't just help yourself."

I focus on the garlic I'm chopping. I can feel Mae's eyes on me. If I look up and intercept her disappointment, what's left of this blue pill will disappear completely.

"I was in a lot of pain," Mae deadpans. "It won't happen again." She photographs the two of us for emphasis.

Another person, Uncle Stewart, would probe this. But Rose doesn't want to. She's the kind of person who makes decisions about people and then any new information is bent around accordingly. It's a nice quality. It will take a lot to get her to finally hate me.

The phone rings. It's Mom. She's standing in a phone booth, pressing the receiver to her wet ear.

Stewart holds the cordless against his vested chest. His mouth is not quite synced up with the sound. "Charlie for you," the words come at a delay. I look down at my garlic and keep mincing it. Something clenches, nausea. Out of the corner of my eye I see him holding out the phone to me, but I don't take it.

"For God sakes," Rose finally says. "Tell him she isn't home."

"You tell him." Stewart is above playing games. He has an empire to run. He has to get back to the study and set his toy soldiers up in the Battle of Austerlitz. The man is demented. I knocked them all down once and the next day they were all set up again just how they were.

"…She doesn't wish to speak to you," Rose is saying into the phone.

I go outside and vomit into the azaleas.

Dear God, I think, I sound like a horse. And then, Dear God. And then just, God. Are you watching me do all of this?

No, but Mae is, through the lens of her camera. Neither of us acknowledge that she has lied for me.

"Take a picture, it'll last longer," I finally say and wipe my hand on the slick grass.

Rose removed the mirror on the medicine cabinet in my bathroom so I wouldn't have to look at myself. Of course, she couldn't protect me from all reflective surfaces. In the evening, with the lights on in my room, I would glimpse my bandaged face in the hand-blown glass of the windows or in the shiny copper pots hanging over the island in the kitchen. Out of curiosity, I asked Rose once to show me what I looked like when she was changing my bandages. She didn't want to, but eventually she gave me her powder compact. Of course, it was horrifying. It was before the cartilage in my nose was reconstructed, and everything else was still so blistered, red, and shiny with the thick ointment. Despite all that, I don't think I thought much about what I saw. There've been times since then when the sight of my bare face has filled me with despair, but that summer it felt like a small price to pay for my freedom. However disfigured, my face was finally my own.

And I liked that it kept people at a distance. I liked this about my camera too. Looking through the viewfinder I could never get sucked in emotionally again, as I had with my dad. The world now was flattened and circumscribed. The only times I felt a strong stirring in my chest was when I looked at the ocean. I photographed it constantly, hoping it would eventually lose this power, but also hoping it wouldn't. Rose took me on early morning walks on the beach. She'd hold a parasol over us as I photographed the water curving along the horizon. I wasn't thinking about that first trip to the beach with Dad and Edie. I wasn't thinking about Mom's body at the bottom of the Gulf. I wasn't thinking about any of the particulars of my own situation, that it would be a long time before my skin would heal enough for me to go swimming in the salt water, for example. No. I was aware only that the ocean was enormous and that I was very small.

It was mostly these photos of the ocean that I printed that summer. I kept all the undeveloped rolls of film in an old straw hat that I recognized from a picture Rose had in The Dad Room. In the picture, Dad is sitting on a riverbank and the straw hat casts a shadow over the top half of his face. A cigarette hangs out of the corner of his mouth and a wisp of smoke curls towards the camera. I believe it was Mom who took the picture. Seeing that younger version of him did not fill me with the same kind of lust that it had before. The hat was just a hat.

For a long time I photographed compulsively, but it wasn't art. When I was getting ready to apply to art schools I went into the city and met with Rivka, my dad's old girlfriend. She sifted through the stacks of photos—really generic stuff—blurry photos of the ocean, my cat, my feet. It was kind of her to meet with me and take me seriously.

She looked at my work, then looked at me and finally said:

ART IS NOT A SHIELD.

IT IS A KNIFE.

YOU HAVE TO BLEED!

Of course, she was right. I was not letting any of myself into the work. It was not expressing anything. It was just a way of making the world more manageable. I wasn't ready then to bleed. That came later.

## RIVKA

I saw a video installation in the Whitney Biennial that haunted me for weeks. A dollhouse nightmare, like a modern Hieronymus Bosch shot on grainy Super 8 film. I watched it and felt immediately transported to a memory that felt like my own but wasn't.

It was the piece everyone was talking about. There was a long, stupid write-up for it in *Art in America*. The critic understood it to be a metaphor for the Jungian conception of childhood. So bloodless and reductive. The film was not a metaphor, it was personal, and yet I didn't understand how personal until I met the artist in her studio.

It was a very hot day and she wasn't wearing the balaclava that had become her signature. Her skin was thick and clotted, but her gray eyes were so clear and unaffected that it made everything surrounding them look like a mask. I remember wondering if it was all part of some elaborate performance piece. I remember also that one of her ears was perfectly formed, smooth and intact, not affected at all by the burns.

She welcomed me. "Rivka," she said, "you haven't changed at all, still ugly as ever." I wasn't offended, not when it was coming out of a face that looked like hers. We caught up for a while. She thanked me for something inspirational I had said to her years ago, which I did not remember saying and which did not really sound like the sort of thing I would say.

She was getting ready for an exhibition at LACMA and offered to show me her new work. It didn't use dolls or props like her previous films. She called it the Hat series. It used old, often damaged, pictures she had taken as a kid right after recovering from the fire. The pictures still held the charge of what must have been a very difficult time.

The most striking piece was a collage of a room filled with her sister, who was wispy and much sadder-looking than I remembered. The sister was included in duplication—sitting at the foot of the bed, lying on the floor, pacing near the door, looking out the window at the ocean. A ghost in a fur coat, circling the viewer.

"Haunting," I said.

"Yes," she said. "I suppose."

"Do you have any pictures of your father?" I asked. I suddenly had a strong urge to see him as he had been, to remember that time period in my life.

"No," she said. "I don't."

Even with her burnt face it had somehow not occurred to me until then that the films were autobiographical—that gentle Dennis Lomack was the monstrous love object. This was before the televised lawsuit where Dennis was wheeled out, drooling and silent, by the awful woman he married.

## Edith (1997)

I knock on the door to the darkroom. "Spooks? Can I come in?"

"Hold on." I hear her banging around, then the click of the lock.

She pulls me into the room and quickly locks the door behind me. It takes a moment for my eyes to adjust to the dim red bulb hanging over us. There are trays of liquids set up in the bathtub and an enlarger on a little side table. Cronus is lying in the sink, paws fanned out, watching us. He likes the cool porcelain against his belly. I rub him behind the ears.

"Dennis and Amanda are downstairs. Everyone's getting ready to go to the beach," I say.

Mae doesn't seem to hear me. She hits a button on the enlarger and a square of light appears for a few seconds, then beeps when it shuts off. She takes the blank piece of paper out of the machine and drops it into the first tray in the bathtub.

I sit on the toilet. Cronus and I watch her work. She looks like she's in a trance as she rocks the tray back and forth, back and forth. The chemicals smell like vinegar and feet. Suddenly an eye emerges on the page out of nowhere, then a beak—a seagull.

"Magic!" Mae says. Each time a picture shows up she seems delighted like a little kid. I worry that the fire did something to her brain.

"Cool," I say.

Mae picks the photo of the bird up with her tongs and watches it drip into the tray, then drops it into the next tray. "The eyes always appear first. I wonder why that is."

"Dennis looks weird," I say, changing the subject. "Gaunt. Like he lost a bunch of weight."

She ignores me. The only thing she ever wants to talk about is the photographic process. She leaves the seagull in the middle tray and takes another print out of the last tray.

"This is fixer," she says. "After a photo sits in here for a while, it can be exposed to light without getting damaged. It's toxic though, so I have to be really careful it doesn't go down the drain."

"Cool," I nod, trying to look interested. It's better than her not talking to me at all, I guess, which is how it was until recently. She takes the dripping paper out of the fixer and rinses it under the spout, then hangs it up on the clothesline by the blacked-out window. I look over her shoulder at the picture. A gray rectangle.

"What is that?" I ask her.

"The ocean."

I look closer and see some white caps. Waves. The other pictures hanging up look identical. I don't really get it—why the pictures interest her, why she takes them over and over.

She scratches her arm with the back of the tongs. I think she winces though it's hard to tell through that ski mask of gauze.

"Does it itch? Do you want me to tell Rose to apply some more cream?"

"Why don't you go on to the beach without me," she says. My fussing irritates her. In here I think she forgets for a while about her body, and she doesn't like me reminding her. She's not going to tell me anything I want to know anyway. "Hold on, let me just cover the paper so it doesn't get ruined." She puts lids over the chemical trays and hides her paper in a special plastic bag. "Go ahead," she says.

"Do you want me to tell Dennis anything?" I try as she gently pushes me out of her darkroom and locks the door.

I wait on the other side for a response, but all I get is the sound of my own breath and faint voices from downstairs. "Okay then, I'll see you later," I say.

I pass Dennis on the stairs. He is heading up to see my sister. I crouch, out of view.

"Mae? Mae, darling?" I hear him say. "Maybe we can talk? Can I come in, please? There's something I wanted to tell you."

I creep back up the steps and catch sight of him, leaning his forehead against her door. When he sees me he straightens up.

"Ready to go to the beach?" he asks me. I nod. What did he want to tell her? Nobody tells me anything.

"See you when we get back then," he says through the door and follows me back to the kitchen where Uncle Stewart and Amanda are talking about alumni funds and academic excellence while Rose is carefully finishing loading up the picnic basket.

We file out the back door and down the bluff to the club's private beach. The wind is whipping sand against our legs. The men we pass stare at me even though the top of my bikini lies flat against my chest—that's something at least one of these rich lobsters, soused at the 4th of July party, has offered to have fixed. When the men realize I'm with this group of middle-aged people that they know, they stop eye-fucking me and wave at Uncle Stewart. "Happy Labor Day!" they shout. He waves back but keeps walking. He's trying to keep up with Amanda who is plodding through the sand like a determined cow. They make quite the pair in their stupid sun hats. Why don't they know they should be embarrassed? Her white back is covered in moles. It's disgusting. I don't understand why Dennis has brought her. He's wearing mirrored sunglasses so I can't see his eyes. Why is he with that repulsive woman? I am sure somehow that she is responsible for what my sister has done to herself.

I slow down at the tiki bar set up on the sand. The bartender is making something with ice cubes and cherries that smells like hairspray. I can imagine sipping it and that pleasant heat spreading through my chest, making this excursion a little more bearable.

"Club soda?" the bartender says. He's wearing a bowtie and a vest, even though it's hot and he's on a beach.

Rose has stopped and is looking back at me, waving for me to keep walking. I shake my head at the bartender though I'm in no rush to catch up with Rose. I don't need a drink now, it's fine. I'll have one later. I'll take a few sips of the wine Rose uses for cooking. Uncle Stewart changed the lock on the wine cellar.

We keep walking farther, past the people, towards the deserted end of the beach, until we get to the lighthouse. In the sun, its walls are blindingly white. Desert bones like in the Georgia O'Keeffe paintings Mom likes. Is that where she went, maybe? Out West? I squint at the sand, ignoring the ocean for a moment—this is what the desert must be like. I picture Mom's head sticking out of the sand. What if I'd almost stepped on her? I have to blink several times to remove the feeling of her face under my foot. Ick. Ick. Ick.

"Can you give me a hand?" Dennis is struggling with the beach umbrella in the wind. I hold the top of it as he buries the base. I'm watching Stewart apply globs of sunscreen on Amanda and Rose. Why doesn't it even occur to him to rub it in properly? I can't stand to see it smeared like that on Rose's back. When Dennis is finished burying the umbrella, I go up to her and rub in the white smears. She jumps slightly at my touch, surprised, but then leans into it a little too gratefully. Last night she gave me a bracelet that belonged to her mother. She took me aside and tearfully told me that I was as close to a daughter as she has ever had. The bracelet is nice, thin silver chains held together with a mother-of-pearl clasp, but it seems unfair to Mae, not that Mae cares.

"The water might be warm enough for a dip." Rose looks at

me anxiously, waiting for me to smile back. I do, but I wish she'd stop handing me a knife to cut her with. It's only a matter of time before I'm not able to resist.

Stewart offers me the sunblock, but I shake my head. "I put some on at the house already. Why don't you put some more on Amanda."

Rose opens the basket, takes out a loaf of bread and a Tupperware container full of butter.

"I'm all set," Amanda says. She arranges her hand casually, flashing a diamond ring at me. They're married? Her and Dennis? And that coy twat thinks I'll ask her about it? I'd rather die.

"*Are* you set?" I say. "I'm sure you could use some more. Maybe nobody has ever told you, but your back is covered in disgusting black moles. It's truly revolting. You should get it checked out by a dermatologist."

Amanda snorts and takes a magazine out of her beach bag.

"What a thing to say!" Uncle Stewart says, then looks at Dennis, waiting for him to reprimand me. Of course Dennis does no such thing.

"Does anyone want some herring?" Rose asks, trying to change the subject.

"Edith, that's unkind," Uncle Stewart says to me slowly, like I'm an imbecile. He ignores the jar of herring Rose is pushing on him. "It's unkind and you're better than that."

Am I? Well, I'm sure skin problems are a sore (!) subject for him. Amanda turns the page of the magazine, pretending to be reading it, her dumb ring glittering in the sunlight. Behind her, three seagulls land and begin tearing apart an abandoned bagel. One bird manages to hook what's left with its beak and take off. The other two are left behind, squawking stupidly.

"We talked about this," Stewart is saying to Rose as if I can't hear him. "She needs boundaries and discipline."

I stand and the sand from my lap scatters onto their faces.

"I'm just concerned about her health is all," I say sweetly as they blink and spit. Then I walk down to the water. They can play house without me. I'll give them their fresh start.

A wave crashes and the cold foam rushes over my feet, then sucks the sand out from under me. A moment of vertigo, steadied by an arm on my shoulder. Dennis.

"Want to go for a walk?" he says.

I shrug though already we are walking.

"How are you doing?" he asks me.

"Great, Dennis. I'm doing great." What does he think?

"Oh yeah?" he says, pulling on my arm so I'll turn around and face him.

"Mae told me everything," I lie.

"Everything," he repeats.

"Yeah. So, I know."

He nods. "Know what?"

"What you did."

"Okay, and what was that?"

It must have been something horrible. "You know," I say.

He nods.

"Is it true?"

"It's probably true. Why would your sister lie?" Dennis bends down and picks up a seashell. Holds it up to the sky. It's partly translucent in pearly layers.

"She wouldn't."

He throws the shell back in the water. We turn back. I step on a pile of seaweed and the tendrils squish under my feet. I don't know what Dennis did or didn't do, but when I left, Mae was fine. If I hadn't left, she'd still be fine.

I glance at Amanda, who's sitting in the shade of the umbrella. "She's pregnant, isn't she?" I ask. It seems obvious as soon as I say it.

"She is," Dennis says.

"Oh," I say. That's why he's marrying her. "So, you're having a baby?"

"That's the hope, yes." He smiles, but I don't smile back. This baby will be his do-over, his second chance. Mae and I are the first pancake. The shriveled one that gets thrown out.

Dennis pulls off his shirt and sunglasses and tosses them inland. "Want to take a dip?" he asks. His eyes are squinty. His chest hair is gray now. It wasn't gray before.

I follow him into the water, still stunned. Oh, it's so cold, so cold. I suck my stomach in, trying to keep it warm as I go in up to my waist.

"OO—OOO—OO. eee—eeee—eeeee," Dennis says of the cold.

I take another step and suddenly the water is pulling me. Moments ago it was flat but now it's going vertical. A wave is forming in the distance. A big one. I hesitate, taking a step back towards shore, but my knees are water-locked.

"Dive under," Dennis shouts. The wave crests above us. "Dive!" Dennis shouts again before he disappears under the wave, while I am frozen. A wall of water comes at me. It hits me in the chest, knocks me down, pulls me underneath.

I'm being dragged along the ocean bottom, the sand scraping my back and legs. I'm being buried under water. I unclench my eyes and see a cloud of sand, hair. My mother's hair.

And then I'm standing again, waist-deep, coughing. My top has been knocked sideways, my bottoms are full of sand. My nasal passages are on fire. A mop of seaweed bobs along the surface.

Dennis is a few feet away. "You all right?" He floats towards me. Behind him I can see another wave beginning to form, and this time, I don't let it hit me. I turn and run, or try to anyway, using my hands as paddles. I can hear the wave breaking behind me, but it doesn't knock me off my feet. Instead it helps me along, pushing me towards the shore where Aunt Rose is waiting for me with a towel.

"Are you all right?" she says, wrapping the towel around my shoulders. Snot is streaming over my lips. I'm shivering. She tries to lead me back to our blanket, but I lie down in the hot sand where we're standing. She fusses, a long heavy pear, an armless goose. She kneels by me, clucks, clucks, gives me a sandwich. I eat it flat on my back without opening my eyes. Every few bites, a grain of sand gristles against my teeth.

# PART III

## MARIANNE

physicists say that some particles exist only when they are being watched. an electron that isn't leaping from one orbit to another like a flea, or that isn't being prodded by a scientist, ceases to be. i think this is what happened to me. i ceased to exist.

& then I reappeared one day, inside of ruth day's gaze. she was a nun without a convent. god told her to leave the order & start a farm. she saw me walking along the highway & pulled over.

"i found you," she said & i felt found.

i can't account for the hole I crawled out of. i don't know how much time went by. i'd lost language. i repeated other people's words but could not form any of my own. words were just tricks for my tongue, nothing more. there was a pretty name for this condition, this meaningless repetition. *echolalia*. doesn't it sound like a lullaby or a type of bird?

there were twelve of us, ruth day's apostles, living together on a farm & subsisting mostly on the food we grew. we had morning meditations & afternoon prayers & evening meditations & night rituals. in between we did things to maintain the farm. we grew chard & spinach & kale & cauliflower & cabbage. we had

an apple orchard & we raised sheep & bees. we sold unpasteur-
ized sheep's milk & honey & hammocks & wind chimes at the
farmer's market.

the land belonged to a mathematician. he lived with us &
tended to the honey bees & drew complicated maps on dead
leaves, which we gave away to people at the farmer's market
when they bought a hammock or a wind chime.

every day the people on the farm would put their hands on
me & pray. i'd feel a warmth in my liver, in my spleen, in the
bowels in between. this was grace that was moving through me.

eventually, meanings reattached themselves to words. i felt
like adam.

i'd watch the herd of sheep & think: sheep!

i'd watch the swarm of bees & think: bees!

i'd go into the barn & look at the tigers & think: tigers... poor
tigers.

we'd bought two tigers from a man in a motel. he'd been
unable to care for them. those tigers had been in hell—mangy,
underfed, hepatitic. they were happy living in the barn. they
hunted mice: little meats, quick heartbeats. we brought them
arrow-pierced deer. they liked their food injured but alive. the
smell of fear helped aid salivation & promote digestion. we
watched them run in circles for our evening meditations. their
stripes moved like the view outside a train. a wordless incan-
tation. one would catch the other—creep, creep, pounce. then
both would yawn, stretch out their pink spiny tongues.

once, one escaped & ripped open my ewes & ate the lambs
inside. it was spring. for days he belched wool & passed soft
lamb bones in his stool. how i hated him after this. i avoided that
side of the farm.

poor cat, poor cat. i have done things in my desperation, that
were uglier than that...

i try not to dwell on those things. my life is split into before

I met ruth day: darkness, misery. & after: surrender, light. as marianne i have hurt & failed many people. i had wanted so desperately to die & i did.

& i was reborn.

my problem had been in my units of measurement. working with the bees, i could see that the hive had a soul even if the individual bees did not. i was not meant to be a modern person. i have always been a fragment, seeking wholeness in a hole. on the farm, i surrendered. each of us surrendered & became a stitch on god's mantle, a hair on his head.

in the afternoon, we pray by the hives. the bees form a cloud & settle on our faces, hands & feet. eye to eyes, so many eyes. their feet are pinchy as they grip our skin. when they sting it keeps us present. "ouch, ouch, ouch, we're here," we sing. "we're here." we hum our hymns into their roar. their roar is louder than a tiger's. their roar enters & purifies us. when we're clean, ruth day feeds us honey like a sacrament.

eat his light, not his body, she says.

& we fill with god's light.

**PART IV:**
*Los Angeles, 2012*

I kiss Hugh as he wipes his hands on a dishtowel. The guests are all here for my baby shower but I don't care. I want to crawl inside his mouth. I try to press against him, though I have to do it sidesaddle because of my belly. He gently pulls away.

"Hi," he says, to someone behind me. I turn around and it's Mae.

"Surprise!" she says. "Oh, it actually worked. You're surprised."

Mae! "I am!"

I'm so happy to see her. She looks so good. She's wearing a blue silk caftan and a veil. Her beautiful eyes are exposed, outlined with kohl and blinking like gray buttons. Her eyebrows are painted on. Perfect arches.

"I thought you were only coming next week for LACMA."

"I lied about the dates," she says. The part of the scarf that covers her mouth is damp, a darker blue. "Hugh and I conspired." She steps back. "God, you are incredibly pregnant. Let me get a picture, please—"

Her assistant, Paul, hands her a camera and she photographs my enormous stomach.

"It feels like I'm carrying around a pot of stew," I say.

One of Hugh's friends, a woman named Agnes, is clinking on a glass, making an announcement about the baby shower games she has organized.

"Each jar has a pureed fruit," she is saying. "Taste the baby food, write down your guess as to what it is on the attached notecard, initial it, and pass it along."

I couldn't possibly think of anything I would rather do less.

"I'm going to show Mae the nursery," I say as everyone else is sitting down. I pull Mae into what used to be the guest room and shut the door.

"Please take it off," I say, pointing to her veil. "It's too hot and I miss your face."

Hugh painted the walls pale gray recently and the smell has lingered. I slide open the window. The parts for the crib Rose got us are leaning against the closet door. We haven't gotten around yet to putting it together.

Mae sits on the edge of the bed and reaches inside her gauzy veil to loosen the inside ties.

"The room looks nice." She pushes the veil up and flips it over her head. And there's her shy face. Red and uneven, but still hers. I can't help myself. I descend on her with kisses, smudging her eyeliner. I try to fix it by rubbing it with my thumb. "Remember when Mom got annoyed if we kissed her too much?"

"No," Mae says, laughing. "I don't remember *trying* to kiss her."

"She'd say: Let *me* kiss *you*. You don't need to kiss me back." I take her hand and put it on my belly. "God. I can't believe you're here. I'm so happy to see you."

We sit like that for a minute, quietly. I can hear people laughing in the other room.

"What's with the geode?" she asks, pointing to the huge crystal on the bedside table.

"Hugh bought it at a prop sale after going to a workshop on energy," I say. "Touch it."

I know she doesn't believe in this stuff, but she puts her free hand on it next to mine.

"It's feels like a rock," she says.

"Right…" I say. "That's because it's a rock!"

We both giggle.

"I like it, I guess," she says.

I pat her bumpy cheek. I wasn't sure until now if I was going to do this: "There's something I want to show you," I say.

"Okay."

I go over to the bookshelf and squat down.

"Hugh's brother seems like he's drunk already," Mae says, getting up to go look out the window.

"Jack? Of course he's drunk. He's a drunk." Hugh's brother is a compartment I prefer to keep closed.

"Are those parrots?" she asks, looking out at the lemon tree.

I reach my hand behind *Goodnight Moon* and grope around. I could've sworn I hid it on this shelf.

"Probably. There's a flock of wild parrots that flies around."

Oh, found it. *The Iowa Review*, Spring 2010.

"Can I read you a poem?" I ask her.

She drops the slats of the blinds back into place with a clink. Squints at the lit mag in my hands. Notices the broken spine, no doubt. "Since when do you read poetry?" I know what she's asking me. Why haven't you moved on?

"Just, can I read it?"

She nods. "Sure." She sits back down on the bed, puts her hand on the geode. I scoot back on the floor to lean against the wall, clear my throat.


*in my life before, i'd stood with my*
*face pressed to a wall, plaster to eye,*
*i did not know that i could turn my head*
*& there'd be space, light & air. when I wed*

*the wall, white gown & all, i did not know*
*there was a room behind me—with rugs & a window,*
*high ceilings, tables, chairs, a door.*


I feel triumphant, finally hearing it out loud. "Tell me you don't think this sounds like her," I say. But when I look at Mae, her face looks blank. She thinks I'm crazy.

"It just seems a little random," she says carefully, petting the geode like it's a cat. "Who does it say wrote it?"

"Ruth Day. But I think that's a pen name. The bio is blank." I flip to the back of the magazine to show her the blank space.

"What makes you think it's her? It sounds like it could be any angsty housewife."

It just is. It's her. "It's not capitalized and she uses those ampersands."

"That seems a little thin..." She takes out her phone and types something in, then shows me a Google image search for "Ruth Day." A stream of apple-cheeked women. Like she thinks I haven't done that already. "It could be any of these Ruths," she says.

"Wait. There's more," I say. "That was just the opening. The poem talks about living on a farm and tigers and beekeeping and all this stuff. Anyway, listen to this part. This is how it ends:


*before there was no day,*
*just night.*
*driving & pacing. insomniac light—*
*the color of puss trickling out of an ear.*

*swimmer's ear—*
*my older got it twice a year.*
*did she even know how to swim?*

*i'm not sure.*
*my younger was scared of the water.*
*my younger was scared of me.*
*i gave her every reason to be.*
*do i think about my daughters now?*
*rarely.*

*i avoid raspberries too.*
*they remind me too much (of you two)*
*arms thorn-torn, shirts baskets, mouths rushes*
*of rubies.*


Her eyes are closed. She opens them and stares at me.

"I don't know, Edie." She does too know! "All kids get ear infections and eat raspberries."

She's only arguing with me because that's her role.

"I wrote the magazine to try to get in touch with her, but it hasn't gotten me anywhere."

"Honey, are you ready for the surprise? Everyone's waiting..." Hugh leans in through the doorway. I slide the magazine out of view and Mae quickly flips her veil back down over her face. "Oh..." He seems flustered at the sight of Mae exposed.

"Can you give us a minute?" I ask.

"Of course." He hesitates, turns around, but doesn't leave.

I haven't told Hugh about the poems. Until I know for certain, I don't really want his input. It's not that he wouldn't be supportive, he would. Too supportive. Pitying. I don't like to open my mother up to other people's judgments, even if those judgments aren't inaccurate.

"So, do you think it's her?" I ask Mae. She stands, straightens out her dress, tightens her veil.

"I've thought I've seen her places too. I think that's pretty natural. Walking on the street. Or going by in a car. I was actually thinking about doing a piece about this..." she trails off.

This is not really what I'm talking about.

"Does it help you to believe it's her?" she asks.

"Yes," I say quickly. "It does."

Hugh leans in through the door again. "I don't want to give away too much," he says, "but this surprise is time-sensitive."

"Okay." I smile at him and he helps me up.

Out on the deck our hippie neighbor, Seagull Carl, is playing a tiny organ. There is a large object on the table. A centerpiece covered with a sheet. Even if it's a pile of old shoes under there, I'd be happy. But it won't be. Knowing Hugh, it will be something amazing.

"Tada!" Hugh says, and with a flourish and flick of his wrist he pulls off the sheet and exposes... What exactly?

A jewel? No, better. A block of ice he carved into a sculpture of me holding a baby. We're posed like a Madonna and child. Inside the ice is something pink and yellow. Frozen flowers. Pink carnations and yellow daffodils.

"Amazing." I lean in so that me and ice-me are nose to nose. My head is full of flowers mid-float. I kiss the ice-baby on the cheek. Everyone is distorted through the ice, oohing and aahing.

Mae gets up and takes a picture. Paul hands her a different lens.

"Ice," Jack mutters. "What an appropriate medium for our Edith." And when nobody responds he repeats it again, a little louder but with the same studiedly casual intonation.

Hugh ignores his brother. Instead, he tells the story how right after we met, he went on a trip to India to visit Swami Ishwarananda. Sobriety was new to him and his future felt too big. The Swami told him to go down to the Ganges River and pray. "That river is the embodiment of the Shakti," Hugh says, "the primordial cosmic energy, because it's both sacred and destructive. People bathe in it and give birth in it and scatter their dead's ashes in it. I sat by the water and meditated for three days, watched people pray and make offerings, flowers mostly, and by the end of it I knew what I wanted. As soon as I got back into town I called Edie and asked her out on a date. And, well, the rest is history." He quit drinking years ago, but he's never gotten out of the habit of making toasts. Everyone cheers. I go over and sit on his lap, my belly pressing into the edge of the table. I remember that date. Naked piggyback rides through the house, fucking, swimming in the ocean, more fucking, eating tacos. It lasted two days and ended only when he needed to go to a Meeting.

I go back and sit next to Mae. Tillie, sweet Tillie, passes out cupcakes that she and Maria baked for dessert.

"Is that Tillie Holloway?" One of Hugh's friends whispers.

"Is Tillie Holloway your mother??" Agnes asks me.

"No," I say. She just played her in a movie, but I don't feel like explaining this. "She's my boss. I help run her foundation."

"It's like a king cake," Tillie is saying over the whispers. "One lucky one has a little plastic baby inside of it."

Mae's breathing flutters the scarf over her mouth. She sticks the cupcake under her veil and eats it in several greedy bites.

"You could *too* swim," she says, apropos to nothing, her mouth full of cake.

So, she does believe me about the poem then. "I could."

"What kind of mother doesn't know this about her child?" Mae turns to Agnes. "Can you imagine not knowing if your kid could swim?"

"We haven't started swim lessons yet," Agnes says defensively. "I know people say the younger the better, but the chlorine in the pool is so harsh on their skin."

"You're about to have a baby." Mae pokes me in the stomach. "Tell me, you could imagine doing to it what Mom did to us?"

I look down at the hump. "Which part?"

"Any of it. Any of the parts."

Everyone is looking down the table at Mae.

"Of course not," I say. "But that doesn't mean I won't."

"You won't," Mae says dismissively, and takes another cupcake.

I wish I could be so sure. I look down at the high rises in the distance. They're outlined in a light smog. Or maybe just fog. I can feel the baby trying to swim inside me but it has run out of room. Can you imagine every time you try to swim being stopped by someone else's organs? The conversation around us has moved on to the coyotes. Tillie has spotted one up the mountain, watching us from a distance.

"How do you know it's not a dog?" Mae's assistant asks.

"The pointy ears."

Hugh is telling the story of how last week a coyote stood eyeing me through the glass doors, and he'd had to spray it with a fire extinguisher to get it to leave.

"It's because of the drought, I guess," Tillie says. "They're starving and they have nothing to lose."

Maria shyly tells the story of how she saw one the other day, carrying a cat in its mouth. "It was so sad," she says.

Jack coughs, coughs, finally spits something out into his hand, holds it up for everyone to admire. A half-chewed plastic king cake baby.

"Oh dear," Tillie says. She and Maria shuffle over to me. "We should head out."

"I'll see you in court tomorrow," I say. Maria will be testifying against her pimp. He threw her off a balcony and now one of her legs is shorter than the other one.

"You can't do wrong by doing right," Tillie says. It was a line from her movie that she now uses in real life. It's a nice sentiment. Who knows if it's true.

"You can't do wrong by doing right." I say it back to her.

There's a lull in the conversation. Several people have left already. And then... Odd. The subway, rumbling underneath us, except there is no subway. A lemon falls out of the bowl on the table and rolls in an arc at my feet. The neighborhood dogs are barking. One's whining sounds so much like a baby crying that it makes Edie's milk leak. She stands up and laughs, dabs at her dress with a paper towel as the earth shakes under us. And then, just as suddenly, it stops.

An earthquake.

"It's good luck, like rain on a wedding day," Edie says to her tall husband and kisses him wetly.

Paul looks very pale. "Was that an earthquake?" he asks.

"Don't worry," Edie tells him. "That was a 2.0 at most. It's nothing. It's kind of fun!"

I laugh. Her kind of fun. Not Paul's kind of fun.

"What about the aftershock?" Paul asks me nervously. He doesn't believe in leaving New York. This is confirming all his suspicions.

"What about it? Oh, look, the power's out," Edie says.

It's true. The porch light is off, but because we're outside, I hadn't noticed. The sky is dimming. What's the word, gloaming?

Edie leans over the side of the deck to yell down the mountain. "Yoohoo! Blackout! Come get your candles! We have extra! 474 Glen Albyn Place.

"How exciting," she says, turning back to us, all a-sparkle.

"How exciting," the drunk mimics quietly.

The other guests are dispersing, saying their goodbyes.

Behind them, Hugh is trying to open the fuse box while holding the flashlight in his teeth. I offer to hold it.

"Thank you," Hugh says. He wipes the handle on his shirt before passing it to me.

I tilt the flashlight left then right to look at how the shadows fall on his face. He has a very nice profile.

He puts his hand on mine and brings the flashlight level with the circuit breaker.

"Sorry," I say. "I was looking at the sculptural possibilities of your face."

He grins at me. "Ha," he says. "Everything is possible." I don't know what this means, but I like the sentiment.

He flips the switches one by one. "Let there be light!" he announces dramatically before flipping the last switch.

I hear my laugh. It escapes before I can grab it by its tail and pull it back.

"Dang," he says. "Guess not. Must be out in the whole neighborhood." His smile is clean and pure—the smile clearly designated for his wife's sister. He is a domesticated dog through and through.

What would it be like, I wonder, to have a husband like that and a fuse box and a lemon tree? And now a baby too. I'd always assumed it would be stifling, "a face to the wall," or however Mom put it. But maybe it wouldn't have to be. Maybe this is something I've internalized without questioning. A shard of her left in me that I could pull out.

When Hugh is out of earshot, gone to give an elderly neighbor some candles, the drunk reaches for the ice sculpture and breaks off Edie's ear. He drops it in his glass and stirs it with his finger.

"What?" he says to the table, pleased with his own outrageousness. "It's just gonna melt!"

As if this is their cue, the remaining guests scatter to the wind.

Jack licks his finger and says to me: "Your sister and I used to be in love before she met my brother."

The earth shakes again, but barely, just enough to once more set off the dogs. I look over at Edie.

"It's true." She shrugs.

"Remember when we stole the horses?"

He tries to grab Edie's hand, but she twists out of reach, stacks the dishes on the table. "Yes," she says. "I remember."

I haven't heard this story. "What happened?" I ask him.

"One night, we broke into the stables in Griffith Park and stole two horses. We rode them all the way up to the observatory."

"I fell off the horse. I'm lucky I didn't break my neck," she says.

"It helps to be drunk." The drunk says this very earnestly. "It does. Your body is looser. You don't resist."

"I think that's just for car accidents." I don't know why I'm arguing this point. "With whiplash."

"Don't engage him," Edie says. "Don't get him started."

His eyes are shiny. "You looked so beautiful lying there in the moonlight. I should have bashed your head in with a rock then and there."

"Hey!" I say, surprised. I realize he's weeping.

"Jesus Christ," Edie says. "Let's go for a walk."

"Okay," I say to Paul. "We'll be back. Will you be all right?"

Paul blinks several times, looks at the weeping Jack, nods.

We walk up the hill. Edie holds her lower back like she's pushing herself forward. I look down between the houses at the darkening city below. The only lights are from cars and fire trucks. The air feels charged. I hear the parrots from the tree take off, circle around, and come back, cawing in confusion.

"Hugh wants us to move to India for a while."

"To get you away from Jack?"

"No," she laughs. "I don't think so. He just wants to live abroad. Have an adventurous life."

"Do you want to go?"

"I can't."

"Why not?" I ask even though I know the answer.

Edie looks at me and lies: "Oh, you know, air pollution. Increased rates of asthma and childhood cancers."

I don't press her. We're delicate with each other. How long has she been sitting on that poem before she showed it to me? She's so excited it exists that I don't think she has absorbed what it was saying.

*Rarely*. Edie. If it was even her, she thinks about us *Ra-re-ly*.

"When I first moved here," Edie says, "I'd go on these epically long walks at night when I couldn't sleep."

I think of the walks we used to take with Dad.

"Most nights, I'd pass this pet store on Sunset and I'd see a man sitting inside, in the dark, with birds perched on his shoulders and legs."

"What did he look like?"

"I don't know. I could only see his outline. Bald, I think? Not very big. I was so lonely. He was like my loneliness totem."

We stop at the overlook, glance down at the moonlit city. Edie pulls a fig off the tree we're standing under and pops it in her mouth.

"*Loneliness blows through me. The whistle of an empty house*," I say.

"Yes. Exactly," she says, throwing the stem into the grass. "Where's that from?"

"One of Dad's books."

She turns to look at me. "Have you seen him since the trial?"

"I tried to visit him once, actually, but *she* was there. She wouldn't let me see him."

"She's always there. That deranged cunt. You know when I visited them after Thomas was born, she kicked me out of the house. She said I was going to hurt the baby. Like I would ever… And of course Dennis just went along with it."

"He was doing what he had to do, I guess." It comes out acerbic, but isn't it true? He got his fresh start. For a few years at least. I look up at the moon through the lens of my camera. It looks brighter and sharper because there's no light pollution. I can see its craters.

"What he had to do…?" Edie says, pulling the camera away from my face. She wants me to go places I'm not interested in going.

"I know you want me to be outraged," I say.

"I don't want you to be anything," she says disingenuously. "I want you to be honest. You talk about it to *Marie Claire*, but not to me."

I shrug. I know this hurts her feelings, but I can't talk about it with her. She wants me to see my relationship with Dad the way she does, stripped of any magic. She wants me to see myself as his victim. She thinks admitting this would set me free. There's no use arguing with her because it just makes her angry.

"Okay," Edie says, lifting up her hands. She'll drop it for now. I wrap my arm around her shoulders. Kiss her temple. We walk up the hill in silence.

We both hear the thudding footsteps at the same time. A figure rounds the corner and runs past us down the hill.

"Hey!" Edie calls out but the person doesn't stop. On impulse, I snap a picture. The bright flash goes off and for a moment I can make out an adult with a child's backpack. Was he being chased? By a person? By coyotes? And then, I'm blind.

I blink, walk, blink, walk into a parked car. "Shit."

I wait for the stars to pass.

"Hey!" I hear Edie shout down the hill. No answer.

"Weird," she says, taking my hand.

We walk back to the house, slightly dazed. In the living room, Hugh is on his knees in front of the fireplace, stacking wood. The drunk is playing the piano. He's not bad, actually. Hugh strikes a match on the grate and I feel it inside my spine. I step back quickly, bang my legs on the rocking horse I gave them. It creaks as it swings back and forth.

"Are you all right?" Paul asks from the corner.

"Sure." I sit down next to him, in the chair farthest from the fire. The room glows orange. Edie is on the floor by Hugh, stretching her hands out to the flame.

The drunk starts a new song. It's ragtime. Fast fingers. He must be a professional musician. On the high notes, he gets ambitious, leans too far and almost topples, rights himself slowly and keeps playing.

"Mae, you should sing something," Edie says. "She's very good," she tells Hugh.

"Oh yeah?" He turns to look at me.

"I can't," I say, focusing and unfocusing the camera on the rug. "The smoke damaged my lungs."

"That's horseshit," Edie says.

"Why would I lie about it?"

"Because you don't want to sing."

"Well, there you go."

"Fine," Edie says. "*I'll* sing." This is a threat. As a kid she was so tone deaf she wasn't allowed to sing in the car.

She gets up and sings the entire jingle from the Personal Injury Law Firm commercials we used to mock as kids over the ragtime song the drunk is playing.

"But I've been in-jured on the job," she drawls. "How'm I gonna find a law-yer to get me the settlement that I de-serve?"

I look at her.

"I sa-aid," she says, dancing over to me, "how'm I gonna find a law-yer to get me the settlement that I de-serve?"

"Why, it's just as easy as picking up the phone!" I finally say. She pulls me up from the chair and we dance to the piano music.

When the song's over, I laugh and clap. I wind easily. I sit down. I can feel Paul staring at me.

The drunk starts another song, then gets up abruptly and staggers out of the room. Edie continues dancing by herself, laughing.

"Edie," Hugh says and pulls her down carefully into his lap. "Edie," he says, "settle down." They kiss. I close my eyes again and listen to the sound of the logs burning and my sister kissing her husband and my assistant breathing through his mouth. And then I hear it. A knock. A knock on the front door.

I open my eyes. Did I imagine that?

"I think I'm feeling better," Paul announces.

Another knock. This time more definite. Edie hears it too.

"I got it," Edie says, standing up and smoothing her skirt.

"If it's people looking for candles, there're more in the hall closet," Hugh calls after her.

Edie doesn't seem to have heard him. From where I'm sitting, I can see her profile. She pauses with her hand on the doorknob and for a moment she looks 16 again. Her face is open and hopeful. And there, inside of me, stirs that ancient feeling of dread that I thought had been extinguished years ago.

# Acknowledgements

Thank you to Eric and Eliza for publishing this book. Thank you to Bill Clegg, whose sharp editorial eye made the book better.

Thank you to Washington University's MFA program and the Olin Fellowship program, and particularly to Kathryn Davis who supported my writing and read early versions of this book.

Thank you to the Elizabeth George Foundation for its generous grant and support that allowed me to write for a year and pay for childcare.

Thank you to the Ucross Foundation, where I began writing the book, the Virginia Center for Creative Arts, where I began re-writing the book, and Playa where I finished it.

Thank you also to Jen and Jordan Monroe who gave me a little residency in Catalina Island, to Seth Archer and Amber Caron for our Utah retreat.

Thanks to the Wisconsin Archives—the research that I did there on the Civil Rights Movement helped inform the book, particularly Ann Carter's character.

Thank you to all my friends who read this book and helped get it published—Michael Almereyda, Colin Bassett, Amber Caron, Anton DiSclafani, Randi Ewing, Sara Finnerty, Matt Grice, Anne-Marie Kinney, Zach Lazar, Mimi Lipson, Lisa Locascio, Betsy Medvedovsky, Emily McLaughlin, Emily Robbins, Maura

Roosevelt, Randi Shapiro, J Ryan Stradal and Andrew Wonder. And thank you especially to Lia Silver, Jordan Jacks and Miriam Simun—who have read this book a million times each.

Thank you to Diana Bartlett and Jesse Hutchison for their medical advice.

Thank you to my parents who are nothing like Marianne and Dennis, and to my brother, Matthew Shifrin, my unsolicited copyeditor extraordinaire, and to my daughter, Fais.

And most of all, thank you to David, who supported me through this whole exciting and difficult process. I love you very, very much.

# Two Dollar Radio
## Books too loud to Ignore

**ALSO AVAILABLE** Here are some other titles you might want to dig into.

### THE BLURRY YEARS NOVEL BY **ELEANOR KRISEMAN**

← "Kriseman's is a new voice to celebrate."
—*Publishers Weekly*

THE BLURRY YEARS IS A POWERFUL and unorthodox coming-of-age story from an assured new literary voice, featuring a stirringly twisted mother-daughter relationship, set against the sleazy, vividly-drawn backdrop of late-seventies and early-eighties Florida.

### THE UNDERNEATH NOVEL BY **MELANIE FINN**

← "*The Underneath* is an excellent thriller." —*Star Tribune*

THE UNDERNEATH IS AN INTELLIGENT and considerate exploration of violence—both personal and social—and whether violence may ever be justified. With the assurance and grace of her acclaimed novel *The Gloaming*, Melanie Finn returns with a precisely layered and tense new literary thriller.

### PALACES NOVEL BY **SIMON JACOBS**

← "*Palaces* is robust, both current and clairvoyant… With a pitch-perfect portrayal of the punk scene and idiosyncratic, meaty characters, this is a wonderful novel that takes no prisoners." —*Foreword Reviews*, starred review

WITH INCISIVE PRECISION and a cool detachment, Simon Jacobs has crafted a surreal and spellbinding first novel of horror and intrigue.

### THEY CAN'T KILL US UNTIL THEY KILL US ESSAYS BY **HANIF ABDURRAQIB**

→ **Best Books 2017:** NPR, *Buzzfeed, Paste Magazine, Esquire, Chicago Tribune, Vol. 1 Brooklyn*, CBC (Canada), *Stereogum, National Post* (Canada), *Entropy, Heavy, Book Riot, Chicago Review of Books* (November), *The Los Angeles Review, Michigan Daily*

← "Funny, painful, precise, desperate, and loving throughout. Not a day has sounded the same since I read him."
—Greil Marcus, *Village Voice*

## Thank you for supporting independent culture!
Feel good about yourself.

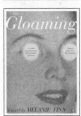

# Books to read

Now available at **TWODOLLARRADIO.com** or your favorite bookseller.

## THE ORANGE EATS CREEPS
### NOVEL BY **GRACE KRILANOVICH**

→ **National Book Foundation '5 Under 35' Award**

← "Breathless, scary, and like nothing I've ever read." —NPR

**A RUNAWAY SEARCHES FOR** her disappeared foster sister along the "Highway That Eats People" haunted by a serial killer named Dactyl.

## SQUARE WAVE NOVEL BY **MARK DE SILVA**

← "Compelling and horrifying." —*Chicago Tribune*

**A GRAND NOVEL OF** ideas and compelling crime mystery, about security states past and present, weather modification science, micro-tonal music, and imperial influences.

## ANCIENT OCEANS OF CENTRAL KENTUCKY
### NOVEL BY **DAVID CONNERLEY NAHM**

→ **Best Books 2014:** NPR, *Flavorwire*

← "Wonderful. Deeply suspenseful." —NPR

**LEAH IS HAUNTED BY** the disappearance of her brother Jacob, when they were children in rural Kentucky. When a mysterious man shows up, claiming to be Jacob, Leah is wrenched back to childhood.

## RADIO IRIS NOVEL BY **ANNE-MARIE KINNEY**

← "[*Radio Iris*] has a dramatic otherworldly payoff that is unexpected and triumphant."
—*New York Times Book Review*, Editors' Choice

**RADIO IRIS IS THE STORY OF** Iris Finch, a socially awkward daydreamer with a job as the receptionist/personal assistant to an eccentric and increasingly absent businessman.

## THE INCANTATIONS OF DANIEL JOHNSTON
### GRAPHIC NOVEL BY **RICARDO CAVOLO**
### WRITTEN BY **SCOTT MCCLANAHAN**

← "Wholly unexpected, grotesque, and poignant." —*The FADER*

**RENOWNED ARTIST RICARDO CAVOLO** and Scott McClanahan combine talents in this dazzling, eye-popping graphic biography of artist and musician Daniel Johnston.

# Books to read

### NOT DARK YET NOVEL BY **BERIT ELLINGSEN**

← "Fascinating, surreal, gorgeously written."
—*BuzzFeed*

ON THE VERGE OF a self-inflicted apocalypse, a former military sniper is enlisted by a former lover for an eco-terrorist action that threatens the quiet life he built for himself in the mountains.

### THE ABSOLUTION OF ROBERTO ACESTES LAING NOVEL BY **NICHOLAS ROMBES**

← **One of the Best Books of 2014:** *Flavorwire*

"Kafka directed by David Lynch doesn't even come close. It is the most hauntingly original book I've read in a very long time. [This book] is a strong contender for novel of the year." —*3:AM Magazine*

### HOW TO GET INTO THE TWIN PALMS NOVEL BY **KAROLINA WACLAWIAK**

← "Reinvents the immigration story." —*New York Times Book Review*

ANYA IS A YOUNG WOMAN living in a Russian neighborhood in L.A., torn between her parents' Polish heritage and trying to assimilate in the U.S. She decides instead to try and assimilate in her Russian community, embodied by the nightclub, the Twin Palms.

### MIRA CORPORA NOVEL BY **JEFF JACKSON**

→ *Los Angeles Times* **Book Prize Finalist**

← "A piercing howl of a book." —*Slate*

A COMING OF AGE story for people who hate coming of age stories, featuring a colony of outcast children, teenage oracles, amusement parks haunted by gibbons, and mysterious cassette tapes.

### HAINTS STAY NOVEL BY **COLIN WINNETTE**

← "In his astonishing portrait of American violence, Colin Winnette makes use of the Western genre to stunning effect." —*Los Angeles Times*

HAINTS STAY IS A NEW Acid Western in the tradition of Rudolph Wurlitzer, *Meek's Cutoff*, and Jim Jarmusch's *Dead Man*: meaning it is brutal, surreal, and possesses an unsettling humor.